ALSO BY DARRYL BOLLINGER

The Medicine Game

A
CASE OF
REVENGE

A Novel

DARRYL BOLLINGER

JNB Press

JNB Press
Tallahassee, FL

www.jnbpress.com

Printed in the United States of America

First Trade Edition: October 2012

ISBN 978-0-9848432-2-0

In memory of my aunt, Necie Bollinger Brown,
who never judged.

Chapter 1

Brian Jennings was tired. It was late Tuesday night, around one a.m., technically Wednesday morning. It had been a long day. He walked to his truck in the parking garage of the hospital where he worked.

It was an almost cool evening in Fort Myers, cool being a relative term. He'd been putting the finishing touches on his board presentation for tomorrow. Brian was the Chief Executive Officer or CEO at Rivers Community Hospital in Fort Myers, FL. People were surprised to learn the CEO drove a pickup, though it was a late model Ford F150 King Ranch Edition, costing as much or more than many luxury sedans on the road.

Brian had always driven trucks. It reflected his practical nature and, unlike many truck owners, he used his as a utility vehicle. Trips to the home supply store were frequent as well as stops at the landscape center to pick up plants and supplies for the yard.

He pulled out of the parking garage and headed south on Cleveland Avenue. Cleveland Avenue, or US 41, was one of the main north-south routes through Fort Myers. Traffic was light this time of night, so he made good time.

He was going home to his house on Sanibel Island. It was a long commute, especially during season.

Season in Fort Myers referred to that joyous time of year between Labor Day and Easter when hordes of snowbirds made their way to southwest Florida, clogging up the roads and choking restaurants and stores. There were only two seasons in Fort Myers. Neither related to the weather.

The commute was worth it. He and his wife, Dorothy, had bought a house on the bay side of Sanibel over twenty years ago when he was promoted to the top position at the hospital. Only the wealthy could afford anything on the Gulf of Mexico side, so that had been out of the question at the time. A small place on the bay had just come on the market. The real estate agent had taken them to see it as quickly as possible. She told them it was priced right and wouldn't last the day. They figured it was sales talk, but as soon as they drove in the secluded driveway and saw the house, it was love at first sight. They made an offer at the asking price and it had been home since.

Despite the drive, they loved it out there. It was quiet and peaceful. They had a dock out back with a small flats boat they used for fishing and riding around in Pine Island Sound, which separated Sanibel from the mainland.

At Colonial Boulevard, he turned right. He was going west to pick up McGregor Boulevard, which would take him all the way out to the Sanibel Causeway. During season and at rush hour, he would never consider going this way. It was a welcome change of scenery.

Before long, Brian was approaching the toll booth, signifying the end of McGregor Boulevard and the official start of the Sanibel Causeway. He stayed in the left lane, which was for electronic tolls, eliminating a stop. Slowing down as he passed through the toll booth, the device on his windshield beeped to confirm the toll was paid.

The Causeway was three miles long, the only link connecting Sanibel Island with the mainland of Florida just south of Fort Myers. It consisted of three bridges and two man-made islands.

Leaving the toll booth and back up to highway speed, Brian had just come over the first bridge, the tallest at seventy feet high. At the bottom of the bridge, the road lands on the first island and makes a sweeping turn to the left. Brian was headed toward that turn when he noticed his steering wheel wasn't responding. He applied more pressure, trying to turn the wheel to the left, but the full-size pickup acted as if it had a mind of its own and resisted his efforts.

He glanced at the speedometer and saw he was going seventy miles an hour, the needle still climbing. Realizing the steering wheel wasn't effective, he moved his right foot from the accelerator to the brake. He pumped the brake, but could tell it had no effect.

With growing horror, he sensed the brake, just like the steering wheel, was obeying someone other than himself. Moving his foot back to the accelerator pedal, he pumped it as well, hoping it was stuck and the force would dislodge it. Nothing. The truck was continuing to gain speed. He glanced at his rear view mirror and saw only the receding view of the bridge. No cars were behind him. He was now going ninety. Looking ahead and to his left, he saw no one approaching in the opposite lane. His situation made no sense at all. It was as if the accelerator and brake and steering wheel had been disconnected.

There was no guardrail on his side of the road, only a narrow stretch of sand between the pavement and the water. Still gaining speed, he logically understood he was going to go straight, over the sand and into the water. Rationally, his mind knew the sand wouldn't stop him or even slow him at this speed. But the survival instinct in mankind outranks the logical mind, so Brian thought that somehow this time would be different.

At the bottom of the bridge, the truck first veered left. He heard the tires squeal and looked in shock as he thought he was going off the opposite side of the Causeway. Then, the truck turned back to the right, straight toward the bay as if taking aim on the broad expanse of water. Time had run out. He'd failed to solve the problem. He never panicked. It was more like the illogicality of it paralyzed him.

Brian could feel the truck bouncing off the pavement and over the sand. Even as the large vehicle ploughed into the water head-on, at a speed police later calculated at over ninety miles an hour, he was still trying to figure it out. He felt the impact of the crash and heard the explosion of the charge activating the airbag. Immediately, the airbag was in his face and he was unable to see. The two and one-half ton vehicle nosedived into the water.

Suddenly it was quiet, and he had a short-lived sensation of weightlessness as the truck briefly lost contact with the earth, flipping upside-down and submerging the cab. Just before he lost consciousness, he felt the warm waters of the Caloosahatchee River flooding the inside of his truck. That was the last conscious thought Brian Jennings registered.

No one paid attention to the young man sitting in the beat-up red truck in the parking lot at the public boat ramp on the north side of the causeway, just before the first bridge. It was a popular spot, vehicles always parked there, with people coming and going at all hours. Had anyone looked closer, they would have seen he had a laptop out in the dark cab, but he was parked away from the other vehicles on purpose. The laptop display was dimmed to its lowest setting so as not to impede his night vision nor attract attention.

He didn't see the result of the crash. But looking at the map on the computer screen, he knew Jennings's truck was somewhere in the water on this side of the first island. He allowed himself a smile of satisfaction. The program had worked flawlessly. Just a matter of ones and 0s, he thought.

Pleased with the outcome, he logged off and shut the laptop down. He closed the screen, put it back into its case, and set it on the floor on the passenger side.

He cranked the engine and pulled out of the parking lot, heading east, back toward Fort Myers.

Chapter 2

More asleep than awake, Carly Nelson fumbled in the dark to find the buzzing phone on the nightstand. Through clouded eyes, she glanced at the clock; 4:09. Pressing the correct button on the second try, she held the phone to her ear and hoarsely whispered, "Hello?" She didn't want to wake Eric, sleeping next to her.

"Carly?" It was a female voice on the other end.

"Yes?"

"It's Helen. Sorry to bother you."

Helen? Who the hell was Helen? She shook her head. Helen from the hospital. Must be.

"That's okay. What is it?"

There was a pause. "Brian. He's gone."

Carly struggled to understand. "Gone?"

"There was an accident. They brought him in an hour ago, but he was dead when the ambulance arrived."

The word "dead" quickly lifted the fog of semi-consciousness from Carly's head. She got out of the bed and stumbled into the bathroom, closing the door behind her and flipping on the light.

"Brian's dead?" Carly wanted to confirm she wasn't dreaming.

Helen was sniffling. "Yes, I knew you'd want to know as soon as possible."

"Oh my God! Let me get dressed and I'll be there in thirty minutes." She hung up the phone without waiting for a reply. Setting it on the counter, she splashed some water on her face. Her mind was starting to race.

She stared into the mirror at the forty-three-year-old woman looking back at her. *What now?* Carly was the Chief Operating Officer at the hospital where she worked. Brian Jennings, her boss and mentor, was the CEO. Many still thought of the position as administrator, the title when Brian had first taken the role years ago. Brian didn't care what the position was called. He never bothered to correct anyone who still introduced him as the administrator at Rivers Community Hospital. Everyone knew he ran the hospital and that was all that mattered.

Carly splashed more water on her face and tried brushing her short brown hair. There wasn't much she could do with it. She skipped any makeup, walked into her closet, and grabbed some slacks, a shirt, and athletic shoes. Quickly, she dressed, grabbed her phone, and turned out the light.

She opened the bathroom door, tiptoed out, and almost tripped over Bo, their black Lab sitting right outside the door. She reached down to pat his head, then walked out of the bedroom, Bo following close, as they went to the kitchen.

She opened the door to the garage and pressed the button on the wall to raise the garage door. They walked to the entrance of the garage where she stood while Bo did his business on the grass at the side of the driveway. After sniffing a few places, satisfied his territory was secure, he came back into the garage with Carly. She opened the door to the kitchen, let Bo into the house, and closed it. Opening the door to her BMW, she climbed in, cranked it, and left for the hospital.

Mornings were comfortable this time of year. She lowered the window, hoping the fresh air would help clear the cobwebs. There was little traffic on McGregor Boulevard as she drove downtown. She wondered what kind of an accident, wishing she'd thought to ask on the phone. Fifteen minutes later, she swiped her badge and pulled into the employee parking lot at the hospital. She found an empty spot one row away from the employee entrance and parked.

She nodded, but didn't speak to the few people she passed en route to the Emergency Department. When she walked through the doors, she looked around for Helen Farmer, the Vice President of Nursing. She was over at the triage desk, talking to a small group of people gathered around. Helen looked up and saw her just before she got there.

Without a word, Helen walked over and threw her arms around her, squeezing her hard. Carly returned the hug, staring at the red-eyed people standing there.

Finally, Helen pulled back.

Carly looked at the small group. Not knowing what to say, she looked back at Helen.

"What happened?" Carly asked.

"Apparently, he was in his office here until after midnight. The night owl, you know how he is. He was on his way home and ran off the Sanibel Causeway. A car came by after it happened, saw the truck upside-down in the water, and called 911. EMS got there within ten minutes, but by the time they got him out of his truck, it was too late."

Carly's eyes started to tear up and she shook her head. Brian had been her mentor and a father-figure to her. She couldn't believe he was gone.

"Why did he go off the road?"

"The Highway Patrol officer thinks he fell asleep or had a heart attack. There were no skid marks."

"I can't believe it." Carly looked down at the floor. Tears were sliding down her cheek, dropping onto the gleaming floor at her feet. She wasn't sure she could talk.

"Have they notified Dorothy yet?" Carly asked, her voice breaking.

"George left right before you got here. He rode out with one of his friends in the Sheriff's Office." George Hopkins was the head of security at the hospital.

Carly shook her head, still disbelieving. "Thanks for calling me, Helen. I'm going upstairs. Try to collect my thoughts." She turned and walked away.

Walking down the hall to the elevators, Carly was in a daze. She thought she spoke to a familiar face she passed in the hall, but she wasn't sure. The elevator door opened, she stepped in, then, when the doors opened again, she walked off, barely recognizing the fifth floor. It was dark, with only a single light on in the hall. She didn't remember pushing the button for five.

She put her key into the office door, walked past her assistant's desk, and unlocked the door to her office. In the dark, she sat in her chair and stared out the window.

What to do? For a long time, she just looked, watching but not seeing the lights downtown, the few cars making their way around Fort Myers early in the morning.

Carly felt like she had to do something; if for no other reason than to keep her mind off what happened.

She pulled a note pad out of her top desk drawer and a pen. Probably should make a list of things to do. Where to start? She wrote down the number one and beside it Dorothy. Brian's wife. She would need to call her or go out to see her this morning. She would give George a call in an hour or so and talk to him first.

As the second-in-command, she was responsible for getting the word out. First, she needed to notify corporate. Rivers Community Hospital was owned by HealthAmerica, a publicly-traded health care company based in Atlanta. She looked up the number for the Regional Vice President responsible for Rivers, Paul Leggett. She called his cell phone and it rang straight through to his voice mail. Not surprising, since it was five in the morning. She left him a message asking him to call her ASAP.

Next she wrote down management team. She would get Sandy, her assistant, to call an emergency meeting of the management team first thing this morning. Then they could get the news out to their managers. Of course, Carly knew that nothing was faster at communications than the grapevine at a hospital. Probably half of the employees knew by now.

Beside the number four, she wrote Board. Even though they had a meeting scheduled this afternoon, she would call each of them first, starting with the Chair.

Around six, she called George's cell phone. It went straight to voice mail. She figured he was still with Dorothy, so she left him a message to please call her as soon as he left.

Just before seven, George called her back on her cell phone. He had worked at Rivers as long as Brian and they were old friends. Carly was glad that George had gone out to Brian's house. That would be some comfort to Dorothy, although in a time like this, Carly imagined there was little comfort to be had.

Carly answered the call. "I'm so sorry, George. I know how close you were."

George cleared his throat. "He was a good man. Hard to believe he's gone."

"I know. How's Dorothy?" Carly asked.

"Not bad, considering. Martha's still out there with her." Martha was George's wife. "Dorothy's sister is on her way down from Atlanta and should be here around lunch."

"I want to call her or go see her, but I don't want to impose. What do you think?"

George hesitated. "I know you've got your hands full there, Carly. But I think it would be nice if you could come out, even for a few minutes. I think it'd mean a lot to her."

"Consider it done. I've got a management team meeting set for nine. As soon as it's over, I'll drive out there to see her."

"Thanks, Carly. See you later this morning."

Carly ended the call. As soon as she set the phone down on her desk, it buzzed again.

"Hello?"

"Carly. Paul Leggett."

"Paul. Bad news, I'm afraid. Brian Jennings was in a car accident just after midnight." She paused and took a deep breath. "He didn't make it."

"Oh my God! What happened?"

"He was driving home alone. Lost control on the Sanibel Causeway and went off into the water. They think he either had a heart attack or fell asleep at the wheel. It was too late by the time anyone got there."

"I can't believe it. I'll be down there soon as I can get a flight. Anything you need right now?"

She forced a weak laugh. "Two more hands. Another eight hours in the day."

"I wish I could help you there. Anything else, let me know, okay? I'll call soon as I know my arrangements."

"Thanks, Paul." She ended the call and set the phone down once again.

At ten minutes before nine, Carly walked down to the auditorium for the management meeting. Along the way, she ran into a couple of department heads and walked with them. No one said much. Of course, they had heard the news.

The mood in the auditorium was subdued without the usual chatty buzz that preceded most management meetings. At precisely nine o'clock, she turned on the microphone and adjusted it.

"If everyone would please take their seat," she said. It was the way she usually began the meeting, although this morning it wasn't necessary. Most everyone in the room was seated and waiting for her to start.

"I'm sure some of you have already heard the tragic news from this morning. Brian Jennings was killed earlier today in a single car accident on the Sanibel Causeway."

There was a hushed murmur from the people gathered. She paused a minute to regain her voice.

"He was going home after a long evening at work and ran off the Causeway. The Highway Patrol thinks he may have fallen asleep or possibly had a heart attack, but they're not sure at this point. Funeral arrangements will be announced as soon as they're complete. I'm sure all of us will join together to express our condolences to his wife, Dorothy. That's all. Thank you."

Carly was relieved to have finished her remarks. She wasn't sure she could've said anymore without her voice cracking. George was standing in the back of the room and she walked over to him. The group was slow to disperse as everyone was talking about the news.

"I'll be happy to drive you out there," he said as she walked up.

"Thank you, George, but no. I know you have plenty to do here. I've got my phone if you need me."

He reached out to give Carly a hug, which surprised her. George was a grizzled ex-Marine and retired police officer. He wasn't much on public displays of affection.

"Thank you," he said as she embraced him.

She walked out to the parking lot and got into her car to drive out to the Jennings's home. Driving down Cleveland Avenue, she couldn't help but wonder if Brian had taken this same route earlier today. We never know, she thought. Brian had no clue that would be the last time he made that trip. She picked up the phone and called Eric's cell phone.

"Hi, love. What's up? You left early this morning." His cheerful voice told her he hadn't heard the news.

"Brian's dead. He was—"

"What? Brian Jennings? What happened?" Eric knew how much she liked and respected Brian.

"He was on his way home after midnight. Ran off the Causeway. They think he fell asleep or had a heart attack. He was dead by the time anyone got there."

"My God," was all Eric could say. "I'm so sorry, Carly. I know how much he meant to you."

A tear rolled down her cheek as she fought to maintain control. "I'm on my way out to Sanibel to see Dorothy. I'm sorry, I would've called earlier, but as you can imagine, it's been a hectic morning."

"No, no. I understand. I'm just in shock. Are you okay?"

She was starting to sniffle. "I guess. Trying to keep busy. So much to do." More tears were coming and she couldn't stop them. "I love you."

"I love you, too, Carly."

She hung up and let herself cry, not that she could stop it. Digging a tissue out of her purse, she turned toward the toll booth. She stayed left and went through the express lane, the electronic device on her windshield beeping to confirm its acceptance of her toll payment.

As she came down off the first bridge, she thought about Brian and his last thoughts. There was no sign of anything. No skid marks, his truck had already been removed. There was no indication a person had lost his life there only a few hours ago. She slowed as she rounded the sweeping curve to the left, wondering what had happened. He'd driven this same route thousands of times.

"What happened, Brian?" she asked out loud.

By the time she got to Sanibel and turned right on Periwinkle Way, the tears had stopped for the moment. She turned right again and wound her way back to Brian's house. Taking a quick look in the mirror to check her face before she got out, she took a deep breath and walked up to the front door.

Martha, George's wife, opened the door as she walked up the steps. The two women hugged and the tears started up again. It was a minute before either could speak. They finally separated and Carly followed her back to the lanai where Dorothy was sitting, watching the calm waters of Pine Island Sound. She turned when they entered the room, recognizing Carly.

Clutching her handkerchief, the petite older woman stood to greet her. Reaching up and putting her frail arms around Carly's neck, she hugged her and said, "Thank you for coming, Carly. He loved you like a daughter, you know?"

Carly burst into tears at that. She tried to stop, but couldn't. Dorothy was comforting her, which was so strange. This woman had just lost her husband of forty-three years and here she was comforting Carly.

Carly pulled away, but held Dorothy's hand as they sat. "I'm so sorry, Dorothy. He was my friend and mentor. All I ever wanted was for him to be proud of me. That's what drove me." She dabbed her eyes with the tissue.

"Oh, dear, he was so proud of you," Dorothy said.

She nodded as she held Carly's hand and looked into her eyes. "He watched you grow into that job and was enormously proud of you. I heard him say on more than one occasion that he was more proud of you than anyone he'd ever mentored. You were his star pupil. Don't ever forget that."

She didn't know where they were coming from, but more tears rolled down Carly's face. "Is there anything I—we can do?"

Dorothy shook her head.

"Not at the moment, dear. I'm sure I'll think of things later. My sister Janie, from Atlanta, will be down later today. She'll be a big help. Besides, you have a lot to do back at the hospital." She patted Carly's hand. "I do appreciate so much you coming out here. But I know you need to get back."

Dorothy turned and looked out on the water. "I've decided to have the service on Saturday at one." Looking back at Carly, she said, "Is that okay, you think?"

Carly nodded. "I think that's perfect."

"We'll have it at Saint Luke's. That's where we were married."

Carly shook her head. "I didn't know that. I knew you were married in Fort Myers, but not where."

"I've spoken with Father Cowan. He said that would be fine."

"I'll get the word out at the hospital. I'm sure lots of people will want to pay their respects. He was so well-liked."

Dorothy smiled. "He loved that place—from the beginning. He always said it was where he was meant to be. And I believe it." She squeezed Carly's hand. "Thank you, Carly. Now you go on back to the hospital. They need you there. Don't let it get out of hand. Brian wouldn't be pleased, you know."

Carly couldn't help but smile. "I'll do my best, Dorothy. And please call me if you need anything.

Anything at all." She stood to say goodbye. "I'll call later to check on you."

Dorothy turned Carly's hand loose and returned her gaze out to the water.

Martha walked her out.

Carly gave her a card with her cell phone number on it. "This is my personal cell phone number. Please call me if she needs anything at all. And thank you for coming out here."

Martha hugged her. "Thank you for coming. It meant a lot to her, I could tell."

Carly got back to the hospital just in time for the board meeting. It was a short one, with the Chair deciding to postpone the formal agenda due to the circumstances. Carly spent the rest of the day on the phone and in meetings, putting her schedule on hold while she dealt with the crisis at hand.

That night, when she got home, Eric met her in the kitchen as she walked in. Bo was wagging his tail, glad to see her, and nuzzled her leg as if he understood.

She petted him, not speaking, and walked over to Eric's waiting arms. The tears started flowing as he pulled her close. Neither said a word. Neither had to.

After a few minutes, she pulled away.

"I can't believe I have any tears left," she said.

He handed her another tissue, and she dabbed her eyes.

He shook his head. "I still can't believe it."

"I know. I'm exhausted, but I don't think I can go to sleep just yet. Could we have a glass of wine and go out on the lanai for a few minutes?"

He nodded and turned toward the wine cooler.

"Go on out. I'll bring it to you."

She kicked off her shoes and took off her slacks, draping them over the breakfast bar on her way to the lanai. The lanai, a common fixture in south Florida, was screened and had a pool, functioning as a courtyard, since it was surrounded on three sides by the house. With the tropical climate, it was used as an extension of their living area most of the year.

It felt good to relax and get out of her clothes. She unbuttoned her blouse and sat in the chair at the small table next to the pool. Bo lay down next to her chair. Eric brought out two glasses of red wine, set them on the table, and sat across from her.

"I like that outfit," he commented, looking at her sitting there in panties, bra, and open blouse. Since it was only the two of them at home most of the time, they wore little, if anything, around the house.

She smiled, glad he noticed, but too tired to act on it. She picked up her wine, raised her glass toward him, and took a sip. He did the same.

"Hard day," he said.

Carly just nodded. "Going to see Dorothy was tough. She's so strong. I felt like she was comforting me."

She reached out and took Eric's hand. "I hope to God I never have to go through what she's going through. I know that's selfish, but I hope and pray I go before you."

He shook his head. "My vote is we get to go out together. I don't want to find out what it's like without you."

They talked about the events and the schedule for the rest of the week. Carly began to unwind, and by the time she finished her wine, she was exhausted and ready for bed.

Chapter 3

The next morning, when the alarm clock sounded, Carly shut it off and rolled over. Six o'clock came early. The gym was calling. She felt like she already had a workout. Yesterday had been a long day and she hadn't slept well. She'd been dreaming when the clock went off. It was one of those dreams where something was chasing her, gaining ground and she couldn't escape.

But she made herself get up, feeling like it would do her good to exercise. She was careful not to wake Eric. Still groggy, she made her way to the bathroom and splashed some cold water on her face. After putting on underwear, a loose fitting t-shirt, and baggy shorts, she took her shoes downstairs, Bo trailing close.

He sat on the floor next to her and watched as she sat at the breakfast table, putting her socks and shoes on. Today she put both socks on first. She put on the left shoe and laced it. Next, she put on the right shoe and laced it. Each morning, she did it in a different order. It was a deliberate ritual.

Yesterday, she put on the left sock and left shoe first, lacing it before moving to the other foot. It was her small way of not falling into a rut, of not being predictable. Silly, she knew. But it was something that was always in the back of her mind.

She was determined not to be like her mother, whose every move was expected. Dinner was the same time every single day. If it was Tuesday, Carly would know what was on the table. When she left home, she vowed she wouldn't be like that. Even after her mother died three years ago, she wouldn't let her guard down, as if the mundane was stalking her, waiting for a weak moment. Of course, her obsession of not being predictable and deliberately doing things different was predictable in itself. Too early to analyze that, she thought.

Carly went to the garage and let Bo out for his morning bathroom trip. A few minutes later, she got into the car. It was just getting light outside as she backed out of the garage into the cul-de-sac. As much as she disliked getting up this early, it was the only way she would exercise on a regular basis.

She pulled into the employee parking lot at the hospital, grabbed her bag, and headed to the gym attached to the hospital. Five mornings a week she worked out. It helped her maintain her weight and figure. Besides, it was also a wonderful stress reliever. The usual regulars were in the gym and she spoke to them as she turned on her iPod and plugged her earbuds in. Most of the people watched the talking heads on the numerous flat panel television screens scattered around the bright airy facility, but Carly preferred her choice of music. This morning she went for Fleetwood Mac, preferring something easy in the classic rock category. She did her thirty minutes on the elliptical machine, then went over to the weights to do some upper body work.

Carly was sweating as she finished her routine and made her way to the locker room. She showered and dressed for work, which was convenient since it was in the building next door. She made it to her office by eight and started on the pile of work in the middle of her desk left over from the day before.

Around nine, a heavy-set, well-dressed man with grayish-brown hair walked in. He was wearing the business uniform—dark suit, pale blue shirt with a blue and gold striped tie. Paul Leggett was the Southern Region Vice President with HealthAmerica. Brian's boss, now hers, she thought. Carly had never seen him in anything but a suit and tie.

She didn't have much of an opinion of Paul. He'd been nice enough to her, though her exposure to him had been somewhat limited. All she knew was what Brian had told her—Paul was a corporate minion, not to be trusted.

"Morning, Carly. Good to see you. I just wish it was under more pleasant circumstances. I'm sorry to hear about Brian." He sat in one of the chairs facing her desk.

"I know, still hard to believe. When did you get in?"

"Late last night. I was hoping to get in earlier yesterday, but just didn't happen. I understand the funeral's tomorrow?" he asked.

Since Paul was high enough up the corporate ladder to have use of the corporate jets, she wondered why he couldn't come yesterday. Whatever. She nodded and said, "One o'clock at Saint Luke's Episcopal."

"I'll be there. Probably won't be able to stay longer, though. How's his wife—Dorothy, is she—holding up?"

"Good, considering. I went out to see her yesterday. She's a strong woman, but it has to be tough losing someone after that long."

"I'm sure." Paul shifted in his chair. "How long had they been married?"

"Forty-three years."

His eyes opened wide. "Wow. Long time." He shook his head, then continued, changing the subject.

"I wanted to talk to you about Brian's job. It's no secret that I want to promote you to his position. You're clearly everyone's choice. But I need to run it by Carter first and he's on vacation on his boat somewhere in the Mediterranean." Carter Freeman was the President of HealthAmerica and Paul's boss. "I'm sure you understand."

Carly nodded without saying anything.

"He's scheduled to be back next week, so we should be able to move pretty fast. I'll let you know soon as I talk with him."

He leaned forward and put his hand on the desk. "I'm going to make the rounds. Have you got dinner plans tonight?"

"I'm supposed to have dinner with one of our docs, Forrest Langford. You're welcome to join us if you like."

Paul laughed. "I think I'll pass. My last meeting with Doctor Know-it-all was pretty tense, so I think I'll keep out of your way this trip. Maybe next time."

He got up to leave. "I'll check back with you later this afternoon."

Carly started back on her emails and her cell phone buzzed. It was a text message from Michelle, her daughter.

B home at 5 2mrw LU

Adopting the abbreviated text language, she responded.

K LU 2

Carly was old school and still had problems with the text shorthand. We're creating a world of illiterates, she thought, but had to confess, she was slipping into it more and more. If she wanted to communicate with her daughter, then she'd better get with the program. Texting was the future, and the future was now. Carly would have to get used to it.

Michelle, her only child, was a senior at the University of Florida in Gainesville, four hours away. At least Carly thought she was a senior. When pressed about her class standing, Michelle gave slightly different interpretations of exactly where she was, depending on the day. The best Carly could figure is she was a late Junior or early Senior, hopefully graduating within the next twelve months.

Michelle was coming home between semesters, though Carly knew she would be spending most of her time with friends and out at the beach. But that was to be expected, Carly thought. Although she wanted more of Michelle's time, she couldn't complain. Michelle had turned out to be a pretty good kid and Carly was proud of her. She was the product of Carly's marriage to Dr. Forrest Langford, a supremely talented neurosurgeon in Fort Myers. Now divorced, their relationship had remained civil for two reasons.

First was Michelle. Carly had been determined she wouldn't be a vindictive shrew of an ex-wife. Many times, her tongue had bled, but she was determined she wouldn't bash him in public or in front of Michelle. What had happened between them was personal, and she intended to keep it that way. Forrest had remarried, twice, and was currently with his latest trophy, a twenty-something skinny platinum blonde young enough to be his daughter.

The second reason behind their amiable peace was work-related. Langford was the top admitter at Rivers Hospital. Doctors drove the hospital of choice for patients. Having a heavyweight like Langford pushing all of his admissions to Rivers meant big business for the hospital. Of course, he knew that and relished using his power to get his way. Professionally, just as personally, she found herself constantly biting her tongue in the numerous confrontations with the egotistical surgeon. But that came with the territory, and she dealt with it.

Carly took a deep breath, thinking about her meeting with Forrest this evening; never an easy task.

The afternoon went by in a blur. Paul stopped by on his way out and said he was having dinner with Rich, the CFO. He suggested he and Carly get together for brunch tomorrow before the funeral.

Between more meetings and phone calls, the time had flown and it was almost seven. She finished the document she was working on and logged off her computer.

Leaving the hospital, she made her way to L'Auberge on Bay Street, probably the nicest restaurant in Fort Myers. It was only two blocks away and she walked in at seven on the dot.

Of course, Forrest wasn't there yet. She told the hostess she was expecting someone and asked to be seated. Although they were to meet at seven, he was late as usual. She ordered a glass of wine and fifteen minutes later, a tall, slim, distinguished man with dark blond hair and receding hairline strode over to the table. Carly decided not to even bother with saying anything about his tardiness, preferring to pick her battles.

Forrest Langford walked over and gave her a perfunctory kiss on the cheek when he got to her table.

"I'm sorry to hear about Brian. He was a nice person and a good CEO," he said as he seated himself. "One of the few people who knew what he was doing."

Carly ignored the last remark and softened at the mention of her mentor's name. "Yes, he was both. He'll be sorely missed."

"So, are they going to promote you?" Langford was direct and didn't waste time getting to the point.

She shook her head and looked at him with pity. "I have no idea, Forrest. Hasn't crossed my mind." She wasn't about to mention her conversation with Paul Leggett. It wasn't any of Forrest's business, and besides, nothing was ever final in the corporate world until it was announced.

He picked up the menu and asked, "How have you been?" moving on to his next agenda item.

"Fine, thanks. And you?"

"Busy. Thanks for meeting with me this evening. With my schedule, it's difficult to get any time during the day."

He was such a pompous ass. She wanted to add, *for someone as important as you*, but instead said, "No problem. What's on your mind?"

Small talk out of the way, he got to his reason for wanting to have dinner.

"You need to do something with your OR manager, Carly. I was late getting out two days last week, all because their turnover time is totally unacceptable. He should be fired. You need to get somebody in there who knows what he's doing."

Carly was expecting this. Keith, the Operating Room manager, had already warned her about Forrest's explosion last week. Forrest's office had added on two cases one day and one the next, so the delays were unavoidable. She took a bite of her salad before responding, choosing her words with care.

"I heard you were late getting out both days. But in all fairness, adding on cases at the last minute is probably going to result in delays. We can't create time."

"If your scheduling system doesn't allow for add-ons, then maybe I need to consider other options."

She watched him attacking his entree, working himself up for a fight. He didn't waste any time playing the threat card. With two large hospitals in town, the big-hitters were always threatening to take their business to the other facility. This wasn't the first time they'd done this dance. But she wasn't going to bite, and ignored his comment.

"Forrest, you know we give you the best block schedules on the calendar. My people bend over backward to accommodate you. Always have, always will. It's no secret that you do a lot of business in our hospital and we appreciate it."

He slowed down a bit, receiving her acknowledgment with aplomb.

"I'll talk with Keith and go over what happened to make sure we continue to do all that we can to make things work as smoothly as possible," she said.

Now that his ego had been stroked, he grunted and appeared satisfied. He pointed his fork at her and said, "Well, if it happens again, I'll be back in your office. And I will expect him to be replaced."

He was bluffing and she knew it. This was one of those times she bit her tongue. He had to get in the last word, which she let pass. She considered it closed and changed the subject.

"Are you going to be able to spend any time with Michelle while she's home on break?"

"Tonya and I are thinking about flying down to the Keys for a few days. Thought maybe Michelle would like to go."

Tonya was the latest goddess, only a few years older than Michelle. Carly wasn't about to weigh in on a cozy trip for the three of them and try to speak for her daughter. Michelle was old enough to make her own decisions.

"I'm sure she'd like that," Carly said.

Forrest had his own plane that he used for short trips, mostly to Key West, where he owned a beautiful waterfront home. Must be nice, she thought. Although she knew he was a competent pilot—he succeeded at everything he did—she still wasn't keen on the idea of her only child getting on an airplane with him at the controls. She always thought flying was something better left to professionals.

"We're probably going to fly down next Thursday and come back Sunday," he said. "Is she home yet?" Forrest never was good at keeping up with anyone else's schedule but his own.

"She gets home tomorrow afternoon. I'm not sure when she has to be back in Gainesville, but she has a week or so before next semester."

"Good, that should work out. I'll give her a call tomorrow."

"I'll let her know you'll be calling."

They finished a quick dinner and Forrest excused himself. "Sorry to eat and run, but I have another engagement. Thanks for dinner." They both stood and he gave her a peck on the cheek, but it was for show. There was no emotion there, and they both knew it.

"No problem, I understand." She gave him an air kiss, which was more than she felt like. She thought, *after all, you're a very important person. I wouldn't expect you to be saddled with me*. She watched him walk out of the restaurant and leaned back to finish her coffee.

When she got home, the kitchen was dark except for the light over the stove. Slamming her purse on the kitchen island, she went upstairs to find Eric reading in bed and Bo sleeping on his rug in the corner.

Bo raised his head, evaluating whether or not there would be scratches. He concluded there would be and got up and padded over to Carly.

Eric put his book down and smiled at her. "You must have had a meeting with the eminent doctor."

She reached down to give Bo a few scratches behind his ears. Satisfied, he trotted back over to his rug and lay down.

Her thoughts returning to Langford, Carly glared at Eric as she started taking off her jewelry. "And what makes you think that?"

"When I hear you slam your purse down in the kitchen that's a pretty good indicator you've had a close encounter." He reached out to her.

She walked over and sat on the bed. "He's such an arrogant asshole. What did I ever see in him?"

"Modest, caring, sensitive . . ."

She took her hand away and slapped his arm. "You're no help," she said, laughing. "Damn, he's such a pig."

She stood, pulled the dress over her head, and stood there in her underwear.

Eric licked his lips in an exaggerated fashion. She still had a nice figure. "His loss is my gain. Need some help getting undressed?"

She smiled, appreciating his sense of humor and attention. She unhooked her bra and threw it at him.

"No, but you better have that book closed by the time I get back in here," she said as she walked toward the bathroom. "I'm just going to have to take out my frustration on you tonight."

Chapter 4

When Carly got home from work the next day, Michelle was sitting at the breakfast room table, busy on her iPad with Bo lying at her feet. As soon as she looked up and saw Carly, she jumped up to hug her mom.

"Hi, Mom. I'm glad to see you."

Carly hugged her daughter. She was glad to see her. They were close, always had been, and seemed to get closer as Michelle got older.

"Glad to see you, too. What time did you get in?"

"About an hour ago. Eric still at work?"

"He should be home soon. How was your drive?"

"Not bad. Of course, I-75 is always jammed. Good day?"

"Okay. Just a bad week." Carly had called Michelle on Wednesday to tell her the news about Brian.

Michelle hugged her tighter than usual.

"I know. I'm so sorry, Mom. I know how close you were."

"I had dinner with your father last night," Carly said, changing the subject.

"Why?"

Carly laughed. In spite of her efforts not to disparage Forrest publicly, their perceptive daughter knew there was no love lost between her mom and dad.

"Hospital business. He wants you to go to the Keys with him next weekend," Carly said.

"Is Barbie going?" Michelle didn't care for the latest Ms. Langford.

"I think so, but you'll have to take that up with him. He said he'd call you."

Michelle shrugged. "Whatever."

The door bell rang. Michelle ran to get it, Bo right next to her, tail wagging. "It's Anna. We're going bowling tonight." She threw open the door and Anna, Michelle's best friend, walked in.

They had been best friends since they were five or six years old. Most of the pictures of Michelle included Anna. School, dance recitals, sports; they had been inseparable. Although other friends had come and gone, their friendship had stayed intact over the years.

Looking at them, Carly was still struck by how much alike they looked. Slender, but not too thin. Long brown hair framing an oval face. Brown eyes, tanned complexion and slightly upturned nose completed the picture. No tattoos, at least that Carly could see, on either one. Both were about Carly's height, but not tall enough to be a serious threat on a basketball court. They could pass for sisters. In fact, many people assumed they were.

After giving Bo a brief cuddle, Anna came over and hugged Carly.

"Hi, Ms. C."

Anna was like one of the family and had always called her that. Carly knew Michelle received a similar reception at Anna's house.

"Hi, Anna. How've you been?" she asked, as she hugged her "second" daughter.

"Good, thanks. Studying hard."

"How's school going?" Anna was going to school in Tampa at the University of South Florida. Carly always figured the two would end up at the same college, but Anna had her heart set on USF and Michelle was equally determined to go to Gainesville. College was one of the few things the two had differed on.

"Good. Two more semesters, then maybe I can talk Michelle into grad school in Tampa."

Carly turned to Michelle. "Oh, really?"

Michelle sidestepped her mom's question and started dragging Anna back out the door before Carly could grill them further.

"We won't be late, Mom. Later." Michelle waved over her shoulder and they were gone.

Carly made a mental note to ask Michelle when she was finishing her undergrad coursework and went upstairs to change. Eric wasn't home yet, and she decided to surprise him and cook dinner. She loved cooking, but didn't do it much anymore. Between her schedule and Eric's, they rarely had the time.

She came back downstairs and walked into the kitchen thinking about what to prepare. It was too late to make a trip to the market, so she'd have to make do with what was in the pantry. Opening the door, she stood there and stared at the well-stocked shelves, hoping something would speak to her. The linguine beckoned. You could never go wrong with pasta, she thought, as she took the package of linguine off the shelf.

She rummaged around a bit before she found what she was looking for, a jar of Chef Ricardo's Mediterranean Tomato Sauce. Perfect. Throw in a tossed salad, a bottle of Chianti, some bread, and voilá—dinner. Not exactly her best effort, but it would have to do.

As the pasta was cooking, she heard the garage door. Eric, a math professor at Florida Gulf Coast University, was home. Bo, who'd already heard him pull into the driveway, was standing at the garage door, tail wagging.

He walked into the kitchen, gave Bo a quick pet, and kissed Carly. That was one of the things she loved about him. Even after six years together, he still kissed her as soon as he saw her. Every time, regardless of where they were. Somehow she knew he'd do that twenty years from now.

"Something smells good," he said.

"Wish I could take credit, but Chef Ricardo bailed me out tonight. I decided to cook for us at the last minute and had to make do with what was here."

"Works for me. Anything I can do?"

"Pour us some wine after you change."

He laughed. "That I can do," he said as he went upstairs to change clothes. Carly finished making the salad and checked the sauce she had warming in the pot. She buttered the bread and put it into the oven.

Eric came back down stairs and put his arms around her waist. He nuzzled her neck, causing her to tingle. It felt good. She never got tired of him touching her.

She reached up and put her hand on his face. "If you expect me to get dinner on the table, then you better open the wine. Otherwise you're subject to be attacked." She could feel the grin spreading on his face.

"Ohh. I'm sooo scared. Promises, promises," he said as he pulled himself away from her and walked over to the wine cooler under the counter.

He pulled out a bottle of Chianti, opened it, and poured a small amount to taste. After swirling it around the glass and swishing it inside his mouth, he pronounced it acceptable and poured two generous servings. He handed one to Carly and raised his glass. "To the love of my life."

She touched her glass to his and repeated, "To the love of my life." She watched him over the top of her glass as she drank.

Damn, she thought, he's the sexiest man on the planet and she was so in love with him. With scruffy blond hair, blue eyes and ever-present tan, Eric had that "California surfer" look. He had on that ratty California t-shirt with "Cal" in the trademark script of the University of California, Berkeley, where he received his PhD. Well worn flip-flops and tattered shorts completed his wardrobe. But forget the clothes; she could devour him.

Carly had been involved in serious relationships with two of the brightest men she'd ever met. Both had IQ's off the chart. But the similarities ended there.

Forrest Langford felt compelled to constantly remind everyone of how smart he was. He was brilliant. If someone didn't believe it, all they had to do was ask and he'd confirm it. He had an opinion on every subject and was quick to make it known. Always right, he seldom had the patience to listen to anyone else's ideas.

Eric Taylor was just as intelligent. But to someone meeting him, they would never know it. It wasn't as though he came across as dull; quite the opposite. He was a great conversationalist and engaging. It was just that he never felt the need to bombard people with it at every opportunity. And he was genuinely interested in whoever he talked to. He actually listened, tending to keep his opinions to himself unless asked.

She served their plates and they retreated to the dining room, where she had lit candles for no reason at all, which was the best reason.

"I'm impressed. You could easily spoil me, you know?" he said as he sat at the table.

She pursed her lips. "I thought I already had?"

"You have, my love, you have." He reached out and touched her hand, and it was electric. "After dinner, maybe I can show you?"

Carly blushed as she smiled and said, "You're on."

Content dessert was settled, he said, "I see Michelle made it home."

She had a puzzled look, then remembered Michelle's car was parked in the driveway.

"Yes, about an hour ago. She and Anna left to go bowling just before you got home."

Eric laughed. "I don't expect we'll see much of her during her break except in passing. She has to catch up with her friends."

"Maybe we can corral her for dinner one night. I didn't get a chance to tell you last night, but Paul Leggett's in town for the funeral. He stopped by the office yesterday, said they want to promote me as soon as he can clear it with Carter Freeman."

"That's great news. You deserve it."

"I just feel kinda strange about it, getting promoted this way. I mean, I thought it would happen one day, but only when Brian retired."

"Love, fate played a hand in it. I know you're sad about Brian's death, but things happen. And Brian would have wanted you to take his position if something happened."

Carly shrugged. "Well, it's not final yet."

"Sounds like a formality. We'll have to celebrate when it's official."

"We're meeting Paul for brunch in the morning. Hope that's okay."

"Sure, I'd blocked out tomorrow anyway."

They continued chatting about their respective days as they ate, enjoying each other's company as always. That was another thing about Eric, Carly thought. He's my best friend.

Chapter 5

Saint Luke's Episcopal Church was packed. It was a beautiful old church only a few doors down from Thomas Edison's winter home. The oldest church in Fort Myers, and one of the largest, it was standing room only. They had made arrangements for the service to be shown on video screens set up in the auditorium next to the church to accommodate the overflow, and it, too, was packed.

Along with Paul Leggett, Carly, Eric, Michelle, and Anna sat in the row behind the family where Dorothy and her sister Janie sat. George and Martha sat in the pew on the other side of Dorothy. The Jennings had no children, and Carly knew of no other living family.

Father Cowan had just started his sermon. Although he wasn't the one who had married Dorothy and Brian Jennings some forty-three years ago in this very church, he related the story to the audience. It was a touching account about a beloved couple who had been a cornerstone of this community for so many years. Father Cowan told the story well, and by the time he was finished, there wasn't a dry eye in the place.

The fact that so many people were at the service was a testimony to how well liked Brian Jennings was. Carly still couldn't believe that he was gone. He'd played such an important part in her life, and in the blink of an eye he was dead. She squeezed Eric's hand a little harder as if to confirm that he wouldn't meet the same fate.

Dorothy held her head up high. As George had said, she was stronger than she looked. She smiled as Father Cowan told the story of their marriage, no doubt thinking back to the fond memories of that day.

Carly hoped she and Eric would have the kind of relationship Brian and Dorothy had. She'd always been envious of the couple, and it was only when she met Eric that she started to understand what true love really meant. It was a selfish thought, but if they couldn't die together, then she hoped she passed away before Eric. Carly couldn't imagine confronting what Dorothy was facing.

After the service, the family stood outside the church and greeted the throngs of people who'd come to pay their last respects. Dorothy was gracious as she accepted the condolences of everyone who stopped. When she saw Carly, she put her arms around the younger woman as if to comfort her once more.

"He was so proud of you, Carly. Don't forget that."

Carly couldn't help but start sniffling as the widow held her. She tried to speak, but all she could get out between sobs was, "I'm so sorry, Dorothy."

"I know, sweetie. We'll make it, though. That's what he'd want us to do."

Carly nodded and pulled away from her, almost ashamed of taking so much of the new widow's time. She walked down the steps to compose herself.

Paul soon joined them. "Nice service." He looked around at the crowd. "Lot of people here."

"He was very well liked and respected. We're going to miss him," Carly said.

"I hate to run, but I have to catch a plane. Enjoyed the brunch this morning. Let me know if you need anything, Carly. I'll be in touch next week." He turned to shake Eric's hand. "Nice to see you again, Eric."

They stood there as Paul walked away. Michelle and Anna walked up behind them. Michelle put an arm around Carly's waist and Anna did likewise on the other side. Carly hugged them both, grateful for their support and concern.

"You okay?" Michelle asked.

Carly nodded, still holding both the girls.

"It's been a long week. I'm glad that part is over."

"His wife seems to be doing well," Michelle said.

"She is such a sweet lady," Anna said, holding Carly close.

"Yes, Dorothy's a strong woman. But the reality will set in soon, after all the commotion is over. That's when it'll hit her the hardest."

"We're probably going out to the beach. I was going to spend the night at Anna's, if that's okay. Maybe we could do brunch tomorrow?" Michelle said. She and Anna hadn't gone out with them earlier.

"That'd be nice. You girls be careful. Remember the rule."

"No problem," they said in unison.

They each gave Eric a hug and walked away, neither needing to be reminded. The rule, as it was called, referred to something that Carly and Eric had drilled into their heads from the moment the girls got their driver's licenses. No drinking and driving, and no riding with someone driving who'd been drinking. If they needed a ride, all they had to do was call—anytime, no questions asked.

As the crowd started to thin out, George walked up to her. Eric excused himself to chat with a fellow faculty member he spotted a few yards away.

"What a turnout, huh? Good thing they set up in the auditorium," George said.

"I know. I don't think I've ever seen so many people at a funeral before. Father Cowan did an excellent job."

"Yes, he did." George's eyes were moist. "I don't think the reality has set in yet. I keep thinking he's just away or something and we'll see him again tomorrow or the next day."

Carly felt her eyes tear up. "I know what you mean, George. I feel the same way. I wasn't ready for this."

They stood there silently next to each other for a few minutes. Neither could say anything, not that anything else needed to be said.

George broke the silence. "I should be getting back to Martha and Dorothy. I think they're about ready for the graveside service."

Dorothy had requested a private interment for family only, which of course included Martha and George. It wasn't a matter of excluding others, but more a practical limitation of little room in the columbarium and an easy way of paring the invited list.

Carly leaned over and hugged George. "Damn, this is hard. I miss him."

George hugged her back with equal intensity. "So do I." He pulled back and walked away, unable to look at her.

Eric walked over and, knowing what to do, took her in his arms. The dam burst and tears flowed once again on his shoulder as he patted her back.

"It's all right, love. I know you miss him."

After a few minutes, the tears stopped. She was still amazed there were any left. They said their final goodbyes to the dwindling crowd and made their way to the car. Eric drove and Carly held his hand the entire way home.

When they got home, they went out to the lanai and sat beside the pool. Eric poured them each a glass of wine.

"I'm glad the funeral is over. Good thing it's Saturday; I'm wiped out. I just feel like sitting out here all afternoon," she said.

"Well, then, you should." He put his hand over hers. "Take the afternoon off. We didn't have anything planned. I'll fix us some dinner later and we can sit out here as long as you like."

She squeezed his hand and nodded. They sat there for the longest time without saying a word. Bo was stretched out with his head down between his paws watching the waterfall in the pool. But it was a comfortable silence, the kind that occurs between the best of friends, with neither feeling compelled to fill the void with idle chatter.

After a while, Eric got up. "I'm going to start dinner."

Out of habit, Carly started to get up to join him.

"Sit," he commanded. "You're off today, remember?" He stood over her as she slid back down into the lounge chair.

"Yes, sir," she replied, a thin smile crossing her lips.

He returned the smile, leaned down, and kissed her forehead, then walked into the kitchen.

She must have drifted off to sleep, because the next thing she knew, Eric was bringing plates out to the small table on the lanai. The table had been set with a bottle of Sauvignon Blanc in the middle.

"Ah, I see you're awake. Must be the smell of this delicious dinner I prepared." He laughed.

Carly inhaled, and indeed, did get a whiff of something good. "What are we having?" she asked.

"Grouper Mediterranean. My secret recipe. And you thought I couldn't cook, didn't you?"

She laughed. Eric wasn't known for his prowess in the kitchen. But she appreciated his effort. She got up, moved over to the table, and sat down. On the plate was a sautéed piece of fresh grouper with Kalamata olives over rice. It looked yummy. She didn't realize how hungry she was. She picked up the bottle of wine and looked at Eric with a wary eye.

"I'm going to pretend that this is the only bottle you opened this afternoon. Otherwise, I might get the idea that you're plying me with alcohol to take advantage of me."

He looked at her and grinned. "But of course. We've only had a glass so far. But I still reserve the right to try to take advantage of you."

Turning her attention to the food, she said, "This looks wonderful." She put a forkful into her mouth. "Mmmm, Eric, this is delicious! You've been holding out on me. You can cook!"

"Glad you like it. Just following an old adage of a chef friend of mine—get them hungry enough and they'll like anything you feed them."

They finished dinner, with Eric insisting on cleaning up. Carly had to admit, it was nice being pampered. It did her more good than she realized. After he'd finished cleaning up, they retired to the lounge chairs where they proceeded to finish the bottle of wine.

When they went to bed, Eric was prepared to let her go to sleep. He knew it had been a stressful and exhausting day, despite her earlier comments. But after a few minutes of cuddling, she realized she wanted him, needed him. She whispered into his ear, "Make love to me."

And he did. It was the most tender and caring lovemaking she could remember.

Chapter 6

Michelle and Anna were in Michelle's car on their way to Fort Myers Beach. They were headed to the Tiki Hut, a popular beach bar for the college crowd, where they were meeting Joshua and Ryan, the two boys they'd met last night.

The girls had gone bowling at Gator Lanes. Crowded, as usual, on a Friday night, there was a long wait for a lane. They met a couple of guys who were also waiting and decided to bowl together as soon as either twosome could get a lane.

It turned out to be a great evening. They hit it off with the boys and ended up having a wonderful time. At the end of the evening, they agreed to meet at the beach the next night.

Typical on the beach, parking was a problem, especially on a Saturday night. After driving around for fifteen minutes, they found a spot in a pay lot a block away. It was the best they could do without paying for valet parking, which was too expensive.

They walked through the small parking lot in front of the Tiki Hut. It was jammed, valet parking only, and the kids in khaki shorts and white shirts were running back and forth, taking and delivering cars to the front entrance.

The Hut, as the locals called it, had been there for years. It was an institution on Fort Myers Beach. Several years ago, they built a new building on Estero Boulevard to attract an older and more moneyed crowd. It was air-conditioned, with a separate restaurant and new bar equipped with flat-screen televisions throughout. They also added a new menu, with more items and higher prices.

The old Tiki Hut, nothing but a dumpy outdoor beach bar, was still standing, located between the new building and the beach. They had live music Wednesday through Saturday nights, and it was still the hangout of choice for the younger set. But other than the beach, there was no way to get to the original bar without first going through the new building. Presumably, this was to tempt patrons into eating in the restaurant.

Michelle and Anna just pointed back to the beach when they walked in and were greeted by the hostess, who nodded and moved on to assist the next group. They went through the glass doors and found themselves on the deck of the bar. It was early for college students, but the place was already crowded. Anna went to claim two stools they spotted on the rail facing the beach, and Michelle muscled her way to the bar to get them a couple of beers.

She caught the eye of Mike, one of the bartenders she knew, and raised two fingers.

He brought over two Coronas and Michelle handed him a ten.

"Hey, Michelle. How are you?" the stocky, well-muscled young man with spiked hair asked.

"Good, thanks." She pointed over to the rail where Anna waved. "Anna went to grab a couple of seats. Busy already, huh?"

"Yeah, you know how it is. No complaints. How's school?"

"Good. You still thinking about going back?"

"Maybe next semester. Still trying to save up a few bucks."

"Good luck." Michelle grabbed the two beers and turned away. "Later. Thanks, Mike."

Michelle and Anna had been there often enough that Mike knew the difference was his tip, which was also why he didn't bother to check IDs. He knew they were legal.

She sat on the stool next to Anna. After clinking the cans—no bottles, this was a true beach bar—they both took a swallow. They had interpreted the rule to mean one drink, which they normally followed, and took turns being the designated driver. One partied while the other nursed her drink the entire evening. Tonight was Michelle's turn to drive, so this beer would have to last a while. She glanced back at the crowd and saw Joshua and Ryan making their way over to them.

"Don't look—they're here," Michelle said to Anna.

The guys walked up and greeted them. No stools were available, so the boys stood and chatted until they managed to commandeer two more stools. They picked up where they left off last night. Ryan and Anna were getting along well, which was good. That gave Michelle and Joshua a chance to get to know each other without having to worry about their pals.

Anna and the two guys finished their beer and the guys got up to get another round. Joshua asked Michelle if she was ready for another. She said no and explained that she was the designated driver tonight.

"That's cool," Joshua said. "I respect that." When Ryan brought the fresh beers, Joshua nursed his along with Michelle to show his support. Facing no restraints and knowing they had someone sober to take care of them, Ryan and Anna didn't hold back.

It was after one by the time they left. After an evening of dancing and walking on the beach, the boys walked them to their car with promises to get in touch later.

Sunday morning, Michelle got home around ten. Eric and Carly were waiting and the three of them left for brunch. They went to Karsten's, a downtown Fort Myers landmark on the river just a few blocks from the Edison home. The restaurant was in an old house and retained the charm of a bygone era. A popular spot, Carly got special consideration based on her position at the hospital and was able to get them a table at the last minute.

They were seated at a table in the glass-enclosed courtyard. For the last half hour, including the drive from the house, all Michelle had talked about was Joshua. She told them how they met and everything she knew about her latest crush, even including the part of him observing the rule with her.

"He's smart." Michelle looked at Eric. "You'd like him."

"So where's he from?" Eric asked.

"Fort Myers. He grew up here. Went off to the University of Florida, graduated, and came back home. He works at the Toyota place."

"So when do we get to meet this Joshua?" Carly asked.

"I don't know—maybe before I go back to school. We'll see."

"Does he have family still here?"

"Not sure. He doesn't talk much about it. I think maybe his mom still lives here—I don't know. His dad passed away some time ago."

"No brothers or sisters?"

"An aunt, in Tampa, I think. They're not close."

Carly decided to take advantage of the opening. "Speaking of Tampa, what was that Anna was saying about you going to grad school in Tampa?"

Michelle looked from Carly to Eric and back. "Just Anna talking, that's all."

"Does that mean you're going to be finished in two semesters?" Carly asked.

"Um, close, I think."

"Can we be a little more specific?" Carly was getting tired of this routine.

Michelle looked at Eric, hoping for some help. He obliged.

"So sometime next year, for sure?" he asked.

"Oh, yes," she said, thankful for the lifeline. "I mean, I may have one more semester after the next two. Something about one of my credits for my major. I'm supposed to meet with my advisor when I get back to Gainesville."

About that time, the server brought their food, further saving the day for Michelle. Eric deftly changed the subject, telling them a story about one of his students not being able to answer a simple math question.

"The first day of class, I asked a student what's unique about the number two? Now this is an advanced class, mind you. Of course, everyone in the class was shaking their heads, rolling their eyes, and anxious to answer."

"Well, duh," Michelle said. "Even I know the answer to that. It's the only even prime number."

"Very good. I'm proud of you; maybe you need to change your major. Would you believe he never did give me the correct answer?"

"I'm not sure I would've known the answer to that," Carly said.

"But you're not a math major," Eric said. "Any math major knows the answer."

"Oh, I forgot to tell you—my car's been acting funny," Michelle said.

"Acting funny?" Eric asked.

"Yeah, sometimes the speedometer quits working. All the gauges do. Then in a few minutes, it starts working again."

"How often has it happened?"

"Uh, once, maybe twice, I think."

"Sounds like we need to take it in and have it checked."

"Yeah, I told Joshua about it. He said if we brought it in, he'd look at it himself."

"Well, I'll call tomorrow and make an appointment. I can take it in, get a ride back to the hospital, and you can pick it up tomorrow afternoon," Carly said.

"That'll work. I think Anna and I are going to the beach tomorrow, so I'll get her to pick me up."

"You talk to your dad about going to the Keys?"

Michelle rolled her eyes. "Yeah, he called. I told him I'd go. And yes, Barbie's going. He said we'd leave Thursday or Friday and be back Sunday afternoon."

"Good. You'll have a good time, and I know he's looking forward to it."

Michelle shrugged. "I'll be glad to see him. And it is nice down there."

Chapter 7

Monday morning, Carly took Michelle's car by the Toyota dealer on the way to work. The service advisor, a young black man, came out with his clipboard as soon as she pulled up under the service canopy and waited for her to exit the vehicle.

"Good morning, ma'am. Welcome to Gulf Toyota." He stuck his hand out. "I'm Frank Bowman."

Carly shook his hand and introduced herself.

"Carly Nelson."

"Ms. Nelson, what could I do for you today?"

"I called earlier and made an appointment for my daughter's car," she said, gesturing to the maroon Camry next to her. "She said the gauges occasionally quit working."

"Okay. Let me get a little information from you. We'll get it in and taken care of." He flipped through the pages on his clipboard, found the form he was looking for, and made some notes. "What's the best number to get in touch with you?"

Carly gave him her cell number. He verified her address, then looked at the VIN through the windshield and verified it against what was on the form. Frank switched the car on to get the mileage. After he entered it on the form, he presented it to her and indicated where she should sign, authorizing the work.

"Will you need a ride this morning?" he asked as she was signing the work order.

"Yes, just downtown to Rivers Hospital."

"No problem. If you want to follow me to the courtesy lounge, our driver will be leaving soon. You can get a cup of coffee while you wait, though it shouldn't be long."

Carly followed him inside and he showed her where the coffee was located.

Frank handed her his card. "We'll give you a call just as soon as it's done."

She thanked him and helped herself to a cup of coffee. Noticing a stack of current *USA Today* newspapers, she picked one up and sat in a comfortable looking chair. The only other person in the lounge was a middle-aged man sitting across the room on the sofa talking on his cell phone. She took a sip of her coffee, placed it on the table next to her chair, and started reading the front page.

Half a cup later, a neatly dressed older gentleman wearing a knit shirt with the dealer logo on it walked into the room and announced the shuttle was leaving for those needing a ride. Carly folded her paper and picked up her coffee cup. As she followed the man out to the waiting van, she noticed the other man was still on the phone, apparently having made other arrangements or waiting on his vehicle. He was still talking as she walked out the door.

The shuttle driver opened the rear right-side door of the van and offered his hand as she stepped up into the nicely appointed vehicle. He gently shut the door and walked around to the driver's side. Buckling his seatbelt and closing his door, he spoke. "Looks like you get private limo service this morning. Where may I take you?"

"Downtown to Rivers Hospital. The main entrance, thank you."

The driver said no more, content to concentrate on his driving. Carly opened the newspaper and continued reading where she had left off in the courtesy lounge. She was still reading when fifteen minutes later she realized the van had pulled up to the main entrance of the hospital. As before, the elderly man left the van running while he walked around to open the door for her. She took his hand as she stepped out and thanked him for the ride.

"Will you need transportation back to the dealership later today?" he asked.

"No, thank you. My daughter is picking me up. At least she's supposed to." Carly laughed.

The man laughed at her comment and handed her a business card. "Just in case. That's my cell phone if you need a ride."

She looked at the card. Matthew Giden. "Thank you, Matthew. Have a good day."

Carly turned and walked into the main entrance. She liked to go in that way sometimes just to see it from a visitor's perspective. Something she'd learned from Brian, she thought.

Volunteers manned the front desk, and they acknowledged her as she walked past. The lobby, though bustling with people, was clean and attractive. She reminded herself to compliment the head of housekeeping for a job well done.

She got off the elevator and walked into her office. Sandy was on the phone and waved at her as she walked past. As soon as she sat in her chair, she pulled up her calendar. The morning was full of meetings and the afternoon didn't look much better. Looking at the clock on the screen, she realized she had half an hour before her first meeting, and she decided to go through her email.

Carly was thinking about Paul Leggett's implied promise to promote her. Like she told Eric, she knew she could handle it and it was her goal. She just figured it would happen when Brian Jennings retired. She knew it was silly, but it somehow seemed tainted this way.

Her thoughts were interrupted when a young man appeared in Carly's office door. He was average height and thin, with a dark brown ponytail. She glanced at the name on her computerized appointment book and back at the kid.

"Hello, Wayne. Come on in and have a seat." The kid in the doorway hesitated and walked into Carly's office without speaking. Carly met him halfway and shook his hand. Upon closer examination, she could swear the kid had acne. Carly noticed a scraggly goatee on his chin.

Wayne sat and fidgeted. He crossed his legs and uncrossed them. He opened his notebook and looked up at Carly.

"Ms. Nelson, Ron had an out of town commitment today and couldn't be here. He called and asked your assistant if it would be all right for me to come in his place, and she said it would be." Wayne spoke as if he were reading from a rehearsed script.

"Please, call me Carly. This is nothing formal." Carly tried to put him at ease.

"I'm sure Ron explained to you that I meet with each of the department heads periodically just to get a face-to-face update on what's going on. It's not a trial." Carly laughed, hoping the nervous young man in front of her would relax.

Wayne turned loose a little smile before tensing again. He looked down at his notebook and got right down to business.

"The EMR project is on schedule, with the pilot unit, Two East, on track to—"

Carly interrupted. "Wayne, before we get down to business, tell me a little about you. I've seen you around the hospital before, but we haven't had the chance to get to know one another." Carly was determined to get him to lighten up a bit.

Wayne looked up from his notebook and glanced to each side, as if making sure the question was indeed directed to him. He paused, as if uncertain how to answer.

"Uh, I, I've been working here at the hospital for about a year."

Carly jumped in with a couple of questions to help him out.

"So, were you in Fort Myers? Or did you move here? Where did you work before you came here?"

Wayne twisted in his seat a bit. "I moved when I got the job here at Rivers. I was working in Orlando for a computer support vendor. They got bought out by another company and I wanted to make a change."

Talking about something more comfortable relaxed him, and it showed.

Carly threw out another question to keep the momentum going. "What do you do outside work? Any hobbies?"

"I build computers. I'm basically just a computer geek." He smiled as he said the words.

"Build computers? Wow, I'm impressed. I can barely operate one."

"It's not that hard." Wayne sat up a little straighter in his chair. "But I like doing it. Plus, it's a lot cheaper than buying one. I could never afford to buy one like I can build."

"Now I know who to call when I need help with my home computer." Carly laughed, watching the kid across from him finally laugh a bit, more at ease now.

"How did you learn to do that?" she asked.

"Some classes. Mostly just taking things apart and putting them back together. Trial and error."

"The problem I have when I do that is I always have some extra parts left over," she said. They both laughed out loud.

"How do you like working at Rivers so far?" Carly steered the conversation back to work.

"Oh, I like it a lot. The people are nice and the hospital has some cool projects going on."

"That's good to hear, Wayne. I'm glad it was a good move for you. I know Ron's glad to have someone with your experience and skills in his group. So tell me a little about what's going on with some of these cool projects."

Wayne started to look back at his prepared notes.

"Don't bother with the notes, Wayne. Just talk to me. Tell me in your own words. I get enough formal feedback in the management meetings and status reports. Like I said, this is more like a chat at lunch or walking down the hall kind of thing, nothing more. No hidden agenda, I promise."

Wayne started talking about some of the projects that the Information Technology Department was working on. Some of it was information that Carly had already heard through other channels, but a few tidbits surfaced that she filed away for future reference. Issues or potential issues surfaced in these meetings, which was why Carly continued Brian's tradition of doing them. The thought of Brian caused Carly to drift away. Wayne's voice brought him back.

"Ms. Nelson?" The kid wasn't going to call her by her first name, so she gave up.

"I'm sorry, Wayne. Something just reminded me of Brian Jennings, and I lost my focus there for a minute. I apologize. You were saying?"

At the mention of Brian, the young man seemed to shrink in front of Carly's eyes. He looked down at his shoes.

"I'm sorry about Mr. Jennings. He was a nice man."

"Yes, he was. Like most everyone else here, I miss him."

"Do they know what happened?"

"The police think he either had a heart attack or just fell asleep driving home. His truck veered off the causeway into the water."

Wayne looked out the window past Carly.

"He really was a nice man. I'm sorry he's gone."

Carly was surprised at how sad the young man looked. "You sound like you knew him?"

Wayne turned his attention back to Carly. "I'm sorry, what?"

"You sound like you knew him."

"Not really. I was just thinking about when I first moved to Fort Myers. I was walking back to my apartment late one afternoon after work. My truck had broken down, and I didn't have the money to get it fixed. I'd just moved here, so I spent all I had on deposits and stuff and hadn't got my first check yet.

"Like I said, I was walking home from the hospital, and this big pickup truck pulls over, and the old man driving offered me a lift. He didn't even ask where I was going, just pulled over and said he was headed my way and asked did I want a ride. I didn't think about it at the time; it was hot, and I was just glad to get a ride.

"Anyway, he asked where he could take me and I told him the name of the apartment complex, and he said that was right on his way. So he starts talking to me, asking me about myself and what I was doing in Fort Myers, you know, that kind of stuff. I told him I had just started working at the hospital and had moved here from Orlando and my pickup was broke and everything. He was easy to talk to, real friendly and all.

"We get to my apartment, and as I start to get out, he hands me a hundred dollar bill! Says it's to help me get my feet on the ground. I tell him that, no, I can't take that, the ride was plenty, and I appreciated his help. Well, he insists, then I start wondering, like you know, what's the catch? And he insists I take the money, just tells me that someone helped him out before when he was down and he just wants to keep it going, that's all. So I take the money, and he holds out his hand to shake mine and says his name is Brian Jennings. And then he drives off. Never said anything at all about who he was. Then a couple of weeks later, at our department meeting, this guy walks in and Ron introduces him as the CEO! It was him, the same guy who gave me a ride and a hundred bucks! I about crapped in my pants!"

Carly's eyes moistened as she listened to the young man's story. "That sounds just like him, Wayne. I've known Brian—knew him, for eight years and he was always doing stuff like that. I'm glad you got to meet him. He was the real deal. Thanks for sharing that story." Carly thought she noticed Wayne's eyes glisten a bit, too.

They went back to talking about IT projects, with Carly making mental notes. Wayne mentioned a couple of things that Carly wanted to follow-up on with Ron, Wayne's boss. Carly waited until Wayne left to write down her notes, since she didn't want to disturb the informal atmosphere.

Mid-afternoon her cell phone on the corner of her desk buzzed. She picked it up, but didn't recognize the number.

"Hello?" she answered.

"Ms. Nelson? This is Frank Bowman at Gulf Toyota."

"Oh, hi."

"I was calling about your Toyota Camry. Your car is ready to go."

"Great, thank you. What time do you close?"

"Six o'clock."

"Okay, my daughter will be there to pick it up before then."

"You're welcome. We appreciate your business. When she comes in, tell her to just go straight to the cashier's window next to the customer lounge. They'll have the keys."

Carly pressed End and looked at the clock on her screen. It was 4:10. She called Michelle.

"Hey, Mom."

"Hey, Sweetie. They just called and your car is ready. Do you want to come by and pick me up? They close at six."

"Sure. What time is it now?"

"Ten after four."

"Can I go by and pick it up on my way into town? We're out at the beach. I rode with Anna, so we have to go by the Toyota place anyway. Then I could just come get you in my car."

It made sense, Carly thought. "Sure. Just make sure you get there by six. Go to the Service Department and look for the Cashier's window next to the Customer Lounge."

"No problem. See you later."

At six thirty, Michelle walked into Carly's office.

"Hi, Mom. Ready to leave?"

"In a few. Car okay?"

"Yeah. I talked to Josh. He said it was some instrument panel module. Nothing major. Anyway, they replaced it, shouldn't have anymore problems."

"Great. Give me a few minutes to wrap up a couple of things and I'll be ready."

After Carly got to a stopping point, she logged off her computer and gathered her belongings. Michelle drove them home.

Eric's car was in the garage when they drove up. They walked in and Carly could smell something cooking. He was standing at the stove in his usual shorts and t-shirt, barefoot.

"What's for dinner?" Carly asked.

"Gourmet Mexican food," he replied and gave Carly a kiss as she walked up.

"Tacos?" She looked at the box next to the pan on the stove.

"But that's not all. We have tortilla chips, salsa, guacamole and—my famous margaritas!"

Carly and Michelle both laughed.

"Sounds good to me," Michelle said.

"I like the margarita part," Carly said. "Will you make me one while I go change?"

"Absolutely."

She left Michelle and Eric chatting about the day as she went upstairs to change. The two had always gotten along. It was a difficult role as a step parent, but Eric handled it well. He had given Michelle her space and let her warm to him. He treated her with respect without trying to be her "bud," and it had paid off. Carly knew Michelle loved her dad, but thought she was probably closer to Eric.

Changed into shorts and a tank top, Carly made her way back into the kitchen. She smiled when she heard the laughter of her daughter's voice and wondered what that was about. They were sitting at the breakfast table with a salt-rimmed margarita in front of Eric. A second glass was on the table waiting for Carly.

"You two sound like you're having too good of a time. What was so funny?" Carly asked.

Michelle was still laughing. "Mom, Eric was telling me about this math problem he gave his students. Even I knew the answer."

They both started chuckling again as they thought about it.

"Let's move into the dining room. Everything's on the table," Eric said. "And Michelle can tell you the story as soon as she can quit laughing."

With that, Michelle broke out in even more laughter, tears in her eyes. Carly couldn't wait to hear this one.

"So, Mom. If it takes five cats five minutes to catch five mice, how long will it take one hundred cats to catch one hundred mice?"

Carly looked at the two of them, both grinning. Her initial answer, which she thankfully didn't verbalize, was one hundred minutes. Then she realized the answer was still five minutes.

"Five minutes, of course," she said, smiling.

Michelle held up her fist for a fist bump. "Way to go, Mom. Can you believe out of a class full of math majors, only two got it right?"

Eric shook his head. "Pretty sad, huh? I've got my work cut out for me this semester."

As they were finishing dinner, Michelle's phone rang. She looked at her phone and cocked her head sideways. Getting up from the table, she answered it.

"Hello?" she said. When she heard the voice on the other end, she broke out into a big grin and looked at her mom.

"Oh, hey. Yeah, a little surprised."

Carly could tell it was someone Michelle didn't know well, but was glad to hear from, judging from the size of the grin on her face.

"Don't know. Anna's coming over and we thought about going to a movie. Sure. Okay. See you later." Michelle hung up and put the phone down. "That was Josh. He wanted to know what I was doing tonight, and it looks like he and Ryan are going to the movies with us."

Carly noticed that Joshua had become Josh. "Sounds like everyone has become fast friends."

Michelle shrugged. "Yeah, they're fun to hang out with."

"So . . . when do we get to meet Josh?"

"I dunno, soon."

Carly wanted to ask more, but when Michelle changed the subject, she didn't want to pry. She wasn't being nosy; it was just that Michelle had a tendency to fall hard, so Carly was a bit concerned. At least Josh had a good job, more than she could say for the last one, an unemployed musician. She just didn't want Michelle to get hurt.

Chapter 8

Keith Davis, the Operating Room manager, was sitting in Carly's office for their monthly meeting. They were almost done when she remembered her meeting with Langford.

"I almost forgot. Langford jumped me at dinner the other night. About getting out of the OR late," Carly said.

Keith shook his head. "I warned you. I'm sure he made it out to be my fault."

Carly laughed. "Of course. You don't think that Doctor Langford had any culpability, do you?"

"He added three—"

Carly held her hand up and interrupted. "You don't have to defend yourself, Keith. Believe me. I know what an ass he can be. Remember, I was once married to him. A fact I'm not proud of, by the way."

This time Keith laughed. "He's such a prima donna. We try our best to accommodate him, but you can only do so much."

"I understand. I think you and your staff do a great job. And I know you bend over backwards to take care of him. I was just filling you in. What else is going on?"

Keith had already covered everything on his list and started to get up to leave.

"That's about it. Unless you can help me get my identity fixed."

"What do you mean?" Carly asked.

"Yesterday my bank called. Someone lifted my credit card number and went shopping."

"That's scary. Do you know how it happened?"

"Not a clue. I'm usually pretty careful about that sort of stuff. Fortunately, your liability is limited on credit cards. But it's still a hassle, cancelling the old card, getting a new card."

She shook her head. "I can imagine. Good luck," she said.

"Thanks." Keith walked out and Carly turned her attention to her computer screen to check her next appointment.

Around three, her cell phone buzzed. She picked it up and read the text from Michelle.

Date w J 2nite PMU @8 Wil u b there?

Guess that means they're not staying for dinner, Carly thought. She let Michelle know she'd be home, and less than a minute later, Michelle texted back.

K CU then

Well, at least she was going to meet Josh. Michelle had been out with him the last three days and seemed to be taken with him. He sounded like a mature and responsible young man, unlike the musician. Fortunately, Michelle's attention span seemed to wane quickly, so Carly wasn't too worried.

She called Eric, preferring the old-fashioned way of communicating with him.

"Hey, love. What's up?" he answered.

"Just heard from Michelle. Josh's picking her up at eight tonight and she wanted to know if we were going to be home. I think this is our shot at an official meet and greet."

There was silence on the line. Eric was checking his schedule, Carly knew.

"Cool. That should work. I've got a six o'clock, but shouldn't last more than an hour. Should be home by seven thirty at the latest," he said.

"Good. She wants us to meet him, and I want to meet him, too."

"I understand," Eric said. He could take a hint. "I'll be there. See you later."

Carly pressed End and set the phone on her desk. She looked at her calendar to see if she could get out of the office a little early. She wanted to tidy up a bit. Not that the house was a wreck or anything, but she just wanted to check and make sure it was neat.

Her last appointment was also at six, so that worked out well. With any luck, she should be home just after seven.

When she pulled into the garage at seven fifteen, Eric's car was already there. He was standing in the kitchen sorting through the mail, saw Carly, and walked over to give her a kiss. Bo came over to Carly, hoping to get some pets.

"I can't believe you beat me home," she said to Eric, reaching down to scratch Bo.

"I got the drift. This is important, so I left immediately after my meeting."

She kissed him again. "Thanks. I'm just a bit sensitive when it comes to someone seeing my little girl."

Eric laughed. "I understand. Hey, I claim her as my daughter, too. So I've prepared a few questions for the young man." He pulled a thick folder out of his backpack and held it up.

Carly cracked up. "Oh, yes, that will endear us both to Michelle." She knew Eric was kidding about the folder, but not about his feelings for Michelle. Josh was going to be grilled, even if it was subtle.

They scurried about the house, picking up and arranging various things in their appropriate spots. Thirty minutes later, Michelle walked in. Bo appeared from nowhere and was glued to her side.

"Hi, guys. What's going on?" she asked, as she watched Carly and Eric walking around the house.

"Just tidying up a bit," Carly answered. "Didn't want the place to look like a dump."

Eric looked at Michelle and threw up his hands. Michelle grinned and shook her head.

"It's no big deal. He's just coming by to pick me up."

Carly looked at her daughter and could tell that, although she was protesting, she was pleased that her mom and stepdad were there and wanted to make a good impression.

"So where are you two going?" Carly asked.

"Don't know, probably just out to the Tiki Hut. They've got a new band tonight and Josh knows the lead singer. We'll probably stop and get a bite to eat first. I've got to change. He'll be here soon."

Michelle went to her room, while Eric poured him and Carly a glass of wine. Bo followed them as they walked out to the lanai. They sat at the table while Bo lay down at their feet between them.

Carly started telling Eric about her conversation with Wayne. Bo raised his head up and started toward the front door. About that time, the door chime sounded, announcing the arrival of Josh. Michelle peeked through the curtain in her bedroom, which faced the lanai, and pointed toward the front of the house. Carly just nodded and got up to answer the door.

At the door, she saw Bo stiffen and glimpsed his teeth. He couldn't bark—the result of abuse when he was a puppy before Carly and Eric had rescued him from the animal shelter. But she could tell he wasn't happy.

She looked out the peephole in the door and saw a clean cut, blond young man standing in front of the door. He was dressed in plaid shorts, an Abercrombie t-shirt and flip-flops. Neat, but sufficiently hip.

Carly cracked the door and Bo stuck his nose through the crack. She was surprised. Although loyal and protective, Bo was more likely to lick a stranger to death than attack, yet he appeared ready to go after Josh.

"Bo. Stay." He followed Carly's command, but sat as lightly as he could, as if waiting for any excuse to go after the young man on the other side of the door.

"Bo is acting up a bit, so just ignore him. Sometimes he gets that way with strangers," Carly lied as she opened the door farther. She kept her left hand on Bo's collar as she extended her right hand.

"I'm Carly, Michelle's mom. Nice to meet you, Joshua. Come on in."

"Josh Mills. Everybody calls me Josh. Nice to meet you, Ms. Nelson." He eyed the big black dog as he walked through the door, careful not to get too close.

Carly could feel Bo tense against his collar.

"I didn't hear him bark," he said.

"He's a rescue dog. His voice box was damaged when he was a puppy. He can't bark," she said. She kept a tight grip on Bo's collar as she walked out to the lanai.

Josh followed Carly out to the lanai, keeping an eye on the dog. He hesitated as Eric rose, then stuck out his hand and introduced himself.

"Josh Mills."

"Eric Taylor, Michelle's stepdad."

"Nice to meet you, sir. Michelle tells me you're a professor out at Gulf Coast."

Carly picked up on the sir. She led Bo over next to Eric and told him to lie down. He complied, but still kept his alert eyes on Josh.

"Yes, I am. Have a seat," Eric said. "Michelle should just be a few minutes."

After they all sat around the small table, Eric picked up the conversation.

"So, are you from Fort Myers?" Eric asked. His manner was relaxed and inviting, but Carly knew the interrogation had begun. She was glad Eric was doing it. He had a way of disarming people from the beginning. She would have been more obvious.

They chatted for five or ten minutes, learning that Josh was from Fort Myers, his father had passed away almost seven years ago, he was an only child and worked as a Senior Technician at Gulf Toyota, where he had worked for two years since graduating from the University of Florida.

Before they could learn anything else, Michelle appeared and rescued him.

"I'm sure they got your life history," Michelle said as she looked at her mother.

Josh shrugged. "I think we finished the first five pages."

Everyone laughed. Carly was glad to see he had a sense of humor.

"She's my favorite daughter."

"Mom, you've been saying that since I was little. I'm your only daughter."

Carly put her arm around her daughter. "So?"

Eric shook Josh's hand. "Nice to meet you, Josh. Have a good time, but be careful." The tone was friendly enough, but the point was made, father to suitor. Carly didn't miss it and neither did Josh.

The kids walked out. Eric and Carly sat back down and gave the reviews.

"You first, Mom," Eric said.

"He's cute. Polite, but also playing to the audience, I think. Seems to be bright. You got in a lot of questions for a short period of time. And I caught your threat at the end."

"What threat?" Eric looked innocent.

Carly ignored his question. "He heard you, trust me. Must be a father-daughter thing, because it went right over Michelle's head." She reached out and took Eric's hand. "And thank you."

Eric opened his mouth to say something, then closed it.

"So what did you think, professor?" Carly asked.

"Same as you. He's bright, observant. I like him, but would like to spend more time with him. He has his story down, but I'd like to know a little more about what really makes him tick."

Carly frowned. "Are you concerned about something?"

Eric smiled and shook his head. "No. If you're asking did I pick up on anything, no. Just curious, that's all. My take is there's more to Josh than the little intro we got tonight. Not in a bad way, just more than meets the eye. He's pretty smooth."

"Well, you know how Michelle is. In a month, by the time she goes back to school, she'll be on to someone else."

Eric laughed. "True. But that's better than getting too serious. What was going on with Bo?"

She looked at the dog, now relaxed and stretched out between them. "Not sure. He wanted to go after him at the front door, though. I've never seen him act like that."

"Probably smelled another dog or something on Josh." Eric shrugged. "Who knows?"

Chapter 9

Her last morning appointment had just left, and Carly decided to grab something to eat before the afternoon meetings cranked up.

"I'm going down to the cafeteria for a quick bite," she said to Sandy as she was walking out the door. She always ate in the cafeteria whenever she could, mingling with the employees, yet another habit she'd picked up from Brian.

She got through the serving line and looked for a place to sit. It was well after the lunch hour rush, so it wasn't too crowded. She looked over to her left and saw the young computer guy sitting over at a table by himself. What was his name? Carly tried to remember. Wayne, that was it, Wayne. Carly headed over to the table.

"Hi, Wayne. Mind if I join you?" Wayne looked up and almost swallowed his last mouthful of lunch when he saw who it was. Talk about a deer in the headlights look.

"Uh, no, uh, sure. I'm almost finished, though." Wayne looked down at his plate as if willing the food to disappear as quickly as possible. Carly set her tray down at the seat opposite Wayne and pulled out the chair.

"How've you been? Still building your own computers?"

Wayne seemed surprised that she remembered him. "Yeah, just finished adding some things to mine. More memory, video accelerator, doubled my cache, some other stuff."

Carly had no clue what he was saying. He might as well have been speaking Russian.

"Cool. You'd probably be embarrassed to see my computer at home. I'm just glad it still works! When it dies and I have to replace it, I'll get you to help me out."

"Sure, Ms. Nelson. I'd be glad to, just let me know."

They continued to chat as they finished their lunch, with Wayne settling down and opening up to Carly. One of the nurse managers whom Carly hadn't seen in several weeks stopped by the table on her way out of the cafeteria, boxed lunch in hand. She put her free hand on Carly's shoulder.

"I'm sorry about Mr. Jennings. I know how close you two were, and I know it's hard. It's hard for all of us. He was such a fixture around here."

Glancing at the nurse's badge, Carly responded. "Thanks, Sue. I appreciate that. I miss him. And I know everyone does."

"Well, I've got to get back upstairs."

"Have a good afternoon."

Carly looked back at Wayne. He was looking down and rearranging the last few bites of his food on his plate. "You okay?"

Wayne looked up. "Just makes me sad thinking about Mr. Jennings. Did they ever find out what happened?"

Something about Wayne's question struck Carly as odd. "No, just what was in the newspaper. It was late at night, and he apparently fell asleep at the wheel."

Wayne started to say something, then changed his mind. "I've got to get back, Ms. Nelson. Nice talking to you." Wayne rose from his chair and grabbed his tray.

"Good talking to you, Wayne. See you around."

Carly watched as he walked off. Something was bothering that kid.

Did they ever figure out what happened? That was the second time today that someone had asked that. Then it hit Carly. Wayne. Wayne had also asked her that question a few weeks ago, right after Brian's accident. Then, today at lunch, Wayne had asked her again, the same question, almost word for word. That's strange, Carly thought. Why was Wayne so interested in knowing what happened?

She filed it away for future reference and finished her lunch. Back in her office, she checked her emails and responded to as many as possible before her next meeting.

Later that afternoon, she got a call from Helen Farmer.

"Carly? Helen. I need to talk with you about a situation. You have a few minutes this afternoon?"

Carly looked at her calendar. It was full, but Helen never called unless it was important. "Can you come up around two?"

"Thanks, see you then."

Carly hung up the phone, wondering what that was about. Just what she needed—more problems.

Five minutes before two, Helen knocked on the door. Carly motioned her in and Helen closed the door, walked over, and sat in one of the chairs in front of Carly's desk.

"We've got a problem and I wanted to talk it through with you. It concerns one of our nurses, Darci Edwards."

Carly spread her hands and nodded, a puzzled look on her face. "I don't think I know her."

Helen continued. "She works on Three West. Worked in the OR for about twelve months, then decided she wanted to get back on the floor about a year ago. She's been with us for almost six years."

"So, what's the problem?"

"Two nights ago, we had a patient up there on Levophed, 1 ml/min drip rate. It was Darci's patient. Well, after shift change, the nurse on the next shift checked right after shift change, and it was set to 2 ml/min. She looked on the computer and the patient had been getting 2 ml/min since Darci had come on duty. Almost killed the patient."

Carly interrupted. "Is the patient okay?"

"Looks like he will be. Of course, his doctor is furious. The family doesn't know yet and probably won't as long as he pulls through. But it's on the chart, plain as day.

"I called Darci at home and asked her what happened. She swears she set it at 1 ml/min, checked it every hour as required and it was on 1 ml/min. Darci doesn't normally make mistakes—she's one of my best nurses. Never had any problem with her at all. So I had biomed check the IV pump. Even though it's interfaced to our electronic medical record system, it has a log file on it as well. They called me this morning and said everything was fine, pump is working exactly like it's supposed to. At the beginning of Darci's shift, the log file shows it was set to 2 ml/min and not changed until the following shift, when the new person caught it."

Carly nodded. "Okay, she made a mistake. I know that happens, so what's the problem?"

"Well, last night, same thing happens, but a different patient, different drug, different pump—but same nurse. Again, Darci insists she set it right and checked it through her shift. Once again, biomed checked the log file. It doesn't agree with what she said."

Helen paused and shook her head. "I don't know what's going on, but we can't afford this. She's endangered two patients, and I told her if it happens once more, she's gone. I don't have a choice, Carly."

"Damn, Helen, this is serious. Doesn't she understand?" Now Carly understood the dilemma. Darci was a good nurse, one of their best. She had no blemishes on her record; she was well regarded by both physicians and her peers. As Helen pointed out, this was serious and couldn't be tolerated.

"It gets worse. Both patients were Langford's."

"Great," Carly said. "He's been on the warpath lately, so I guess I can expect another call from him." She asked, "What's going on with Edwards? Is she having some sort of personal crisis? Drugs?"

"Not sure. When I broached the subject, she got angry and defensive. She stands by her story that somehow the equipment is to blame."

"What're you proposing?"

"DA in her file. Reassignment. She's not going to like it, but . . ."

Carly nodded. A written disciplinary action was serious business.

"I agree. You have no choice."

Helen got up to leave. "Thanks for listening. I know you've got a lot on your plate, but I wanted to bounce it off you. I hate it, but I couldn't see any other way. Plus, there's always the chance it could blow up into something."

"No, you did the right thing. And I appreciate you bringing it to me. Just keep me posted on any developments."

Helen walked out and Carly sat back in her chair. She was tempted to call Darci Edwards and talk to her, but she didn't want to get in the middle of something. Let Helen handle it and don't interfere. She smiled as she thought of Brian telling her on more than one occasion *that's why we get paid the big bucks.*

After work, Carly decided to stop by the Fort Myers Sportsman's Club on her way home. Several years ago, she had gotten interested in shooting and joined the FMSC. In a strange way, she found it relaxing and a great stress reliever. She had honed her skills and was known at the club as one of the more accurate shooters around.

She wasn't a gun fanatic and didn't openly advertise her hobby, but at the same time, she wasn't ashamed of it. She'd learned that guns were an emotional topic, and one best avoided, much like politics and religion. Her father had been in the military, so guns weren't an issue with her.

She never thought she would go as far as carrying one, but when her old college roommate was shot in a robbery attempt, she took the class and acquired her concealed weapon permit.

When she got to the parking lot at the club, she took the 9mm Glock 19 out of her purse and unloaded it. FMSC, like most shooting ranges, required all weapons to be unloaded before going inside. She put the pistol inside her small range bag, which also contained her eye and ear protection.

Once inside, she stopped at the desk to sign in and presented her pistol for inspection. She also bought some ammunition and a few paper targets.

She shot a hundred rounds and walked out of the range to the lounge area to inspect her targets more closely. She was pleased with the results. On the last target, all of the shots were within a three-inch circle. Satisfied with the tight groupings, she threw the targets away before leaving. Going to the range a couple of times a month to maintain her proficiency had paid off.

That evening at home, Eric was working on his lesson plan for the week. Carly decided to get on the desktop computer in the bedroom they used as an office. The office had two desks, one for each of them, and two computers, with a printer in the middle they shared.

Bo was lying down between them, content to be in the same room. They'd talked about getting laptops so they could work in other rooms around the house, but decided that would discourage communications between the two and make it easy to spend too much time on the computer. This way, it was easier to contain it.

She turned on her computer and waited for it to boot up. She was checking her email when the screen locked up. No error message, no warning, just nothing worked, not even the failsafe Ctrl-Alt-Del.

"Shit," she said. "Sometimes I hate computers."

Eric looked over at her. "What's a matter?"

"I don't have a clue. Damn thing just locked up. Nothing works, not even trying to reboot it." She reached down and pressed the power button to switch it off, waited a few seconds, then pressed it again to turn it back on.

This time, a dancing bear appeared on the screen. "What the hell? Look at this."

Eric backed the chair away from his desk and rolled up behind her. He couldn't help but laugh. A cartoon-like bear was dancing across the green screen, first one direction, then the other.

"Not funny," she said, then started laughing herself. It was pretty humorous.

"Did you update your anti-virus software?"

She shook her head. "I'm not a blonde, you know. Of course I did. It's set on automatic update."

Eric put his hands up, palms out. "Just checking. Looks like you've got a virus somehow."

"You think? Just what I needed. Are you going to fix it for me?" Eric was a lot more computer savvy than Carly.

"Sorry, love. That's out of my area of expertise. You're going to need the pros for this one."

She reached down and turned off the computer. "Well, so much for working on the computer tonight. I think I'll go to bed and read. Coming to bed soon?"

Eric had rolled back to his desk. "Not too much longer. I want to finish this section, then I'll be in. Probably another thirty minutes or so."

Bo had his head up, looking from one to the other. He took one last glance at Eric and made his decision, following Carly to the bedroom.

She got ready for bed and pulled back the covers. Bo settled on his rug in the corner. She opened her Kindle and turned it on. The Michael Connelly book she was reading came up on the screen, but she was still thinking about the computer and what to do about it. Maybe she would take it to the computer store, or one of the big-box stores in town. Then, she thought about Wayne, the computer geek at the hospital. He'd know what to do. Satisfied she'd come up with a plan, she turned her full attention to her book.

Chapter 10

The next morning, Carly was on her way to a meeting when her cell phone rang. She stopped in the hall and looked at the number on the phone—Forrest Langford. That didn't take long.

"Hello, Forrest."

"What the hell is going on down there? You people have no sense at all. Unbelievable."

Carly took a breath and composed her thoughts. She knew why he was calling, but asked anyway.

"What are you talking about?"

"Your hospital just wrote up one of your best nurses, that's what. I just ran into Darci Edwards and, when I asked her how she was doing, she burst into tears and told me she'd received a disciplinary action because your damn IV pumps malfunctioned."

Thank goodness Helen gave her a heads-up on this yesterday afternoon. Nothing worse than being blind-sided by a physician on the warpath.

"Forrest. Calm down. Obviously, you only know part of the story." She paused to let him settle down. She started to qualify her statement about privacy, but realized that would set him off again. Sometimes she had to bend the rules. She ducked into a nearby alcove and lowered her voice.

"She was involved in two separate incidents over three days. Different patients—both yours by the way, different meds and different equipment. We had biomed check out both the pumps and not only was there no problem found, the log files on the pumps didn't substantiate her story."

The line was quiet. Carly continued.

"We realize she's a good nurse and don't know what happened, but the equipment checked out. That's why we gave her the benefit of the doubt and only gave her a written reprimand. Anybody else would've been fired." She started to add that Darci almost killed one of the patients, but kept quiet.

His pause told her he didn't know the details, but he was determined to save face and get the last word.

"Of course I know they're both my patients. But I also know Darci. She worked with me in the OR and is one of the best nurses I've seen. In fact, I begged her to stay there when she transferred back to the floor. Since going back to the unit, she's handled all of my patients—at my request—and she's been outstanding."

Carly noticed that his voice was a little calmer.

"Maybe she was tired or stressed out or something," he said.

"Helen and I discussed that. Again, Helen—we—decided to give her the benefit of the doubt and temporarily reassign her. Forrest, you of all people should realize how serious those errors are. I don't know what happened, but nothing points to the equipment."

"Fine. I've got to run." The line went dead.

Carly put the phone down and shook her head. This was going to be a long day.

When she got back to her office, she got on her computer and looked up Wayne's extension. She picked up her phone and called.

"Wayne?"

"Yes?"

"Hi, it's Carly Nelson."

"Oh, hi, Ms. Nelson."

She shook her head. Might as well give up on getting him to call her Carly.

"Hey, I've got a problem with my computer at home and wondered if you might be able to help me?"

"If I can. What's the problem?"

She explained what had happened yesterday evening, and when she got to the part about the dancing bear, he chuckled.

"Yeah, that's a good one. It's making the rounds right now. Fortunately, it's relatively harmless."

"So how can I get it fixed? Is there someone in town you'd recommend?"

"I'll be happy to come over and fix it for you. It'll take an hour or so. It's not that bad as far as viruses go. Could've been lots worse. When you want me to come by?"

"You tell me. Your convenience. I'll be home tonight and tomorrow evening, if either of those works for you. You sure you have time?"

Wayne laughed. "Remember, I told you computers are my life. I'll be happy to come over this evening and take care of it."

She gave him her address. "Why don't you come around seven and have dinner with us? I can't promise anything special to eat, but you can meet my husband."

Wayne hesitated. "I don't want to intrude, Ms. Nelson."

"You're the one doing me a favor. The least I can do is feed you. We'll see you at seven."

After hesitating again, he said, "Okay. Thanks, Ms. Nelson."

"Thank you. Give me a call if you have any trouble finding us."

After she hung up, she called Eric to tell him they would be having company for dinner. Carly finished her work, at least what she intended to, and headed home.

Pulling into the driveway at quarter of seven, she was surprised to see Michelle's car there.

Wagging his tail, Bo greeted her at the door. She heard Eric and Michelle laughing out on the lanai as she walked that direction.

When she got outside, Michelle stood and hugged her.

"Glad to see you here—that's a nice surprise," Carly said.

"Anna and I are going out to the beach later. I thought we could all have dinner together?"

Carly went over and kissed Eric. "Hey, love. This is nice, having you both here when I get home."

She turned back to Michelle. "Having dinner together would be great. I'm not sure what we can cobble together, but we'll figure it out. Did Eric tell you we're having company?"

"Yeah, he said some computer guy at the hospital. That's cool."

"I've already taken care of dinner," Eric said.

Carly looked surprised. "Don't tell me you've cooked something again? Maybe I should sit down."

Eric and Michelle both laughed.

"No, but I did order pizza in. Should be here in ten or fifteen minutes."

"Good. That gives me time to change. I'll be right back."

Bo stood, torn between following Carly or staying out on the lanai with Eric and Michelle. He nuzzled up against Michelle, and when she reached out to scratch him behind the ears, the decision was easy.

Carly changed into shorts, blouse, and flip-flops. Walking toward the lanai, she heard the doorbell ring.

"I've got it," she yelled and grabbed her purse on the way to the door. Bo followed her, curious as to who was at the door.

She opened it and a college-age kid was standing there with a pizza box, salad, and a large container of Coke. She paid him, giving him a generous tip, and took everything out to the lanai. Michelle had already set the table with paper plates and utensils.

Before Carly could sit down, the doorbell rang again.

"That must be Wayne. I'll get it," she said.

A few minutes later, Carly walked out on the lanai with the awkward young man behind her. She introduced Wayne to Eric and Michelle, almost forgetting Bo, who was sniffing Wayne's leg.

Wayne reached out his hand to let Bo check him out, then scratched the Lab behind his ears. Bo responded by wagging his tail.

"Well, looks like you've got a friend for life," Carly said. "This is Bo."

Wayne smiled as he continued scratching Bo's head. "Hello, Bo. You like that, don't you?" Looking up to Carly, he said, "He reminds me of a Lab I used to have."

"He's a rescue dog. Part of our family," Carly said. "His voice box was damaged when he was a puppy, and he can't bark."

"Poor fellow," Wayne said. He patted the big dog's side and pulled out a chair.

As they sat, Bo staked out a spot between Michelle and Wayne, somehow sensing they were his best bet for a tidbit.

After the first few minutes, Wayne seemed to relax, Carly noticed. Eric and Michelle took turns carrying the conversation, asking Wayne lots of questions along the way, but he seemed not to mind.

"Carly said you're familiar with the dancing bear virus?" Eric asked Wayne. Everyone at the table snickered.

"Hey, I don't know what it's called; I just know what I saw on her screen. And it was funny," Eric said.

"Yeah, it is funny," Wayne said. "It's called the db virus and it's going around. I should be able to figure it out pretty quickly. The good news is that it's fairly harmless."

Michelle looked at Wayne. "You may know a friend of mine. Josh Mills? He's from Fort Myers, works at Gulf Toyota. He knows a lot about computers, too."

Wayne tilted his head and thought. "Josh Mills?" He shook his head. "No, I don't believe I know him. But I've only been in Fort Myers a year, so I don't know a lot of people here."

When they finished the pizza, Eric offered to take Wayne into the study so he could look at the computer. Eric came back out to the lanai to talk with the girls while Wayne fixed Carly's computer. He asked Michelle about her day.

"Anna and I met Josh and his friend Ryan out at the beach and hung out. Josh is like, so smart. He finished Florida with a 4.0. Can you imagine?"

Carly looked at Eric and smiled. She was one of the few people who knew he finished Berkeley with a 4.0 grade point average. Although Michelle was smart, Carly could understand her amazement at someone getting a 4.0. Michelle would never be in that club.

She went on to tell how he knew all about cars, too. When the check engine light on her car came on, he hooked his computer up to it and turned it off. Apparently the fault was something minor.

"So when are you bringing him over?" Carly asked.

She looked at her mom and rolled her eyes. "Before I go back to school, I promise."

"Great, but please give me a little notice. I don't want him to think we only are capable of take-out here."

"What about his family?" Eric asked. "Didn't he say he grew up around here?"

Michelle looked sad. "His father died when Josh was fifteen. I did find out that his mother is dead, but he's never said anything else about it. He says he has an aunt or something in Tampa, but they haven't spoken to each other in years. He doesn't like to talk about his family, so I don't press."

"Sorry to hear that," Carly said. "What happened to his dad?"

Michelle shrugged. "All he said was that he had a heart attack. I'm not sure what happened to his mother."

"That's tragic," Eric said. "He seems remarkably mature and well-adjusted, though."

Michelle's face lit up again. "Oh, he is. That's one of the things I like about him. He's much more serious than those boys I meet in Gainesville."

"I'm not interrupting, am I?" Wayne was standing at the door. He'd only been gone thirty minutes.

"No, come on out, Wayne," Carly said. "Are you done already?"

Wayne walked over and sat at the table. He got right down to business.

"It was the db virus all right."

"Any way of knowing where it came from?" Carly asked.

"Not really. I mean, you might be able to trace it back, but it would be difficult and take a lot of time. The main thing is that I've deleted it and installed a good virus protection program. You should be fine."

Eric looked at Carly, then back to Wayne. "I thought we had virus protection software installed?"

Before Carly could defend herself, Wayne said, "Well, it wasn't a very good one, and it hadn't been updated in a few months. So I just installed the same one I use on my computer. It's a lot better and it'll update itself so you won't have to worry about it."

"I thought the one we had updated itself?" Carly asked.

"Not really, not on that version. But you're set now."

Carly looked at Eric, rolled her eyes, and shook her head. He smiled, but didn't say anything.

"So, now what?" Carly asked Wayne.

"I'm running a virus scan program that's checking your entire computer. It'll take three or four hours to run, so just leave it be for tonight. I've unplugged your Internet cable just in case, so you'll be without Internet access on that computer for the evening. Just plug it back in tomorrow; it should be fine. If you have anymore problems, let me know and I'll come back over tomorrow after work."

"Yeah, but that won't help me." Michelle looked at her mom. "Dad called this afternoon. I'm going with him and Barbie to the Keys tomorrow. We'll be back Sunday."

Michelle turned to Wayne and said, "My dad has a place in Key West and he wants me to go down with him and my stepmom."

"That's a long trip for just a couple of days," Wayne said.

"Oh, he has his own plane, so it only takes an hour to get there."

Wayne looked impressed. "His own plane? Wow."

Carly spoke, "You may know him from the hospital. Dr. Langford—he's a neurosurgeon."

Wayne nodded. "Yeah, I recognize the name." He turned to Michelle. "So that's your dad?"

"Yep, when he has time."

"Michelle," Carly said, "Be nice. He is paying for your college."

Michelle rolled her eyes and looked at Wayne.

"So no Facebook, tonight, huh?" she asked.

Wayne pointed to her cell phone on the table in front of her.

"You've got that. It's what I use most of the time anyway."

Michelle looked at her cell phone as if it had just appeared. "Oh, guess you're right."

"I could set it up for you, if you'd like. Wouldn't take but a few minutes."

Michelle looked at him and smiled. "Thanks." She handed him her phone. He tapped on it for a few minutes and handed it back.

"You can just tap the Facebook icon. Why don't you go ahead and log in while I'm here in case there's a problem."

She did and brought her Facebook page up. "Cool. Thanks, Wayne."

"No problem. I should be going. Nothing more I can do here. I appreciate the pizza. Nice meeting all of you." Bo stood to say his goodbyes. Wayne leaned down and petted the dog.

"Good night, Bo."

Bo's entire rear end moved back and forth as he wagged his tail.

"Look me up on Facebook. Nice meeting you, Wayne," Michelle said.

"Will do. Same here."

Carly started to get up out of her chair, but Eric beat her to it.

"I'll walk you to the door," he said, as Bo followed him and Wayne into the house.

"What time are you leaving tomorrow?" Carly asked Michelle.

"Dad said to meet them at the airport around one."

"Well, it's good you're going. I know your dad will enjoy having some time with you."

She shrugged. "I guess. Maybe I can tolerate Barbie for a couple of days."

Carly couldn't help but laugh. "Try to be nice. Your dad loves you. And she is his wife."

"I know, but I don't have to like her."

"Nice guy. Glad he came and looked at our computer," Eric said, as he and Bo walked out to rejoin them.

"He was kinda cute," Michelle said. "And smart, too. Where did all of these brainy guys come from all of a sudden?" she said to no one in particular.

Eric and Carly both laughed.

Chapter 11

Page Field, formerly the only airport in Fort Myers, was now the main general aviation airport. Its central location on Cleveland Avenue, not far from downtown, made it convenient and the preference for private aircraft in the area.

Michelle drove out to the airport, parked, and went inside the general aviation terminal, pulling her carry-on. Tonya, Forrest's wife, was sitting inside. When she saw Michelle, she stood to greet her.

"Hi, Michelle." She gave her a hug and air kiss, which Michelle reciprocated with some effort.

"I'm so glad you're coming with us. Forrest is out doing his pre-flight. He's so excited."

"Looking forward to it," Michelle said.

"He said the weather is going to be great. Maybe we can lie out on the beach some, work on our tans."

Tonya gave Michelle the once over. "Looks like you could use a little sun."

Michelle looked back at her father's well-tanned trophy wife and started to say something catty, but changed it at the last minute. "Yeah, too much studying, I guess."

Key West was only 145 miles by air, yet it was a 240 mile drive. In Forrest's plane, that meant a little less than an hour flight.

Michelle looked up to see her dad walking in.

"Hey, you made it." He came over and gave her a hug, holding her tight and kissing her cheek.

"Glad to see you, Dad. Thanks for asking me to come along." Michelle meant what she said. She loved her dad, and despite the sarcastic remarks about the new Ms. Langford, she was glad to see him.

He reached down to take her small roll-aboard. "This all?"

"Yep. Don't need a lot for the Keys."

He looked at Tonya and laughed. "Tell your stepmom that. She brought two suitcases. You'd think she was going to New York for a week."

Tonya just shook her head while Michelle laughed. She grabbed Michelle's hand. "When you're my age, it takes a lot more to look your best."

Michelle couldn't help but roll her eyes. Tonya wasn't that much older than she, and had already enlisted the services of a plastic surgeon. She couldn't figure out what her dad saw in the latest Ms. Langford, except long legs and big boobs.

"We're ready to roll. Anybody need a last stop before we leave?" Forrest said.

Both the girls shook their heads, so he started out the door, leading the way to the blue and white Mooney sitting on the flight line.

The Mooney Ovation was one of the premier single-engine planes. Fast and dependable, it was a popular choice for pilots with the resources to afford it. With a price tag of over half a million dollars, it wasn't cheap.

The cabin seated four, and Tonya insisted that Michelle sit up front with her dad.

Michelle marveled at the interior when she got in and fastened her seatbelt. This was her first flight in the Mooney. Looking at the twin ten-inch LCD screens, she couldn't help but remark to her dad, "This looks like the space shuttle!"

Forrest laughed. "The latest. It's called a glass cockpit. All of the instruments needed to fly the plane are on these two screens."

"That's scary!" Michelle remarked. "I'm not sure about depending on computers."

"Not to worry. This is essentially the same setup you'd see on a commercial airliner. It has dual-battery backup, and you also have the primary flight instruments in the mechanical version," he said, as he pointed to the round gauges off to the right of the computer screens.

"So even if both of the big displays went out, I could still fly it."

She nodded. That made her feel better. She had flown with her dad before and never felt uncomfortable. He was safety conscious and had flown for years without incident. She put the headphones on and watched as her dad turned his attention to the business of flying.

Forrest started the engine, went through his checklist, and taxied to the end of the runway. In a few minutes, they were airborne and headed south toward Key West.

It was a beautiful day for flying as they cruised down the west coast of Florida. Clear, with only a few high clouds, it seemed like she could see forever.

They passed Naples, on their left, and were out over the water, the sunlight reflecting off the Gulf of Mexico. Before long, she could make out the islands of the Florida Keys ahead. In no time, Key West was in sight, and Forrest was setting up his approach to land.

After landing, he taxied to the general aviation area, past the main terminal, where a ramp attendant guided him to a tie-down spot. Forrest shut the engine down, turned everything off, and they exited the plane.

It was warmer here, Michelle thought, almost tropical. Inside the small terminal, Forrest stopped at the desk to make arrangements for leaving the airplane. A driver was waiting and took their luggage to a minivan parked out front where they loaded up for the short trip into town.

They rode down to the pier, where the driver stopped and unloaded. Taking their luggage down to the Sunset Key launch, he helped them board and bade them good afternoon.

Sunset Key, otherwise known as Tank Island, was a private island less than five hundred yards from the island of Key West. Home to less than seventy houses, it was exclusive and could only be reached by boat or the private launch from the Westin in Key West. The recession didn't have much of an impact on the tiny island, where the cottages, as they were called, still fetched several million dollars apiece.

Forrest's cottage was on the far side of the island, on the ocean and facing west. With such an incredible view, it was one of the most expensive on the little island, costing well over five million dollars.

No cars were allowed on the small island, so when they unloaded from the launch, they walked the short distance to the Langford home.

Michelle was still amazed at this place; it was like having a private island. The housekeeper had stocked the house, so when they opened the door and walked in, it was as if they were coming in from a day in town. She texted her mom to let her know they were at the house, and she went to change and put on her bathing suit.

It was only mid-afternoon, so they had plenty of time before dinner. She grabbed a chair out of the closet and walked the few steps to the white-sand beach just out the door. The clear, turquoise water of the keys was incredible. A slight breeze was blowing off the water, just enough to make it comfortable. Key West was truly an island paradise.

Forrest and Tonya soon joined her out on the beach for the sunset, an afternoon ritual in Key West. He'd made margaritas for the three of them, and they sat in a row, watching the large orange orb slowly sink into the ocean at the horizon.

Michelle had never seen the "green flash," an optical phenomenon sometimes seen at sunset, only for a second or two. Her dad and Tonya claimed to have seen it before at this very spot. She stared as the top of the sun was almost to the horizon.

"I saw it!" Michelle said. "The green flash! Too cool!"

Tonya missed it, but her dad saw it.

"Pretty cool, huh?" he said, patting her hand.

"Yes! I thought maybe it was an illusion and wondered if it really existed, but it does! I'm so glad I finally saw it."

Forrest had made dinner reservations at Louie's Backyard, a Key West favorite for many years. Situated on the water in an old Victorian home not far from Mallory Square, it was one of those rare places that offered both ambience and great food.

They had a fabulous dinner, fresh fish and Florida lobster, sitting on the deck overlooking the Atlantic Ocean.

After dinner, they decided to walk back, going a few blocks over to Duval Street and walking its length. Duval, the main street, was always an interesting place for people-watching, something that could be said for Key West in general. Despite the tourists and the occasional cruise ship stop, Key West was still a refuge for the eccentric, a reputation it had since the days of Hemingway. From the vaudeville acts at Mallory Square every day at sunset to the fascinating Conchs, as the locals were called, it was unlike any other place in the country.

Along the way down Duval to the dock to catch the launch back to Sunset Key, they stopped in at The Bull, the oldest open-air bar on the island. They had a couple of drinks and listened to the band playing that night before going back to the house before midnight.

Saturday morning, they took the launch back over to Key West for a day in town. Forrest suggested starting the day at Blue Heaven, an eclectic little restaurant only a couple of blocks off Duval Street. They sat outside, having breakfast with the roosters, watching them roam loose around the yard. All three of them got the pancakes, which are made from scratch.

After breakfast, they leisurely finished their coffee, then walked over to Duval to check out the shops. Tonya, as always, was on the prowl looking for more knickknacks to add to the Key West home. After perusing several different shops, she still hadn't found anything she liked, and Michelle was ready for a break.

"Why don't you guys keep looking?" Michelle said. "I'll catch up with you later."

"We can go somewhere else," Tonya said, trying her best to accommodate the stepdaughter.

Forrest saw the pleading look on Michelle's face, and realized that she wanted to be on her own for a while. He suggested that Michelle do what she wanted for a few hours while he and Tonya continued to shop. They could meet later for lunch. Michelle readily agreed, held up her phone, and told them to call her when they were ready.

Thankful that her dad had picked up on her unspoken request, she headed over to Whitehead Street to the Hemingway house. Although she'd been there numerous times, she always visited the landmark when she came to Key West, where he wrote his only novel set in the United States, *To Have and Have Not*.

She felt as though she could sense the presence of the legend in the well-preserved home, where he lived for eight years. She loved to walk around the grounds, spying the many "Hemingway" cats, which have six toes. Supposedly, Ernest was given a white, six-toed cat by a ship captain and the cats are descendants of that cat, named Snowball. Hemingway named the cats after famous people, a tradition carried on to this day.

She spent several hours there, walking around the house and grounds, trying to absorb as much as she could. It was restorative and a welcome respite from her stepmom. By the time her dad called her for lunch, her mood was better, and she didn't mind hanging around with them the rest of the day.

Sunday came and it was time to return home. At the Key West airport, Michelle and Tonya waited inside as Forrest loaded the plane and did his pre-flight inspection. Before long, they were airborne and heading north toward Fort Myers.

Michelle had to admit she had enjoyed the trip. It was good to spend time with her dad, and "Barbie" hadn't been as tiresome as usual. Of course, the alone time she had at the Hemingway house helped. She was looking out the passenger window and could barely make out the west coast of Florida, coming into view on their right side. All of a sudden, the plane pitched nose-down, jerking her against the shoulder belt.

"What the . . ." Forrest had both hands on the wheel, then started manipulating buttons on the dash with one hand while holding the wheel with the other.

"Forrest! What's happening?" Tonya screamed from the back seat.

He ignored her, obviously concentrating on the situation at hand.

"Mooney niner eight seven two Quebec, this is Fort Myers Center. Please maintain altitude of six thousand, over."

Michelle heard the calm voice of Fort Myers air traffic control through her headset. She watched in horror as the waters of the Gulf seemed to be rushing up to meet them.

"Uh, Fort Myers, I'm having a problem with the autopilot. Trying to disengage, over," Forrest said in response.

She watched as her dad seemed to be fighting the airplane. He was still pushing buttons and flipping switches with his right hand, his left on the wheel. Whatever it was, it was serious, and although she had confidence in her father, the water seemed to be getting too close too fast.

"Seven two Quebec, are you declaring an emergency? Over."

"Negative, not at this time," Forrest said, not even bothering to identify himself.

After what seemed like an eternity, the plane leveled off and Forrest exhaled.

"Fort Myers center, seven two Quebec. I've disengaged the autopilot and going back to six thousand, over."

"Affirmative, seven two Quebec. Everything okay?"

"Affirmative, Fort Myers. Not sure what happened, but the autopilot is completely disengaged and the aircraft is under my control. Requesting priority handling into Page Field, over."

Forrest wasn't taking any chances and wanted to proceed as directly and quickly as possible back to Page Field.

"Seven two Quebec, affirmative. We have you cleared direct approach into Page Field. Maintain six thousand, over."

"Seven two Quebec, six thousand, over."

Forrest looked over to Michelle and back at Tonya.

"Sorry about that. Not sure what happened; the autopilot crapped out and was descending. Took me a minute to disengage it, but everything's fine now."

"Are we going to make it? We're not going to—"

"We're fine, Tonya. Relax, everything's okay." He looked at Michelle. "You okay?"

She nodded. "Scared the shit outta me, though."

He laughed. "Yes, it was a little unnerving." He reached over and patted her hand. "But we're fine now. Don't worry."

Soon, Page Field was in sight. Forrest glanced around the cabin, pointed ahead, and said, "There's home."

Michelle thought she saw a look of relief on his face, though he would never admit it. As he set up his approach to the airport, she saw him tense again, but they landed safely with no further incidents.

After unloading, they went inside the general aviation terminal while Forrest went to find the mechanic to have a little chat with him. Before long, he was back.

"Everyone ready?" he asked.

"I'm just glad we made it. Did you tell someone what happened?" Tonya asked.

Forrest nodded. "They'll check it out from top to bottom tomorrow. I told them I wanted a full report. While it wasn't as dangerous as it seemed, it still shouldn't have happened and I'm not happy about it."

Michelle wasn't as confident as her dad, but relieved he didn't seem too upset. In the parking lot, she stopped to hug him and Tonya before walking to her car.

"Thanks, Dad. I had a good time."

He hugged her. "Me, too. Sorry about the little hiccup, but nothing serious. Your mom will probably freak out, though, so don't make it sound worse than it was."

She laughed. "I'll still fly with you, if that's what you're asking. Don't worry, Mom will be fine. She worries too much."

Tonya gave her a hug and air kiss, then they parted company.

Sorcerer closed the program on his computer and sat back, smiling. He'd stayed up all night working on a program to exploit a weakness in the avionics system on the Mooney. One of his fellow hackers on the Internet had given him some information about a hole in the software, and he'd written the code to take control of the aircraft's autopilot. The access point was Michelle's cell phone. He knew the solution was simple; just disengage the autopilot, but it was still fun.

They had lost less than two thousand feet altitude, although he chuckled as he could picture the three with panic-stricken looks on their faces. He'd heard the blonde bitch's scream when he put the plane into a dive.

He had no intention of killing Forrest Langford in a plane crash; that would be too good for him. The fact that Langford's wife and Michelle were on the plane had nothing to do with it. No, he wanted the doctor to suffer. And suffer he would. Along with everyone else responsible for his mother's death.

Tomorrow was the anniversary of her death. He was sad as he thought back to her death and funeral, every vivid detail etched in his memory forever.

His mother had suffered a stroke and was admitted to Rivers Hospital. He remembered the first meeting with his mother's doctor—Dr. Forrest Langford. What a pretentious, supremely confident prick he was. Langford had assured him that she'd be fine, that there was probably damage, but with time and rehab, there was a good chance she would regain most of her abilities back.

Then, the following night, he got a call at home from the nursing unit. His mother had taken a turn for the worse. He needed to get down there at once. He remembered getting dressed and driving down to the hospital. When he got upstairs, the nurse told him that his mother was in surgery. The doctor had to perform emergency surgery to relieve the pressure on her brain. Don't worry, he remembered her saying, Doctor Langford is one of the best.

He remembered walking down to the surgery waiting room in a daze. Less than twenty-four hours ago, he'd been looking forward to his mother being discharged in a few days and back home. Now, she was undergoing surgery and fighting for her life.

Three hours later, when Langford walked out, still in his scrubs and his head hanging low, the boy knew. The surgeon didn't look so cocky now. He'd lost the battle and was now facing the son to give him the bad news.

The male nurse walking with him, also still in scrubs, stopped at the door on the other side of the red line. Langford paused, nodded back toward the operating suite and kept walking. The nurse turned and went back into the depths of the operating room area.

He remembered wanting to grab Langford by the throat, shove him against the wall, and ask him why? Instead, he stood there like a statue while the surgeon mumbled some bullshit about how sometimes things happen and how sorry he was.

He remembered two days later, sitting alone in the front row of the small funeral home chapel in Labelle, FL, a small town just east of Fort Myers. His mother lay in the casket in front of him. There were maybe ten or twelve people there, most he didn't recognize. He was an only child and had no family left. His father had died seven years ago, the victim of a heart attack. The hospital had sent flowers, but no one even bothered to come to her funeral.

Although Sorcerer had lots of friends in Fort Myers, where he lived and worked, they didn't know about his mother and hadn't been invited to the service. His mother was everything to him, all he had. And now she was gone.

He'd grown up in the rural area east of Fort Myers, about halfway to Labelle. After high school, he'd gone to college and graduated in three years with a degree in Information Technology. He had several job offers with technology companies in California, but he wanted to stay near his mother. Technology jobs were scarce in southwest Florida, so he'd taken a job in Orlando. But that didn't work. He found himself driving to Fort Myers almost every week. His mother had stayed in the modest family home, refusing to move even though her son had offered to buy her a new house near where he lived. So, he left his job in Orlando and found a job in Fort Myers.

He remembered the preacher droning on with his canned funeral service, but he didn't remember anything the preacher said. It didn't matter; it was just words. Besides, the stupid bastard hadn't even known her, and he resented him acting like he did.

He made it through the following week in a daze. Surprisingly, his mother had left a will.

She had left everything to him, of course. She'd worked hard all of her life, saving and sacrificing for her son to go to college. She spent nothing on herself. What she didn't spend on the boy, she put away. Over the years, she had managed to save a fairly decent amount, more than the boy thought possible.

He remembered his boss telling him to take a couple of weeks off, take care of things, and come back when he was ready. He only took a few days off, then came back to work. He didn't need two weeks.

Since the funeral, he'd been plotting. Now he was ready. His soul burned with a passion he'd never known before and his life had purpose again. The people responsible for his mother's death were going to pay, every single one of them. He was going to see to it.

They would experience the pain of loss; what it felt like to lose someone. He was sane enough to know it wouldn't bring her back. But it would even the score.

The fun had begun.

Chapter 12

Well after the main lunch crowd had cleared, Carly was getting something to eat in the cafeteria. As she paid the cashier, she saw Wayne sitting over in the corner, once again by himself.

Michelle told her last night that Wayne had friended her on Facebook and asked her out when she came back to Fort Myers. Of course, that was after Michelle mentioned, all too casually, the incident that happened in Langford's plane on the way back from the Keys. Carly was still worried about that and intended to ask Forrest what happened, even though Michelle assured her it was no big deal.

When Carly asked about Josh, Michelle sounded a little less enthusiastic than before. According to her, they were just friends. Who knew with Michelle?

Carly walked over to Wayne's table.

"Hey, Wayne. You and I must be on the same schedule lately."

He looked up. When he saw who it was, he got that helpless feeling on his face again.

"Oh, hi, Ms. Nelson."

Carly didn't even ask this time as she put her tray on the table, pulled out a chair, and sat across from him.

"Thank you so much for fixing my computer the other evening. Works like a charm now. You're really good with those things."

Wayne relaxed a bit and almost blushed at her compliment. "That was easy. Thanks for the pizza. You have a nice family."

Carly laughed. "A little crazy sometimes, but yeah, they're good." She started to say something about Michelle, but decided not to.

"How've you been? The pilot project for medical records going well?" Carly remembered the status report she'd just finished reading that morning.

"Yeah, not bad. A few minor problems, but so far, so good. Nothing unexpected."

"I hope you don't mind, but I shared your story about Brian Jennings with some people at a meeting the other day. I thought it was a wonderful example of the kind of person Brian was."

Carly watched the young kid for a reaction. Wayne's face sunk at the mention of Brian.

"That's fine. He was a good man."

"Yes, he was. You asked me the other day if they ever figured out what happened."

Wayne's eyes darted around. He looked around as if he were weighing something in his mind. "I was just curious, that's all. Just wondering."

She watched him. His body language said there was more than just curiosity. "I'm not sure they'll ever know for sure. There were no witnesses, no skid marks. They did determine he didn't have a heart attack. So they're sticking to the theory that it was an accident, that he fell asleep. It's the only explanation that makes sense. But I have a hard time believing it. He was always such a careful driver."

Wayne glanced from side to side again, making sure the area surrounding them was clear. He leaned over the table and spoke in a lowered voice. "I don't think it was an accident."

Carly shook her head. "What?"

Wayne looked around and again spoke in a voice not much louder than a whisper.

"I don't think Mr. Jennings's wreck was an accident."

Carly leaned across the table and looked Wayne in the eye.

"What are you talking about, Wayne?"

"Can I come up to your office this afternoon? After everyone has gone? I can't talk here."

"What do you mean, you don't think it was an accident?"

Wayne rose from his seat and picked up his tray. "Not here. Later."

Carly shook her head. He wasn't going to say anything else for now. "What about six thirty?"

"I'll be there. I've got to get back to work."

Carly watched as the young man walked off. What in the hell was this about? Why did he think Brian's wreck wasn't an accident? Now she was spooked. Something was troubling Wayne about Brian Jennings's crash.

When she got back upstairs, Sandy told her that Helen Farmer, the Vice-President, Nursing, had called thirty minutes earlier asking for a few minutes of Carly's time.

Sandy had told Helen to come on up and she'd squeeze her in to see Carly. Helen was waiting in Carly's office.

As the one responsible for all of the various nursing departments, Helen had a big job, one that wasn't easy. And the issue she'd tossed to Carly was a tough one.

"You're sure about this?" Carly asked the petite lady with short chestnut hair sitting across from her.

"I know. I've double-checked everything. I don't know it was Keith, but all I can tell you is that he's the one who signed off on the counts and they didn't match at the end of his shift."

Like many of the nurse managers, Keith occasionally worked on the floor to fill in for someone. It was a way of earning extra money and maintaining other skills. Some Percocet was missing from the unit where Keith worked. Rivers, like many hospitals, had an automated dispensing system for Schedule II drugs, including Percocet. One nurse on each unit for each shift had access to resupply the Schedule II drug cart. All signs pointed to Keith.

"Have you said anything to Keith?" Carly asked.

"No, I wanted to talk to you first. I mean, Keith would be the last one I suspected."

Carly nodded. Keith Davis was one of the best nurses at Rivers. He'd been there ten years and had never had a blip on his record. Doctor Langford, despite his remarks about Keith's inability to handle add-on cases, was one of his biggest supporters. What in the hell was going on? Since Brian's accident, all hell had broken loose. First Darci, now Keith.

"What do you suggest we do?" Carly asked Helen.

She liked for her managers to propose solutions to the problems they presented. More times than not, she went with the ideas from the people on the front line. Unlike the corporate minions in Atlanta, she didn't try to second-guess her managers.

"We can't ignore it. I'd like to have a conference with Keith, of course, with another VP there. Present the facts, document his response. Then sit down, review everything, and finalize our decision on what action to take."

Carly nodded. "That sounds reasonable. When were you thinking?"

"This afternoon. No reason to delay. We need to get this resolved before the grape gets wind of it." Helen was referring to the hospital grapevine.

"Okay. Let me know how it goes. Thanks, Helen. Good work." She started to add that she was sorry it was Keith, but knew that was unnecessary.

Helen rose to leave. "I'll give you a call after the meeting."

At six thirty, Carly heard a knock on her office door. Sandy had gone for the day, so she didn't hear Wayne approach. Carly waved him in, and the shy young man closed Carly's door, came over to her desk and sat down.

"What do you know about Brian's accident?" she asked.

"If I tell you something, will you promise not to repeat it?" he said.

Carly thought before replying. "As long as it doesn't involve something illegal."

Wayne wrinkled his brow and didn't speak for a moment. "I don't know what to do, Ms. Nelson."

"What's going on, Wayne? If you're involved in something, I need to know."

"No, it's not me. I haven't done anything."

"Well, then why can't you tell me?"

"Oh man, I should've never come up here."

Carly sat back in her chair. "Wayne, you have my word I'll do the right thing. If I feel like I have to tell someone, then I'll let you know. I promise." She watched the boy struggle with what to do. Finally, after a period of silence, Wayne spoke up.

"You're the only one I trust. But you can't tell anyone else unless you let me know when and who, okay?"

"Fair enough." Carly waited.

"I spend a lot of time on the computer, right?"

Carly nodded.

"And I'm in these chat groups and game groups and stuff with other people on the Internet, right?" He looked to Carly to make sure that Carly was following him.

"Anyway, there's this dude in one of the geek groups. He calls himself Sorcerer. He's like freaky smart, okay? I mean, I'm pretty good with computers, probably in the ninetieth percentile if I say so myself. I've been doing this since I was eight, and I spend a lot of time with computers. Like I told you, it's my hobby outside of work. But this guy is scary. I mean, he's like a computer god. If I'm in the ninetieth percentile, he's in the ninety-ninth percentile, if not higher. I've never seen anyone like him."

"Does he live around here? Do you know him?"

Wayne looked at Carly like she had stepped off a spaceship.

"No, I don't even know if it's a he, okay? I mean, I've just interacted with this dude online. I have no idea where he, or she, lives, who they really are, like nothing."

Wayne paused for a minute and studied Carly. "You don't spend a lot of time online, do you, Ms. Nelson?"

"Sad to say, email is about the extent of my online interaction. I do have a Facebook page."

Wayne rolled his eyes, then shook his head. "People, like, invent whole personalities online. You don't see anything they don't want you to see. They hide behind the curtain. The smart ones, if they don't want you to know anything about who they really are, you don't know."

"So how do you know this Sorcerer person is really that smart?"

"We share programs and tech tips and stuff like that." He hesitated. "Sometimes we go places we're not supposed to. And trust me, this dude's for real."

"You mean hacking into computers?"

Wayne shrugged and continued.

"Well, one night several of us geeks were online together, and Sorcerer starts talking about hacking car computers."

"Car computers?"

"Yeah, today's cars have hundreds of computers in them. The computers do it all, fuel management, GPS, anti-lock brakes, the works. Anyway, Huffin—Huffin is another of the members of our group. Huffin starts busting his chops and ragging him about BS'ing us. Telling him he doesn't know anything about hacking car computers. You can tell Sorcerer's getting pissed. Finally, Sorcerer says something like, yeah, ask that dude in Fort Myers who went into the water. Tell me what you're driving and you'll do the same."

"Wait a minute, Wayne. You're telling me that someone can hack into a car's computer and cause it to do things? This sounds like something out of a sci-fi novel."

"Haven't you seen the commercials? Like the one where the person has an accident and the car calls the police? Or the one where the dad starts up his car for his daughter with his cell phone?" Wayne looked incredulous. "I'm just telling you, Sorcerer brought this up and threatened Huffin. And he said enough to convince me that he knew what he was talking about.

"Yes, you can hack into a car's computer. Not easy, but if you're good, you can do it. Computer's a computer; they're all nothing but ones and 0s. And today's cars are loaded with them."

Carly shook her head in disbelief.

"Starting a car and unlocking doors is one thing. But making a car run off the road? That's a little far-fetched, isn't it?"

"See, that's the thing. Mr. Jennings drove a big Ford pickup, right?" Wayne asked.

"Yes, he did. So what?"

"Ford pickups are the only full-size trucks with electric power steering. Electric. Which means it has a computer that's hooked into the car's main computer. Most cars have hydraulic power steering, which means it's mechanical, right? No computer. So you could control the brakes and the accelerator with the computer, but not the steering. Change that for electric power steering, and guess what?"

Carly took a deep breath as she pondered the possibilities. Someone hacked into Brian's truck and drove it off the bridge? But why?

"This Sorcerer is bad news. About a year ago, another geek in the group pissed Sorcerer off, big time. A week later, the dude was online, bitching and moaning. His credit cards had been cancelled, his bank account drained, his name showed up on the sex offender list, and an email sent to his boss. His life had been totally screwed over, know what I mean? Totally! And online, Sorcerer was laughing, taunting him. And giving out just enough details to let the dude know it was Sorcerer who screwed him."

"So, what'd you do? What did the other person do? Didn't anybody report it to the authorities?"

"Are you kidding? Think about it. If he could do that to another geek, he's trouble. Trust me. You don't want to mess with him. Anyway, what were we going to report? He didn't leave enough out there to trip him up. Listen to me. I'm good, and I trace people online sometimes, just for fun."

Seeing the puzzled look on Carly's face, he explained.

"You know, tracing them. Finding out where they're logged on, addresses—online information, that kind of stuff. Everybody leaves a trail online. I tried tracing Sorcerer one time, just for kicks. Nothing. He uses aliases on top of aliases behind curtains, spoofing sites, the works. He's like a ghost, better than anyone I've ever seen. I didn't get past square one. He's that good. He could be next door to me or halfway around the world. I don't know. But I do know that I don't want to get on the wrong side of him."

Carly sat back and tried to digest what she'd just heard. Her head was swimming and she was way out of her element.

"I don't understand. Why? Why would Sorcerer deliberately hack Brian's computer and drive him off the bridge?"

Wayne had a look of regret on his face. "I don't know why I said anything, Ms. Nelson. I probably should've kept my mouth shut." He got up to leave. "Just forget I said anything, okay?"

"Hold on, Wayne. I just want to make sure I understand what you told me. You're saying this Sorcerer is capable of hacking into a car's computer and getting it to do something, take control of it?"

Wayne nodded.

"And you think this guy may have had something to do with Brian Jennings's accident?"

"I don't know. All I know is he said enough to convince me maybe he could've."

"Have you told anyone else?"

"Heck no! Took me long enough to get up the nerve to tell you."

"So why did you tell me?"

Wayne was quiet for a moment. When he spoke, it was almost a whisper. "Mr. Jennings was a good man, and he was good to me. He treated me just like an ordinary person, you know? Just like you did that day in your office and at your house the other night. People like me don't have a lot of friends in the real world. Everybody makes fun of us geeks, always have. You get used to it, but it doesn't mean you like it. But you and Mr. Jennings are different. You don't look at us like we're some kind of freaks.

"So, it's been bothering me that somebody may have done something bad to him. I mean, I may trace people and snoop around on other people's computers, stuff like that. But I never hurt anybody, Ms. Nelson. I couldn't do that."

The kid looked at Carly. "What're we going to do, Ms. Nelson?"

Carly exhaled. "I'm not sure, Wayne. We need to turn this information over to the police."

"You said you wouldn't tell anyone unless you told me first."

"I did, and I'll keep my word. But if someone is responsible for Brian's death, that's a criminal act, and we need to turn it over to the authorities. I've just got to process all this for a bit. Let me think about it over the weekend. Why don't I give you a call Monday?"

"Sure. I can give you my cell number." Wayne waited for Carly to pick up a pen and paper.

Carly wrote down the number.

"Thanks, Ms. Nelson."

Carly put her hand to her chin. "Not sure I've done anything yet. I'll call you."

Wayne got up and let himself out the door. Carly sat back in her chair and thought. Shit, what was she going to do? This was way out of her league. Call the police? What exactly was she going to tell them?

She didn't have anything to tell. The speculation of some pimple-faced kid and a forty-something hospital administrator? But what if Wayne was right? What if this Sorcerer did have something to do with Brian's accident? But why? Who would do something like that? Brian didn't have any enemies Carly could think of. Why would anyone do something like that to Brian?

Carly needed to sleep on it. She did better on hard issues when she let her subconscious handle things, the boys in the basement, as Stephen King called it. This was something for the boys in the basement. She was tired. Let the basement work on it tonight.

Chapter 13

Her office phone buzzed, and Carly picked it up to answer.

"This is Carly."

"Carly, Helen. Got a minute?"

"Sure, want to come up?"

"No, I've got something else in a few minutes, but I wanted to get back to you after meeting with Keith late yesterday afternoon."

Carly remembered that Helen had talked about meeting with him and waited for her to continue.

"He went nuts. That's probably an understatement. Said he's never taken drugs and was willing to take a lie-detector test. It was pretty ugly. He stormed out mumbling something about getting an attorney."

Carly shook her head. Just what she needed.

Helen continued. "Anyway, I was wondering if you'd have some time later today to sit down and talk about it?"

Carly looked at her schedule.

"What about two fifteen?"

"Sounds good. I'll see you then."

Carly hung up the phone and typed the entry into her calendar. Before she'd finished, her phone rang again.

"Carly," she said, not bothering to see who was calling.

"Carly, hi. TJ. Got a sec?" TJ Tanner was the hospital attorney.

"Sure, TJ. What's up?"

"I just got a discovery notice on a patient, a Robert Willis, and I wanted to come up and talk to you about it."

Discovery notices from attorneys weren't unusual. Rivers was a big hospital and, as such, was often the target for lawsuits, frivolous or otherwise. Carly looked at her schedule.

"I'm free until ten if you want to come up now."

"Be there in a few."

Ten minutes later, a slightly heavy, silver-haired man in his fifties wearing gold-rimmed glasses knocked on her door and walked in.

"Hey, TJ. How are you?"

"Not bad. Congratulations on your promotion. You doing okay?" TJ sat in a chair across from her desk.

"It's just an interim thing—I'd be more excited if it was permanent. Just trying to get on top of everything. As you can imagine, hectic."

He nodded. "I'll get right to the point." He laid a file on Carly's desk. "We may have a big problem with this one."

Carly looked puzzled and TJ continued.

"I just received a discovery notice from Banks and Middleton."

Carly perked up. Banks and Middleton was a well-known, old-line personal injury law firm in Fort Myers. There had always been an unofficial "gentleman's agreement" between the hospital and the law firm's original partners that they wouldn't sue Rivers. However, Brian had noted a year ago that the last of the original partners had retired, and he wondered how much longer the truce would last.

"They're representing Robert Willis. He's the patient who we had a medication error on last week."

"Shit," Carly said, louder than she realized. This wasn't good. She didn't know the patient's name, but this had to be Darci Edwards's patient. "This was Darci's patient, I take it?"

TJ nodded.

"You talked to Helen?"

"About an hour ago."

"Darci?"

"Not yet. Wanted to talk with you and Helen first."

"What do you think?"

"Not good, as you can imagine. Unfortunately, Willis had a less than desirable outcome, probably would've regardless of the med error. Darci claims she's being setup or the equipment has a problem. She hinted that she may sue us."

"Bad, huh?"

"I've just started looking into it, but yes, so far it looks ugly. We can't deny the error; it's well documented, so the key is going to be proving or disproving relevance. I haven't talked with Dr. B yet." Everyone referred to Dr. Baahir Ravindra, the Medical Director at the hospital, as Dr. B.

"How 'bout the other patient?"

"Doing fine as far as I know."

"Does Langford know yet? Both of the errors were on his patients."

"No, not that I know of, unless they sent discovery notices to him."

Carly looked at TJ and spread her hands, palms up. "So . . ."

"I want to talk to Dr. B, then to Darci. So far, this is just preliminary, but I wanted to let you know. Meantime, I'll gather as much information as I can. I'll keep you posted." TJ rose from his chair.

"Before you leave, I want to talk to you about something else."

TJ looked puzzled as he stood next to the chair. Carly explained the situation with Keith and mentioned that Helen was coming to her office at two fifteen.

"I'd like you to be here for that. Looks like it might also be a messy one."

"When it rains . . ." he said, shaking his head. "I'll see you then."

"Thanks, TJ."

At ten minutes after two, Helen was in Carly's office. TJ walked in, closed the door, and sat at the table. Carly nodded to Helen.

She cleared her throat and said, "I wanted to see how we should proceed with Keith. It looks like it's going to turn ugly."

"Helen, why don't you go back over everything with TJ. I gave him the quick version earlier, but I think it would help for both of us to hear it direct from you."

Helen nodded and took them through the entire story, starting with a short count on the drugs. TJ took notes, but didn't interrupt with any questions, waiting until she finished.

"So no one else had access to the cabinet during Keith's shift?"

Helen hesitated. "Well, obviously, I did. But, no, other than me, no one else on duty had access."

"Did anyone not working come by the unit that day?"

Helen thought about it for a moment, then replied, "No, I asked several of the other nurses. Nobody else."

"Any other recent problems with drugs missing or counts off?"

"No, thank goodness."

TJ nodded and looked at Carly, indicating he was through with his questions.

"So, what do you recommend, TJ?" Carly asked.

He exhaled and looked at his notes before speaking.

"Maybe just a verbal. I mean, it's the first problem on this unit and involving him. No witnesses. And the count was only off by a few pills." He looked at Helen. "No problems since?"

She shook her head.

"Keep an eye on him, but that's about it right now."

"Helen?" Carly asked.

She shrugged. "I'd agree. Not that we should be intimidated, but my guess is that Keith would calm down if it boiled down to nothing more than a verbal warning."

Carly nodded. Although she was prepared to follow TJ and Helen's lead, she was relieved that they suggested this course of action. The last thing she needed was yet another incident resulting in more attorneys and bad publicity.

"Okay. Let's roll with that. I know you will, but Helen, keep a close eye on things. If there is a problem, I want us to be on top of it early."

TJ and Helen nodded, gathered their things, and rose to leave.

"Let me know how it goes with Keith," Carly said as they left.

Later that afternoon, her cell phone buzzed. Forrest. She dreaded answering.

"Hello, Forrest. I was going to call you."

Langford ignored her comment.

"My office just called me about some sort of discovery notice sent by Robert Willis's attorney." His voice was almost calm; for Forrest, that is. "Apparently he's suing the hospital, me and everyone else regarding the medication error the other week."

"That's what I understand. TJ filled me in not too long ago."

"So what do you intend to do? This was your screw-up and I'm not taking any heat for it."

Carly took a deep breath. Forrest didn't waste any time bailing out on Darci Edwards. As always, Forrest was only concerned about Forrest.

"We just got the notice today. TJ's reviewing it and gathering information. That's about all I know at this point. What happened on the flight back from Key West?"

There was a pause on the line as Forrest processed the change in direction and switched gears.

"Just a small problem with the electronic autopilot. Nothing major. I switched it off and flew back to Page Field with no problems."

His tone had changed, and Carly pressed her advantage.

"Well, I hope you get it fixed before you plan on Michelle going with you again."

"Don't worry—the aircraft mechanic is next on my list. And yes, he damn well better have a good explanation."

He jumped back on the offensive.

"I'm calling Michael Wentworth on the Willis case. Tell TJ he can expect to hear from him." Forrest hung up. Michael Wentworth was Forrest's attorney and a member of another big, well-respected law firm in town.

Forrest punched in the number for the aircraft mechanic at Page Field. Not bothering with pleasantries, especially in his foul mood, he launched into the man as soon as he answered.

"I hope the hell you can tell me what happened to the damn autopilot on my half-million dollar plane," Forrest said.

"I'm waiting on a callback from the avionics people. Preliminary analysis indicates it was a software glitch."

Forrest screamed into the phone. "I'm not interested in a fucking preliminary analysis! All I know is the son-of-a-bitch went into a nose dive, with my wife and daughter on board, and I want it fixed!"

"I'll call you as soon as I know something concrete."

Forrest slammed the phone down on the table, breaking the cell phone, his second one in a month. *Shit*, he said. Now he'd have to find someone to call his office administrator and get another phone. He'd get her to call Wentworth. He didn't have time to talk to him anyway.

* * *

On the drive home, Carly thought about the latest development. She knew she'd have to call Paul Leggett in the morning to tell him. Corporate didn't like to be blindsided by things like this. She wondered how much Willis's poor outcome was related to the med error, if at all.

Robert Willis was an older man who had a stroke. Malpractice suits hinged on proving damages and eliciting sympathy. The exposure on an older patient with a stroke was considerably less than that on a young patient with something more definitive. From a purely economic point of view, that was positive. But from a public relations point of view, it was still a problem.

She pulled into the garage next to Eric's car. When she walked in, after kissing Eric and scratching Bo, she asked Eric about going out for dinner. Michelle was out with Anna.

Eric nodded. "I was thinking about Il Palazzo. In the mood for Italian?"

Il Palazzo was their favorite Italian restaurant in Fort Myers. They had known the owner/chef, Carmine, since he'd first come to town a few years ago. His homemade pasta was to die for. It was a small, hole-in-the-wall restaurant, the kind of place they liked.

"Always," Carly replied. "And the way my day went, wine—several glasses."

The tiny restaurant was located in an old strip shopping center south of Page Field on Cleveland Avenue. There were only about a dozen tables, each sporting a red-checked tablecloth. A few posters of Italy hung on the wall and, with tile floors and the lighting leftover from the previous tenant, it left a lot to be desired in the ambience department. But the food couldn't be beat.

After they were seated in the restaurant, Carmine came out and scolded them for not having been in for a couple of weeks. He was a small, portly man, almost bald with black-rimmed glasses. Originally from New York, he had moved to Fort Myers five years ago and opened Il Palazzo. Eric and Carly had been among his first customers and regulars since, something he hadn't forgotten. He chatted with them for a few minutes, stopped at another table, then went back to the kitchen.

They ordered a bottle of wine and Carly told Eric about the lawsuit. He agreed it sounded messy.

"You sure the equipment's working properly?"

"Biomed checked it, though I suppose I could get them to re-check it or have the manufacturer look at it. Oh, and guess whose patient it is?"

Eric smiled. "Langford?"

Carly rolled her eyes and nodded.

"It figures. Might not be a bad idea to get the manufacturer to check the equipment. Just hard to believe a good nurse with no problems made two errors within a few days. But, mathematically, the incidents are separate and the probability is the same for each."

She put her hand over his, laughed, and shook her head. "My mathematician. Is that supposed to make me feel better?"

"Sorry, just trying to provide some insight. This is one of those cases where the logic and emotion differ."

"I've got a bad feeling about this one. TJ said our only defense was the relevance of the med error to the patient's outcome, which is an unknown at this point."

They ordered and, after checking to make sure no one was within earshot, she proceeded to tell him about the situation with Keith and the results of her meeting with Helen and TJ.

Eric shook his head. "It must be a full moon, though it sounds like you may have avoided a major problem on that one."

"Really. The way things are going, I won't have to worry about leaving. HealthAmerica will be taking care of that."

Eric shrugged. "Like I told you, not the end of the world. I just hate that everything seems to be happening at one time."

"Tell me about it."

Becky brought their dinner, and Carly waited for her to leave before she continued.

"I was telling you about my conversation with Wayne from IT," she said. She told him that the computer whiz thought that Brian Jennings's death may not have been an accident. Eric listened to what she told him and asked a few questions as she relayed Wayne's comments.

As a mathematician, Eric was analytical and able to quickly distill the most complex issues down to their core. When she'd finished, he sat back and contemplated what she'd told him.

"It's plausible," he said. "There was an article in *USA Today* last week about hackers unlocking and starting a car with a cell phone, so the premise isn't that farfetched. The big question would be why? Why would someone do that?

"Hacking into bank accounts and company files is one thing, which happens all the time. But hacking into a vehicle and causing an accident is something else. Very malicious. And no monetary gain for the perpetrator. Based on what you've told me, I'm not sure that this Sorcerer person is telling the truth. Being capable of doing something versus actually doing it is a whole different matter.

"You said that Wayne told you people make up personalities, names, etc. He's right—these kids are creative and imaginative. I see that in my classes. So I'm inclined to think maybe Sorcerer made it up."

"I don't follow."

"Well, if Sorcerer commented on it after it hit the news, anyone could've done that. Any way to determine exactly when he mentioned it?"

Carly thought about what Eric said. It was logical and, as usual, cut to the issue. If the time of the accident and the time Sorcerer mentioned it were pretty far apart, then the whole thing blows up.

Eric continued. "Wayne may be on to something, but I sure as heck would want to have a little more information before taking it further," he said.

"Good point. As always, you make a lot of sense."

They finished their dinner, with Eric talking about his day. It was a good way to unwind, and the bottle of Chianti didn't hurt. They passed on dessert, and Becky, the young girl who served them, came over and presented the check. Carly pulled out her credit card and handed it to her without even looking at the tab.

In a few minutes, Becky came back to the table, looking uncomfortable. She leaned over next to Carly as she handed the credit card back. Her voice was almost a whisper.

"I'm sorry, Ms. Nelson. Your card was declined. I ran it again just to make sure and it was declined again."

Carly looked at her and frowned. "I don't understand," she said. "Why was it declined?"

"I don't know. It just tells us accepted or declined, nothing more. I'm sorry."

Carly exhaled and started to dig through her wallet for another card.

Eric just laughed and pulled out his wallet. "Are you sure you paid your bill this month?" He handed his credit card to Becky. "Probably some glitch in their system. We'll check it out when we get home."

Carly shrugged, still confused. The only other time that happened was when she was in San Francisco and made several large purchases. That time, they had called her cell phone to verify she was indeed the one using the card.

She pulled out her cell phone to see if she'd missed a call. Nothing. Putting her phone back into her purse, she shook her head.

"Oh well. Thanks for dinner," she said as they got ready to leave.

Eric smiled. "I'm starting to think I was set up. Maybe this is just a modern version of the 'Oh, I left my wallet at home' story."

Carly punched him. "No, but I'll file it away for future reference," she said, laughing.

When they got home, Carly pulled out her credit card and called the number on the back. After navigating the automated response system and entering her card number, she heard a live voice for the first time.

"This is Jerry. I'll be happy to help you this evening. May I have your name please?"

The accent didn't seem to match a name like Jerry, she thought. After further verifying that she was indeed Carly Nelson, he asked how he could be of assistance.

She explained that her card had been declined when she had tried to use it at dinner.

"I'm sorry, Ms. Nelson, but that account has been temporarily suspended by our fraud department."

"Fraud department?"

Eric put down the papers he was reading to listen.

"Yes ma'am. If you would please hold, I'll be happy to transfer you."

"Thank you."

She got the elevator music, indicating she was on hold. As she was about to explain to Eric what was going on, another voice answered, this time a female.

"This is Breanna with the fraud division. May I have your name please?"

This time, the distinct Southern drawl matched the name. Carly went back through the steps of verifying that it was her.

At last convinced that she was indeed talking to Carly Nelson, Breanna proceeded to explain that they had put a security hold on the account because of suspicious attempted transactions.

"What kind of transactions?" Carly asked.

"There were several large dollar transactions attempted in the Miami area yesterday that were declined when the holder was unable to provide identification.

Were you in that area or did you authorize anyone to use the card for merchants in that area?"

"Miami? Absolutely not, no to both questions. I've not been to Miami in eight or nine months, and I haven't ordered anything from any merchant there."

Breanna asked if the card had been in her possession and proceeded to ask about a couple of specific purchases on her account made over the last week. Carly confirmed the card had been with her and verified the purchases.

Breanna explained that she'd be sending Carly a new credit card that would arrive within two business days. Her current credit card would be cancelled, and she gave Carly a case number to reference for future calls. She apologized for the inconvenience and thanked Carly for her business.

With a bewildered look, Carly hung up the phone and walked over to Eric. She sat next to him and explained what had happened.

"Not unheard of," he said. "Somebody lifted your card number and tried to run up the bill as quickly as they could. Sounds like they were clever enough to use it in south Florida to hopefully stay under the credit card company's radar. Be glad their system caught it, although you're limited to fifty dollars liability."

She shook her head. "I know, but it's just the hassle factor. They're cancelling that card and issuing me a new one. Now I've got to change my info at the gym and everywhere else that's set up on automatic payment. With everything going on, I don't need this."

He gave her a hug. "They'll get it sorted out. Besides, nothing you can do tonight. Come to bed, get a good night's sleep. Be more like Bo," he said, nodding over to the Lab, stretched out and sound asleep on his rug in the corner.

Carly couldn't help but laugh. "For a dog's life. He certainly hit the jackpot with us, didn't he? Not a care in the world."

She gave Eric's knee a squeeze, then lightly ran her fingertips up his leg. "But I think I'd rather sleep up here next to you. I'll be back in a minute." She flashed him a wicked smile and got up to get ready for bed. She unbuttoned her shirt, slipped it off, and tossed it onto the floor as she walked away from him, knowing he was watching.

Chapter 14

She was sitting at her desk when Sandy walked in and laid the newspaper on her desk. Above the fold was the headline "Local Man Sues Rivers, Blames Medication Error."

Carly lowered her head into her hands, elbows on her desk, shaking her head.

"I didn't think you'd seen it yet," Sandy said.

Carly looked up at her assistant. "Is there a black cloud hovering over my head? It sure seems like it."

Sandy snorted. "What do you want me to do?"

"Give me a few minutes to read it and get Paul Leggett on the line for me, please." Might as well get it over with.

Sandy turned and walked out. Carly looked back at the paper and read the article. There it was, in black and white. Robert Willis was suing Rivers Community Hospital and Forrest Langford. He was still partially paralyzed, had trouble speaking, and was deprived of "relations" with his wife of fifty-three years. Right—like they were having sex twice a day before the surgery.

Parks Middleton, Willis's attorney, was quoted as saying "there appeared to be gross negligence involved on the part of the hospital and the physician."

Carly's intercom buzzed. "Paul's on line two."

She winced and picked up the phone. "Hello, Paul. How are you?"

"Good, thanks. I was going to call you today. How are things going in Fort Myers?"

She hesitated. "They could be better. Lots better, actually."

She told him about the lawsuit and the newspaper article. "I'll fax it to you when we hang up. What were you calling about?"

Paul ignored her question and cleared his throat. "This doesn't look good, Carly. You fired the nurse yet?"

"We gave her a written DA."

Paul exploded. "You gave her a fucking DA? She almost killed a patient and all you did was write her up? Shit. You know why I was calling, Carly?"

"No." She started to add, I asked and you ignored my question, but thought better of it.

"I was calling to tell you that Carter had approved your promotion. Now I don't know—we've got to hold off till the dust settles on this."

Carly gripped the phone tighter and clenched her teeth. She was this close to telling Paul Leggett where to stick his damn promotion.

"I'll call you back later," he said, and hung up without waiting for a reply.

She called TJ and told him about the article and the conversation with Paul Leggett. As she hung up, she saw Ron Dawkins standing in her doorway. He was a tall, handsome, black man, dressed impeccably, as always. Without a doubt, he was the best-dressed man in the hospital.

Ron played linebacker at Florida State and still appeared to be in good shape, although that was ten years ago. He was good enough to go pro, but a knee injury his senior year nixed that path. Smart enough to make his education a priority, he got his degree and never looked back.

Carly had forgotten about her monthly meeting with him, but motioned him in anyway. Ron was the IT chief at the hospital and was there for his monthly update.

"Hi, Ron. Come in and have a seat. How are you?"

"Not bad—did I catch you at a bad time?"

Carly shook her head. "Just one of those days. I don't think there's going to be a good time today."

Ron laughed, and it was a deep-throated, hearty laugh. "I know what you mean. I can come back later if you want?"

"No, maybe you can help me get back on track. Just don't tell me you have any disasters in IT."

"No, things are going well. Wayne told me he updated you last month. Sorry to bail, but I had to be out of town."

"Not a problem. He seemed like a nice young man. I think he was a little intimidated."

Ron chuckled and nodded. "He doesn't get out much. Sharp kid, though. Glad to have him. He's a genius with a computer and the main reason the electronic medical records project is going so well. Can't believe he was in Fort Myers, right under our nose."

Carly cocked her head. "Really? I thought he was from Orlando?"

"Nope, right here in river city. He's an only child—his dad died seven or eight years ago, so it was just him and his mom. She passed away around a year ago, but I never did find out what happened."

Carly was thinking back to her first conversation with Wayne. Maybe she misunderstood him, but swore she remembered him saying he was from Orlando.

Ron gave her a quick update on the status of the EMR project. The pilot unit, Three West, was going well; so well that he wanted to accelerate the roll-out to the other units. Physician feedback had been positive overall, with a few exceptions that were anticipated. They were almost completely paperless, with the physician's notes the last thing to be automated. Several of the older doctors were complaining, but most had embraced the system once they had a little experience with it. Everything on the unit, including the medical equipment, had been electronically interfaced, eliminating the manual step of transferring information from one box to another, thus eliminating a big source of error.

Less than an hour later, she got a call from Breanna with the credit card company.

"Is this Carly Nelson?"

"Yes it is."

"I'm sorry, Ms. Nelson, but I need to verify your identity again. Could you please give me the last four digits of your social security number?"

Carly complied and answered the additional security questions, including the case number that Breanna had given her the other evening.

"Clearly your account has been compromised, Ms. Nelson. We're trying to track down how, but in the meantime I have a few more questions for you."

Breanna went on to ask her questions about legitimate places she had used her card, were all of her cards accounted for, had any of them been out of her sight for even a few minutes, etc.

After ten minutes of questions, Breanna said, "I've confirmed that we've cancelled your existing card number and new cards are being sent to you via FedEx. You should have them in the morning. I would suggest you change your login, password, security questions, everything. Have you experienced any problems with any other accounts?"

Carly hadn't thought of that. "No, not that I know of. Why?"

"Well, it seems that the person who used your credit card number had access to some of your personal information, including social security number, security question answers, and the CCV2 code printed on the back of your card. Fortunately, when they tried to use your card number, they couldn't provide matching identification and that's what triggered our involvement. There's good reason to suspect other accounts may be compromised as well. I would suggest filing a police report, checking all of your accounts, and consider freezing your credit reports with all three credit bureaus."

"How did someone get that information?" Carly was getting worried and angry.

"We're not sure, Ms. Nelson. We're checking our systems, but at this point we don't have any indication that our system was breached. Rest assured we're doing everything we can to find out what happened on our end. And we're waiving the fifty dollar liability on your account. You won't be responsible for any of the fraudulent amounts charged to your card. Let me give you my direct number in case you need any further assistance."

Breanna gave her the necessary contact information, and Carly thanked her for her help.

She hung up and before she could check any of her other accounts, Eric called.

"How's your day going?" he asked.

"Horrible. Robert Willis is suing us—front page of *News-Press*, Atlanta chewed me out, and I just got off the phone with the VISA rep. Eric, they think some of my personal data has been compromised. The person using the card had information they shouldn't have had access to."

"That's not good. Have you checked any other accounts?"

"Not yet. I was just about to do that. I just got off the phone with Breanna."

Carly finished the day without anymore major setbacks, but she was still smarting from the phone call from Paul Leggett.

At home, she and Eric cobbled together a dinner of leftovers and sat out on the lanai. She was still angry.

"Can you believe that asshole?" she said, taking a bite of her stir-fried rice. She held up her thumb and index finger. "I came this close to telling him to shove it."

"Better get used to it. Or find another job," Eric added.

She studied Eric's face closely to see if he was kidding.

As if reading her thoughts, he said, "I'm serious."

Carly shook her head. "I know you like it here. You're in line for the department chair."

Eric shrugged. "It doesn't mean much if you're not happy. Start looking for another job. You've got great experience and a good track record."

Bo raised his head and looked up at the two, almost as if he understood what they were talking about.

"But I'd feel like I'm abandoning Brian and his legacy."

"Love, Brian's gone. And with corporate running the show, I'm not sure he would've lasted much longer anyway. That position isn't what it used to be. You know it, and I'm sure that Brian knew it, too. Michelle will be finishing school next year—" He held up his crossed fingers, making Carly laugh. "And I doubt she'll end up in Fort Myers. It'd be a good time to move."

She considered what Eric was saying. Maybe it was time to move on. She didn't want to react to one thing, but she had to admit that this was going to be the norm. She had seen Brian's increasing frustration with Atlanta's incessant meddling. Being female and more junior, she knew she could expect even more of that to come.

She reached over and put her hand over his. "What about you? I thought you liked it here?"

He smiled. "I do, but I can find something else. Don't get me wrong, it's not bad at Gulf Coast, but face it, this isn't Berkeley."

She couldn't help but laugh. "No, I've always thought you could do better."

He squeezed her hand. "The things you do for love."

"I'll think about it, okay?"

"What did you decide to do about Wayne's information?"

"I don't know—to tell you the truth, I haven't had much time to think about it, not with everything else going on. Maybe you're right. I'm probably reading too much into it."

"Why don't you talk to George about it? He's pretty sharp, and with his background, I think he'd be a great person to give you good advice on what to do."

She cocked her head and thought. Probably not a bad idea. She wondered how she could talk to him without divulging Wayne's name.

The next morning, at home, Forrest went into his office to pay some bills on his computer. He turned it on and, instead of booting with the familiar background picture of his ocean-front home in Key West, he was greeted with a dancing bear going across the screen.

"What the hell?"

He banged on the keyboard, tried Ctrl-Alt-Del, but nothing worked. Tonya heard him cursing and went in to see what was going on.

"What's the matter?" she said, as she walked over behind him at his desk.

"Damn computer. Guess it's some sort of virus. I haven't got time to fool with it. Will you call the ComputerTech place and get them to send someone out and fix it today?"

She started giggling when she saw the dancing bear. She put her arms around his neck.

"You have to admit, it's kinda funny."

Forrest just shook his head.

"Nothing funny about it. I was going to pay a few bills before I went to the office and now I can't even use the damn thing.

"I've got to get to the office." He rose, gave her a perfunctory kiss, and grabbed a folder off the desk as he turned to walk out.

"I'll take care of it," she said as he disappeared.

Later that morning, the young kid from ComputerTech showed up. Tonya took him into Forrest's office, after wondering if he even had a driver's license, he looked so young. Everyone seemed to be so young. She noticed that he was sneaking glances at her chest, so she decided to give him a treat and lean over in front of the desk as she asked if he needed anything. She wasn't wearing a bra and knew he could see everything. Although it was harmless flirting, it made her nipples hard as she thought about him looking at her.

The poor boy tried not to stare, but it was impossible to ignore the view she was giving him. Once satisfied that she had totally destroyed his concentration, she left him alone and told him she'd be in the den if he needed anything.

Less than thirty minutes later, he knocked on the den door, interrupting her reading. She held up her hand, finished the page she was on, then put the magazine down and looked up at him.

"Uh, Ms. Langford, it's fixed. I'm going back to the office." He looked around nervously. Tonya smiled as she thought about the effect she had on the young man. She mumbled thanks, waved him off, and returned to her magazine, chalking up his nervousness to being in the presence of an attractive, sexy woman.

The next morning at work, Carly called George and asked him to stop by her office around noon. She had decided against saying anything to Wayne yet. She just wanted to bounce it off George and get his reaction. If he thought there was any need to pursue it, then she could talk to Wayne about it.

At five minutes before noon, she looked up to see George standing in her doorway.

"Busy?" he asked.

"Of course, but come on in. Shut the door, if you don't mind."

He looked curious as he shut the door and walked over to her desk. He still moved with an ease that surprised Carly at times. Although his hair was thinning and he was probably carrying a few more pounds than he should, he hadn't let himself go. He stretched out his tall frame in the chair, making it look a little small as he clasped his hands together and waited for Carly to start.

"Do you think Brian's accident could've been deliberate?" She knew George well enough to get right to the point.

He scrunched up his face and tilted his head as he considered her comment.

"Why do you ask?"

She took a deep breath and proceeded to tell him about her conversation with Wayne, leaving out his name and any details that could lead to his identity. George absorbed what she was saying and didn't interrupt, letting her finish first.

When she was done, he sat there for a moment without saying anything, seeming to process the information and organize it in his mind. She'd told him about Eric's comments, and he started there.

"What do you think?" he asked.

Carly was surprised. It didn't seem to matter what she thought—that's why she wanted to take it to him.

"I honestly don't know. At first, I believed him. I mean, I still do believe that this person is being truthful. I just find it so far-fetched, almost beyond my comprehension. And Eric makes a good point. Why? Why would someone do that? What's the motivation? So that's why I wanted to talk to you. You're the expert in this kind of stuff. I'm surprised you're asking me what I think."

"You're the one who's talked to this person and had a chance to evaluate it. I've found that a person's impressions, especially from someone as reliable and trustworthy as you, are important in evaluating information.

"I have to agree, it does sound pretty remote. I didn't want to believe it either, but Carly, I've considered it and I think it was just what it appeared to be—an accident." He shifted in the chair and paused a minute before continuing.

"I spent a career in law enforcement and learned to be objective, at least as much as possible. I learned when something happens that we don't understand or like, we have a tendency to look for alternate theories—conspiracies, bogey-men and such. That's when you have to go back and look at the facts. And when you look at the facts in Brian's death, they point to an unfortunate accident. Sometimes bad things happen. Not saying with one-hundred percent certainty that something like your friend suggested didn't happen, but highly unlikely."

Carly just nodded, relieved. Her intuition told her that George was right.

"Thanks for your time, George. You've put it in perspective and that's what I needed. Sorry to be a bother."

He stood to leave. "Not a bother. We all struggle to make sense of something like this, but sometimes there's just no explanation." He looked at his watch. "Got to run. See you later."

She watched him walk out. Mentally, she scratched this off her list. She'd call Wayne later and tell him, letting him down gently. He was a good kid, but seeing things. Right now, she had more pressing issues.

It had been a busy morning. She had meetings with Forrest, TJ, and phone calls with corporate, all related to circling the wagons on the Willis suit. Corporate's strategy was obvious—it was Darci Edwards's fault, and they were going to throw her under the bus. The logic was hard to argue with, since she was responsible for the error.

As TJ had surmised, the crux was whether or not the medication error was responsible for Willis's unfortunate outcome. HealthAmerica was already assembling paid experts to go through Willis's medical history with a fine-tooth comb, trying to find weaknesses they could exploit in the plaintiff's case.

Carly was amazed at how quickly the aim shifted from proving right or wrong to sheer evasion. Lawsuits of this nature focused on avoiding blame, nothing more.

She had gone downstairs to the cafeteria to get lunch when she saw Wayne sitting alone again. Now was as good a time as any, she thought, as she made her way over and sat across from him without even asking.

"Hi, Wayne. How are you?"

"Okay." He looked around and, at first, Carly thought he was looking to escape. When he leaned across the table and lowered his voice, she realized he was making sure no one was listening.

"Have you decided what to do, you know, about what we talked about?" His eyes darted about, still making sure they were alone.

She finished her first bite of salad before speaking, deciding not to tell him about talking to George. "Yes, I have. Wayne, I appreciate you telling me. That took a lot of courage, and I realize that. But the fact of the matter is that you—we—don't have anything concrete. For all you know, Sorcerer is just making things up. He could've heard it on the news. We have no way of proving or disproving anything. Unless you've got something else, I'm afraid there's nothing to do."

He looked down as he finished the last bite of his lunch, not saying a word. When he looked up, she couldn't tell if it was relief or disappointment in his eyes. "Okay," he said, putting everything on his tray and preparing to leave.

As he rose, she looked up at him. "I'm sorry, Wayne. I really do appreciate your concern."

"That's fine. I gotta go."

He turned and walked away. She remembered wanting to ask him about Orlando, but he was already across the dining room. Some other time, she thought.

She could tell he was disappointed, and so was she, in a way. It was like George said—sometimes we just don't want to believe bad things happen to good people, but they do.

Chapter 15

Later that afternoon, Carly was back at her desk after a series of meetings around the hospital. Her phone rang and she picked up.

"Carly," she said.

"Carly. Hi, Barry Deaton. Got a minute?" Barry was the head of Biomedical Engineering at Rivers.

"Sure, Barry. What's up?"

"I just got a call from IntelliV. You asked that we send the two IV pumps back to them for analysis, just to make sure there were no problems, remember?"

Carly had to think a minute, shifting gears. "Oh yeah, I remember."

"Interesting news. They said the software on both pumps had been tampered with."

"What?"

"They took a close look at everything after I told them what had happened. Put their best people on it and found what they think is an unauthorized piece of code buried deep inside the manufacturer's program."

"So what does that mean?"

"Well, they're completing their analysis, but said the code exploited a hole in their software. It could give someone control over the pump. What they're trying to figure out is when it was done and how."

Carly sat back and shook her head. What in the hell was going on around here? Did this mean that Darci was right after all, it was an equipment problem?

"When will they be finished?" she asked.

"Probably tomorrow. They just wanted to give me a heads-up."

"Have you told anyone else?"

"Nope. You were my first call."

"Don't say a word to anyone about it. I want to get George involved. Call Sandy and let her know as soon as they're done. We need to sit down and put our heads together on this."

"You got it."

"Thanks, Barry."

She hung up the phone, picked up her pen, and started flipping it back and forth. It was like someone had declared war on the hospital. The timing couldn't have been worse.

She started to call George, but decided to wait until she heard back from Barry.

The next day, Barry called and told her he'd talked to IntelliV again. They had finished their analysis of the two IV pumps he'd sent them. Apparently, the surreptitious code had been added within the last two months and only affected the two pumps. They concluded it was possible someone could've changed the flow rate without changing what was displayed on the pump.

IntelliV was testing a software fix for the pumps and, soon as it was complete, they'd be downloading it to all of their customers. The good news is that it was limited to a specific, older model. Rivers had only six of those pumps and IntelliV advised not using them until the software could be upgraded. What they didn't know is how it was done.

Carly had called a meeting for two that afternoon. The small table in Carly's office was crowded, but she wanted to meet here. This was a huge issue, and she felt more secure discussing it in her office.

Barry, George, TJ, Helen, and Carly were seated around the table. Barry had just given the group an update on the final report from IntelliV on the IV pumps.

There was no way of determining exactly what had happened. The log files appeared to be uncorrupted and contained the correct information. It was impossible to know what had been entered or what was displayed. What was certain is that the master control program for the IV pumps had been compromised, giving the potential for an unauthorized user to take control over the pump.

"So, you're telling me that someone could have overridden the flow rate without it showing anywhere but the log files?" Helen asked.

Barry nodded. "I specifically asked them that question, and the answer was yes."

"And no user has access to the log files?" George asked.

Barry shook his head. "Absolutely not. That's a security feature of the IV pumps. Our people can't even access it."

"But I thought you said the log files differed from what was in the chart?" Helen asked.

"I did. But we had to get IntelliV to log in remotely and print them out for us. We can't do that."

"Damn," TJ said. "So maybe Darci was right? She could've entered the correct rate and thought it was working correctly, when in reality it wasn't?"

"Afraid so," Barry said.

"Any chance that someone from IntelliV could've done it?" George asked.

Barry shook his head again. "I asked that, too. They checked their logs in California. That access has to be from one of their secure servers. They had their network security people check it out—no access either day we had med errors."

"What about someone in your department?" George looked at Barry.

Barry leaned across the table. "Wait a minute—"

George held up his hands. "Just asking, Barry, not accusing. Trying to make sure we explore every avenue."

Accepting George's conciliatory tone, Barry sat back in his chair and nodded. "The thought occurred to me when IntelliV first called. Obviously, we have access to the equipment and people familiar with it. So I snooped around a bit in the department. I've got good people down there, knowledgeable about all kinds of biomedical equipment, and some of them pretty good computer types. But none have the background that would enable them to do something like this. According to the guy at IntelliV, the person who did this was a computer genius, not your run-of-the-mill hacker or biomed tech."

Carly shook her head and asked no one in particular, "Who would do this? And why? How did they get access to the pumps?"

"Not sure," Barry said. "With everything connected . . ."

Carly reached for the phone and buzzed Sandy. "Will you get Ron Dawkins up here, now, please?"

She hung up the phone and explained to the group. "I don't like this. Ron needs to be involved. With all these damn computers around, I'm worried."

In a few minutes, there was a knock on her door, and Ron joined them. The group quickly filled him in on what was going on and solicited his thoughts.

"Yes, the pumps are connected to the EMR on that unit. And, even though we have the most sophisticated firewalls available commercially, as Barry said, everything is connected." Ron shrugged and held his hands out. "I'm not making light of what happened, but it's the world we live in now, good and bad."

Carly shook her head. She was getting a headache. Her credit card accounts, the hospital computers. All of this on top of what Wayne had told her was too much to comprehend. It made her want to unplug every damn computer within reach, even though she knew that was impractical.

"What I'm wondering, is this isolated? Or do we have a bigger problem?" Carly asked the group. "I don't want to overreact, but at the same time, what can we do to insure the integrity of our systems?"

Barry said, "I'm satisfied that the IV pumps are okay. We took the six out of service that haven't been updated, and IntelliV has checked all of the others."

"Fact is, we have hundreds of systems in use. Hard to insure there're no other problems out there. We can't just unplug everything," Ron said. "I suggest that we review our security policies, keep an eye out, but not much more we can do at this point."

Carly agreed with Ron, but she hated being so passive. It wasn't her nature. But he was right, there was only so much that could be done. Just hope and pray nothing else happened.

"Any other comments?" she asked.

"Ron's right," George said. "And I do think we all need to take a fresh look at security, make sure we haven't gotten too complacent. It's easy to do."

Carly nodded. "I agree. I want each of you to do a security review—people, policies, etc. Top priority."

"What about the lawsuits?" TJ asked. "Darci's attorney will be asking for maintenance records. I would, and we'll have to turn this over to them. And the other attorneys, Willis's and Langford's."

"Hold off as long as you can. Let them ask, but don't volunteer anything yet," Carly said.

George nodded. "I've got a meeting later this afternoon with Tony Budzinski, a detective I know with the Fort Myers Police Department. At this juncture, we've got to get law enforcement involved, let them handle it."

Slowly, everyone around the table digested the news and nodded.

"If you think of anything, anything at all that might be helpful, let me know. I'll talk with Tony, and I'm sure they'll open an investigation," George said.

He turned to Carly. "I suggest we get back together Monday morning, probably ask Tony to come in."

Carly nodded and cursed underneath her breath. Paul Leggett would be apoplectic when this broke. She'd have to call him. She probably wouldn't have to worry about a career change. With the way things were going, that decision would be made for her.

"So anything else we need to do?" Barry asked.

"Keep an eye out. Maybe organize your thoughts and any information you may have that could be helpful to the police," George said. "And keep this to yourself. Word will get out soon enough when the police start sniffing around, but let them drive it."

They looked at Carly.

She shook her head. "Wish I had some words of wisdom, but I don't. We'll get back together Monday after George's had a chance to talk with the detective."

As soon as everyone left, Carly closed her door and called Paul Leggett to tell him the news.

"You've got to be kidding me?" he said.

He was calmer than she expected until she told him that George was going over to the Fort Myers Police Department.

"Why in the hell is he doing that? Isn't this a little premature to get the fucking police involved?"

Carly was squeezing the telephone handset hard enough to leave fingerprints. She took a deep breath before answering.

"Paul, we've had two med errors, errors that could've killed patients. We have proof that someone has deliberately tampered with our biomedical equipment! We have no choice but to get the police involved."

"Damn! How long can we keep this out of the news?"

She took another breath. "I honestly don't know. George knows the detective, and they'll do all they can to keep it under wraps, but Fort Myers is a small town." She started to add *maybe a couple of days*, but decided to let it go.

"Shit. Carter's going to blow a gasket on this one." There was silence for a few seconds, then Paul said, "Keep me posted. Call me on my cell if there's anything, *anything* at all. And *nothing* to anyone before you talk to me. Understood?"

"Sure." She hung up before she lost control.

That afternoon, George went to the Fort Myers Police Department to meet with Tony Budzinski, not wanting to arouse any suspicion at the hospital. The sergeant at the front desk recognized George, chatted with him a minute while George signed in, and sent him up to Tony's office without bothering with the required escort.

George knocked on the detective's door.

"Come in," a gruff voice answered.

George opened the door and Budzinski smiled when he saw who was there. He stood to shake his hand.

"George, how are you? Good to see you." Tony knew George from his days at the Lee County Sheriff's Office and had worked several cases with him.

"Doing good, Tony. Likewise. I keep waiting to hear you've retired," George said as he sat in one of the chairs in front of Tony's desk.

Tony laughed as he sat down. "Hell, can't afford to. I need to find me a cush job like you've got."

George nodded. "Most of the time, it is. Not lately, it seems. Got a problem you need to be aware of. Going to need your help on this one."

"What's up?" Tony leaned forward in his chair.

"You saw on the news about the patient suing Rivers? Medication error? Now the nurse, Darci Edwards, is also suing us."

Budzinski nodded. "Yeah, looks like a feeding frenzy for the legal-buzzards."

George laughed. "Got that right. But there's more to it. That's why I'm here."

Tony waited for the hospital security chief to continue.

"There was another error, didn't make the paper—yet. Different patient, different IV pump, but same nurse.

"The nurse claims she checked the settings on the IV pumps and they were set correctly. Yet the log files on the pumps show different. We sent the IV pumps back to the manufacturer for them to take a look, and they found something.

"Someone had hacked into the pumps and slipped unauthorized code into the software. Bottom line is that the nurse could be right—the setting that displayed on the pump could've been different than what the pump actually dispensed."

The detective whistled. "Damn, that's spooky."

George nodded.

"So you're telling me that someone else could've tampered with the settings and nobody would've known?" Tony asked.

"Exactly."

"Any ideas?"

George shook his head. "Not really. The people from IntelliV, the pump manufacturer, said that whoever did it was a computer genius, way above the typical hacker. My first thought was maybe somebody in the biomed department—they maintain the pumps—or someone in the IT department, although there's no way of knowing whether it was someone inside or not. Barry—he's head of biomed—says he's already looked inside his area, and he doesn't think anyone there fits. Haven't looked at IT yet."

"Any ideas on why? Or how?"

"None, but this just broke. I asked everyone to give it some thought this weekend. Told them I was coming to talk to you and we'd get back together Monday."

"You think the nurse is clean?"

George nodded. "I do. She's been there five years, solid as a rock. One of the best, according to everyone I talked to. Unless there's something going on outside, she doesn't look like a fit. It's beyond a prank. According to Helen, the VP of nursing, either of those mistakes could've easily killed someone. That's why I'm here."

The detective scratched his head. "So what's your gut saying?"

George shook his head. "Not sure, but I've got a bad feeling about this one, Tony. Somebody hacked into those pumps, and I have no clue who or why."

"I'll open up a case on it. Do what I can to keep it out of the news. What time are you meeting Monday?"

"You tell me."

Budzinski looked at his watch. Five thirty. It was too late to catch everyone this afternoon. "I'd like to do it first thing."

George stood to leave and shook Tony's hand. "Eight o'clock?"

"That works. I'll be there."

"Thanks. Let me know if you need anything."

"Hey, George? Who knows about what the pump manufacturer found? The software thing?"

George shook his head, then held up his hand and counted fingers. "Me, Barry, Carly Nelson, Helen Farmer, TJ—the hospital attorney, and Ron Dawkins-IT chief. Six, that's it."

"Let's try and keep that quiet, okay? Might prove useful down the road."

George nodded. "I'll call everyone soon as I leave."

Chapter 16

Carly hung up her phone. Michelle was coming home this weekend, unusual so soon after being home for her break. And she had a date with Wayne.

Surprised it was Wayne and not Josh, she pressed her for an explanation. All Michelle would say was that she and Josh were just friends. Carly knew there was more to the story, but figured she'd talk to Michelle this weekend when she was home.

Michelle had always been open with Carly, sometimes divulging more detail than she wanted to know. Carly smiled as she remembered the time Michelle had asked her about having an orgasm, wanting to know if she had them with Eric.

The Willis lawsuit was taking an inordinate amount of her time. The judge had ordered mediation, and the mediation hearing was scheduled in six weeks. Neither side wanted to ask for a delay, so preparation had become everyone's top priority.

Robert Willis hadn't been the picture of health before his stroke. He was overweight, diabetic, and didn't exercise. The defense was going to characterize him as already having one foot in the grave, hinting that a stroke was inevitable and that he was lucky to be alive.

Michael Wentworth, Forrest's attorney, had tried to get the judge to sever him from the suit, but the judge said no. When that failed, Wentworth had started working closer with TJ and corporate counsel.

The hospital, on the advice of corporate counsel, had retained a local law firm to represent them, preferring to keep HealthAmerica and the out-of-town presence to a minimum. Of course, that meant more meetings to bring them up to speed.

Complicating things further, Darci Edwards had retained an attorney and filed suit against the hospital, claiming the equipment was faulty.

Carly shook her head as she pictured the legal bills mounting. At least this would have a positive impact on the local economy, she thought cynically.

When she drove into the garage that evening, Michelle's car was in the driveway. Opening the kitchen door, she saw Bo lying at Michelle's feet. His tail started wagging as soon as he saw Carly.

"Hi, Mom." She rose and gave Carly a hug.

"When did you get in?"

"About an hour ago."

"Thought you had a date with Wayne?"

"I do. He's picking me up at eight."

Carly glanced at the clock on the kitchen wall. Seven o'clock.

Michelle reclaimed her seat at the table and Carly sat next to her.

"So, tell me what's going on with the guys in your life? I thought Josh was it, but sounds like you've cooled a bit on him."

Michelle shrugged and looked up from the iPad. "I don't know. He's got some anger management issues. Besides, I like Wayne, too."

Carly's antennae immediately went up. "Anger management issues?"

"Down, Mom. He hasn't done anything. You know I wouldn't put up with that."

Carly relaxed her shoulders.

"He's just a little too jealous. I mean, when I mentioned to him about Wayne coming over to the house that night to look at your computer, he got all pissy, like he owned me or something. So I decided to cool it with him."

"That's good. I'm proud of you. You don't need that."

Changing the subject, Michelle said, "Wayne and I are going out to The Hut tonight. I thought maybe I could invite him over for dinner tomorrow night, if that's all right with you?"

"Sure, that'd be great. We don't have anything planned. I'll tell Eric—"

Bo rose and walked to the door, tail wagging. Eric was home. The door opened and he walked in, stopping to scratch Bo.

"Hey," he said to Michelle as he walked over and hugged her.

"I guess I've dropped to third," Carly said, smiling as Eric hugged her last and gave her a kiss. "We were just talking about you."

"Oh yeah? Good things, I hope?"

Michelle said, "Always. I just asked Mom about bringing Wayne over tomorrow night for dinner."

"Wayne?" He glanced at Carly, caught her look, and recovered. "Sure, Wayne, from the hospital, right?"

Carly smiled, glad that he had picked up the unspoken message. "Yeah. They're going out to the beach tonight. I told her we didn't have anything planned."

"No, happy to have you around, you know that. Just don't tell me you want me to cook."

Michelle laughed along with her mom. "No, don't worry." She looked at Carly. "I thought maybe you could cook that crabmeat-linguine dish. Wayne likes seafood, and it's one of my favorites."

"Sure. Want to plan on around seven? We'll go out and get everything tomorrow."

"Okay." Michelle turned her attention back to the iPad.

Carly and Eric walked back to their bedroom to change.

"What's that all about?" Eric asked after they were behind closed doors.

As she removed her work clothes, Carly said, "Apparently, Josh is the possessive type. He wasn't too keen on Wayne coming over to the house, so Michelle cooled things with him."

"Good. See? She's a little more savvy than you give her credit for."

Eric was in his boxers and walked over to unhook Carly's bra. "Thought you might need some help." Before she could respond, he had unhooked it and was cupping her breasts in his hands.

"Uh, I wasn't planning on taking it off."

"You complaining?" he said as he put his arms around her and pulled her against his bare chest.

She closed her eyes, enjoying the feel of his body next to hers. "No, but Michelle might start wondering. And Wayne will be here any minute to pick her up."

He ran his hands down inside her panties, touching her with his fingers before he pulled back. "Dessert, maybe?" he whispered in her ear.

She shivered as she willed herself to wait. "You're on. I'm counting on it."

They put casual clothes on and went back out to the kitchen. Michelle was still on her iPad, oblivious to everything.

"So what are we doing for dinner?" Carly asked Eric.

"How 'bout sushi? I've been thinking about it all day."

"Works for me." Eric had introduced Carly to sushi, and they both loved it. They had discovered a great place across the river in Cape Coral, of all places, and went there for dinner at least once a month.

Bo got up and went to the front door about the time they heard a car pull up in the driveway.

Michelle rose to answer the door. In a few minutes, she walked back into the kitchen, Wayne and Bo tagging behind.

"Hello, Wayne," Carly said.

"Ms. Nelson, Eric." He reached over and shook Eric's hand.

"Wayne. Good to see you again. Michelle says you're going out to the beach?"

"Yes sir."

"Okay, well be careful. See you later, hon," Carly said.

"Bye, Mom, bye, Eric." The young couple turned and walked out.

Carly looked at Eric, shook her head, and grinned. "Don't worry. You can grill him tomorrow night at dinner."

Eric grabbed his keys as they walked out the door. "I don't know what you're talking about." But he smiled as he said it.

Michelle and Wayne got lucky and found a parking spot a block from the Hut. The place was already crowded when they walked in. She spotted Anna by the beach and walked over, Wayne behind her.

Ryan was with Anna, and Michelle introduced Wayne. He and Ryan offered to go to the bar for drinks.

"So that's the guy you were telling me about," Anna said, as soon as the guys were out of earshot. "He's cute."

Michelle smiled. "Don't get any ideas. Yeah, he's nice. We've talked a lot since we met, but this is our first date."

"I already like him better than Josh. He was a creeper. I told you that from the start."

Michelle wrinkled her face and shrugged. "He's okay, just a little too possessive for me. How're things going with Ryan?"

Now it was Anna's turn to grin. "Great. I like him a lot. Even my parents like him. He's been over to the house a couple of times already."

"Cool. Wayne's coming over for dinner tomorrow night—our first time, you know, together."

"Uh-oh."

Before Michelle could ask, Josh walked up next to her, a little too close for comfort. "Hey, Anna, Michelle. What's up?"

He had a beer in his hand and was dressed in his preppy attire. Michelle looked at Anna, pleading for help.

"Not much. Out here with Ryan, just hanging out," Anna said.

He nodded and looked at Michelle. "Maybe we could go bowling or something later, what'd you think?"

Michelle took a deep breath. "I'm here with someone."

As if on cue, Wayne and Ryan walked up with drinks in hand. Josh saw Ryan first, smiled, then saw Wayne. The smile faded.

"Josh, this is Wayne," Michelle said.

Wayne set the beers down on the table and stuck out his hand. "Wayne Jensen. Nice to meet you."

Josh hesitated a moment, then shook Wayne's hand. "Josh Mills."

An awkward silence passed. Josh took a swig from his beer, then said, "I gotta run. Good seeing you, Michelle." He turned and walked away without saying another word.

"Sorry," Michelle said to no one in particular.

Wayne picked up his beer and took a swallow. "No problem. Nothing to apologize for."

He turned to Anna. "Michelle tells me you've been friends since you were little. I agree with her mom; you two could pass for sisters."

Anna laughed and Ryan said, "They act like sisters, too."

Everyone laughed, and the conversation picked back up where they left off before the interruption.

* * *

The next evening, Wayne showed up around seven. As Michelle requested, Carly had prepared the crab-linguine dish. The weather was nice, as usual, and they had dinner on the lanai. Bo was in his typical spot when Michelle was home, lying at her feet.

"This is delicious, Ms. Nelson. Michelle told me you were a good cook."

Carly finished her mouthful. "Thank you, Wayne. Glad you're enjoying it. This has always been one of her favorite dishes."

"I can't believe they didn't ask me to cook," Eric said to Wayne.

Michelle and Carly laughed. "In his defense, he makes great tacos," Michelle said.

"Carly tells me you're from Orlando," Eric said.

Wayne said, "I worked there before I came to Rivers."

Carly noticed he didn't answer the question and was puzzled. She looked at Eric and saw that he, too, had picked up on the evasive response. Ron had said Wayne was from Fort Myers, but she decided not to press it.

"So how did you end up at Gulf Coast?" Wayne asked Eric, changing the subject.

"Attended a conference here, liked southwest Florida, and they offered me a job." He looked at Carly. "Of course, meeting Carly at a reception made the decision a lot easier."

"You have family in Florida?" Carly asked.

"No." His eyes seemed to darken a shade, and he asked, "So, how's your computer working? Anymore problems?"

She caught the look from Michelle and went with the flow.

"No, working fine, thanks. I appreciate you fixing it for me."

Eric asked him several questions about computers. After dinner, Michelle announced they were going bowling and the couple left. Carly and Eric were in the kitchen, cleaning up.

"He's reluctant to talk about personal stuff, isn't he?" Carly said.

Eric laughed. "Yeah, I noticed. Every time the conversation drifted that way, he was quick to change the subject."

"I wonder why he doesn't say he's from around here. Ron, his boss, told me he was. And you noticed he didn't really answer your question when you asked if he was from Orlando. That's kinda strange, don't you think?"

Eric shrugged as he finished loading the dishwasher. "Who knows? Maybe something about his childhood he wants to forget."

Wayne brought Michelle home after bowling. They got to the house and he walked her to the door.

"I had a great time tonight. Dinner was good, I enjoyed getting to know your folks," he said.

"Me, too. It was fun, even if you did beat me in bowling."

They both laughed.

"When are you going back to Gainesville?" he asked.

"Tuesday, probably. My Monday class has been cancelled, so I'll probably leave Tuesday around lunch."

He reached out and took her hand. "Want to catch a movie tomorrow night?"

"Sure."

He leaned forward and kissed her, putting his arms around her shoulders. She didn't resist, and was just as enthusiastic about kissing him back.

"I should get inside," she said.

He pulled back and smiled at her, still holding her hand. "Okay. I'll give you a call tomorrow."

"Hey," she said. "Sorry about that little episode at the beach."

Wayne shrugged. "No problem. He seemed a little pissed that you were with me."

"Yeah, we went out a few times and he seemed to think that I belonged to him."

Wayne laughed. "No big deal, don't worry about it. Talk to you tomorrow. Night." He turned and walked back to his car.

Sunday, Michelle and Wayne were driving back from Gulf Coast Town Center in Michelle's car. They were on I-75 heading north, about two miles from their exit.

Wayne was on his phone, texting. Suddenly, the car jerked and started going faster. He looked over at Michelle.

"What're you doing?" he yelled.

Michelle had a look of panic on her face. "I don't know!" she shouted. "It just speeded up on its own!"

"What?" He looked over at the speedometer. They were going seventy-five and the needle was going higher.

"Hit the brakes!"

Michelle was dodging traffic and pumping the brakes. Nothing worked. The speedometer showed eighty-five and was still climbing.

"Shit! The damn brakes don't work!"

Although traffic wasn't that heavy, it was getting harder to dodge cars as Michelle weaved in and out of the lanes. One driver blew the horn and flipped her the finger as she sped past.

Ahead, semis were in the middle and right lanes, and a sedan was next to them in the left lane. Michelle was closing fast, with nowhere to go.

"Turn the ignition off!" Wayne said.

"What?"

"Turn the ignition off! Now!"

In the nick of time, Michelle switched off the ignition and the car slowed. She eased over into the right lane, then, as her speed dropped further, over onto the paved shoulder of the interstate. When the car finally stopped, her hands were shaking.

"What the hell happened?" Wayne said.

Michelle leaned her forehead against the steering wheel, still upset.

"I don't know." She was still trying to catch her breath. "All of a sudden, the car started accelerating. Then the damn brakes wouldn't work."

Wayne shook his head and exhaled. "Scared the shit outta me. Has it ever done that before?"

She shook her head.

"All I could see were those two big trucks in front of us!" He was still talking loud.

After a few minutes, when they had calmed down, they debated what to do. Michelle wanted to call AAA. She wasn't driving the car again until someone checked it.

Wayne suggested that since they were so close to her house, he'd drive it home. Reluctantly, she agreed.

They swapped places, and Wayne drove, carefully watching the cars around them and sensitive to every nuance in Michelle's car. He kept his right hand on the ignition switch the entire time, but nothing else happened.

Carly and Eric were out on the lanai when they got home.

"Mom! My car is possessed!" Michelle said as soon as she and Wayne walked through the door.

They proceeded to tell Carly and Eric what had happened on the way back from the mall.

"Thank God you're all right!" Carly said.

"So, everything was normal the rest of the way home?" Eric asked.

Wayne nodded. "No problem at all. Not even a hiccup."

"Well, I'm not driving that thing to Gainesville in the morning! No way," Michelle said.

"No, you can take my car," Eric said. "I'll take yours by the Toyota place in the morning and get them to thoroughly check it out. That was quick thinking on the ignition switch, Wayne."

The young man shrugged. "Didn't know what else to do."

Michelle turned to Eric, a slight smile on her face. "So you're really going to let me take your car?" Eric drove a Miata convertible.

Carly saw her grin, looked at Eric, and said, "You might not get it back. Now I'm wondering if this whole thing was an imaginative way—"

"Mom!" Michelle said, but now the grin had spread.

Carly held up her hands. "Just kidding. I'm just glad nothing happened, that was dangerous. And no, we wouldn't let you drive it again until we can get it checked out. I'm not even sure that you should be driving it," she said, turning to look at Eric.

"I'll be fine. The biggest problem was the unexpected part of it. Now, it won't come as a surprise, and as Wayne demonstrated, the temporary fix is pretty simple."

Michelle and Wayne got up to leave, and she walked over to Eric and gave him a hug.

"Thanks," she said. "I promise I'll take good care of it."

He laughed. "I'm not worried. I just want them to find out what's wrong with yours."

After they left, Carly looked at Eric.

"That's what Wayne said happened to Brian's truck, remember? Eric, you don't think—"

Eric held his hand up. "Love, don't start jumping to conclusions. We don't know what happened to Brian. Plus, we've had problems with the electronics on Michelle's car—remember the speedometer going out? This was probably related."

She thought about it and had to agree; she was probably overreacting. Like George said, she was just having a hard time accepting that what happened to Brian was an accident.

Chapter 17

Eight o'clock Monday morning, everyone was gathered around the conference table in Brian Jennings's office. Carly hadn't moved into his office and didn't plan to, but his office was larger and more comfortable for the group, so she had decided to hold the meeting there.

As soon as everyone was situated, George introduced Lieutenant Tony Budzinski and turned the meeting over to him.

"Thanks for meeting with me first thing on a Monday. I know you're all busy and have better things to do. Frankly, so do I."

Everyone chuckled. He took a sip of his coffee and continued.

"George came to me late Friday and told me what happened. We're treating this as the highest priority. In fact, I spent the weekend meeting with my people, and we're hitting the ground running.

"I have a few questions for you, but first, I'd like you to share anything you may have thought about over the weekend. I don't know if any of you, other than George, has ever been involved in a criminal investigation, but contrary to what you see on television, it involves a lot of boring and tedious work. It's like putting a puzzle together, so things you may not deem important may indeed be helpful. So why don't we open it up and let me hear what you have to say."

Helen Farmer spoke first. "Obviously, I thought about it a lot over the weekend. It seems to me a lot hinges on Darci Edwards's credibility, so I took a fresh look at that. You know, looking for any indications that she was under outside stress, any different behavior at work. Anyway, I checked that out as thoroughly as I could, and nothing. No different behavior than ever. She's solid, and nothing going on outside in her life that I know of that would possibly be a factor."

"Good, Helen," Budzinski said. "That's exactly the kind of input I need from you. You know the people and the environment better than us, and although we may be going over some of the same territory, this is helpful."

They continued along this vein for almost an hour, with everyone volunteering their thoughts. Budzinski asked questions to familiarize himself with the organization and there was considerable discussion about possible suspects.

"What would be the profile for someone who might do something like this? Or is there one?" TJ asked.

Tony hesitated before answering. "Good question. Hard to say. Clearly, a starting point is a hospital employee, or former one. It doesn't have to be, but a person like that would be a logical candidate, since he would be familiar with the hospital's routine, procedures, etc.

"Based on IntelliV's findings, someone who's a computer whiz, though that may be hard to gauge. Someone who might have a reason, however farfetched, to do something like that. You know, someone who was fired or had a grudge against the patient or hospital. Again, those would be logical places to start. That's why I say there's a lot of dead-ends in an investigation like this. My guess is the person responsible has above-average intelligence, so he's unlikely to leave a lot of obvious tracks."

They continued talking about the incidents, with everyone asking questions. Lieutenant Budzinski told them he expected to start questioning hospital employees that afternoon and reminded everyone this was now a criminal investigation.

When Carly got home that evening, she noticed Michelle's car back in the garage.

"So what did they say about Michelle's car?" she asked Eric, after greeting him with a kiss.

"I talked to the service manager when I took it in. Since it was a safety issue, he made it a top priority. They went over it with a fine tooth comb, got on the phone with Toyota's regional service techs, everything. Nada. No indication of any fault codes and, naturally, they couldn't duplicate the problem. He said they probably drove it over a hundred miles, trying to get it to act up. As a precaution, they replaced the Master Control Unit and updated all of the software. He seemed to think it was some kind of random software error."

"That's too weird. I'm beginning to think the computer gods have declared war on me, with all that's going on. What do you think about her car?"

He shrugged. "I don't have a clue. Cars have gotten so complicated, and there are so many computers in the new ones. I'm convinced they did everything they could."

A chill went through her body as she kept going back to Wayne's comments about Brian Jennings's truck.

"I keep wondering if someone could've done this?"

Eric had a puzzled look on his face as he pondered her question, then shook his head. "You're still thinking about Brian, aren't you?"

She nodded.

"Like I said before, I think you're seeing things. Surely Brian would have had the presence of mind to switch off the ignition, if that's what happened to him."

She considered what Eric said. True, Brian would've known to turn the ignition off. And Michelle had full control of the steering on her car. George was right; we look for things to support our theories when we don't like the outcome.

"You think her car's safe?" she asked.

"As safe as any. I don't know of anything else we could do, other than trading it in. I'd say let's keep an eye on it. If it acts up again, we'll trade it in on something else."

"Michelle will want to trade it on a Miata."

Eric laughed. "So, I'm going to have a hard time getting mine back, you think? What's the latest at work?"

"First things first—what do you want to do for dinner?"

"Il Palazzo?"

"Good, let's go. I'm starving."

* * *

The next day, George was in Carly's office telling her about his latest conversation with Detective Budzinski.

"They have nothing. So far, everyone has checked out. Lots more digging to do. No clues yet, but that's not unusual."

She was frustrated. "So, we're supposed to wait until something else happens?"

"I understand your frustration. Tony says they're exploring every angle. But sometimes these things just take time."

At least TJ had reported to her earlier that the meeting with the plaintiff attorneys had gone well. Nothing else had appeared in the press about the case. TJ had told them about the software being tampered with, and the suits were licking their chops at the prospect of adding a large medical equipment manufacturer to the list of defendants. Right now, she'd take any good news she could get.

Barry Deaton said that IntelliV had updated the software and checked all of the other pumps as a precautionary measure. No more problems had been uncovered.

Helen had met with all of the nurse managers and instructed them to tell their staff to be vigilant about checking IVs. But it was as if everyone was waiting for something else to happen. And no one wanted it to happen on their watch.

The young man took a sip of his beer and watched the young blonde nurse over at the bar by herself. There was nothing to indicate she was a nurse, but he recognized her. Normally, he liked to do everything online, rarely resorting to any interaction with the person. It was safer and less personal that way. Since he didn't plan to have any face-to-face encounter with her, he thought the slight risk was tolerable.

He was only observing. He'd heard the IV pump manufacturer had discovered the code he'd inserted, which was getting Darci Edwards, at the bar, off the hook. That was unfortunate and not planned for. There were already rumors of dismissing her lawsuit against the hospital and wiping her record clean. That was unacceptable, so he'd turned his focus back to her for the moment.

He knew what kind of car she drove and had already transferred his program to the ECU, Electronic Control Unit, in her vehicle. Since her car was an older model and less sophisticated than the new ones, he'd have to be a little closer to her vehicle.

After a few hours, she wasn't having any luck picking up anyone, and he saw her reach into her pocketbook to pay her tab. Since he had paid cash for each beer as delivered, he could leave without attracting any attention.

He took another swallow, then rose to leave ahead of Darci. He walked out to his truck, careful to avoid any potential contact with the woman, not even glancing at her as he walked past the bar. He'd parked on the street, up from the entrance to her parking spot, so he could follow her at a safe distance.

He cranked his truck and turned on the computer sitting on the front seat next to him. It quickly booted up, and he started his monitoring program. The blinking red dot on the map indicated the location of Darci's car.

A few minutes later, he noticed the petite nurse get into her car and pull out of the parking lot. He checked his mirror and pulled out behind her. She crossed the bridge on San Carlos, then turned right on Summerlin Road. Traffic was light on the four-lane divided highway, the perfect place for what he had in mind. He closed the gap, then passed her, going almost sixty. When he pulled back into the lane in front of her, he pressed a key on the computer, then looked in the rearview mirror, watching her car behind him.

It jerked to the right, wheels going off onto the shoulder. She reacted as he thought she would, and yanked the steering wheel back to the left, abruptly bouncing the car back up onto the pavement. In doing so, she lost control, and the small car flipped, rolling over several times.

He had no idea how serious she was hurt, if at all, but didn't care. He knew she didn't have her seatbelt fastened—he'd dropped a dime into the buckle so it wouldn't lock. He could only hope she'd been thrown out of the car when it rolled.

He checked his speed to make sure he wasn't over the posted limit and drove on, closing the laptop.

When Carly got home Friday evening, Michelle was already there. Eric was out on the lanai getting the grill ready. Wayne was coming over at eight to watch a movie, so Carly and Eric had decided to grill burgers.

Eric had already broken the news to Michelle about the car.

"At least I know what to do if it happens again," she said.

"Let's hope it doesn't," Carly said.

"I got a lot of compliments on Eric's car."

Carly laughed. "I'll bet. Don't even think about it. When I see that diploma, then maybe we can talk."

Michelle stood and put her arm around Carly's neck. "Really? Are you serious?" she said as she held her face next to her mom's.

"No promises, but I said we'll talk."

"Hey, that's a start."

"Talk about what?" Eric said as he walked in from the lanai.

"Your daughter is conniving to get your car on a permanent basis." They had dropped the "step" prefix long ago, with Eric calling Michelle his daughter.

Michelle walked over and put her arm around Eric, buttering him up. "Mom says when I graduate, we can talk about me getting one."

"That's not—"

"Sounds good to me," Eric said, as Michelle squealed and kissed his cheek.

"Not fair," Carly said.

Bo raised his head and looked toward the front door.

"Wayne must be here. I'll let him in," Michelle said, as she started toward the front door, Bo next to her.

Carly walked over and gave Eric a deep kiss.

"Wow! What was that for?"

"Do I have to have a reason?" Carly said in mock astonishment.

He smiled. "Not at all. You can do that any time."

"Later," she said, with a wicked grin as Michelle and Wayne walked into the kitchen.

They ate, and as they were finishing dinner, Carly's phone rang. She was tempted to ignore it, but picked it up and saw it was George Hopkins.

"Hello, George."

"Hi, Carly. Sorry to bother you."

"No problem. Just finishing dinner. What's up?"

"Bad news, I'm afraid. Darci Edwards. She was killed in a single-car accident this evening."

"Oh my God! What happened?"

"She'd been out to the beach, had a few drinks, driving home by herself on Summerlin. Car ran off the pavement, and from all accounts, she jerked the wheel back over and the car flipped. She wasn't wearing her seatbelt and was thrown out. She was dead by the time anyone got there."

"Was it the alcohol?"

"Don't know at this point. They'll be checking that, of course. She was definitely drinking, but not sure if that was a factor or not. Anyway, I thought you'd want to know."

"Yes, thanks for calling."

She put the phone down without speaking.

"Everything okay, love?" Eric asked.

Carly shook her head. "That was George. Darci Edwards was killed in a car accident this evening."

Chapter 18

The next day at the hospital, Darci's accident was all everyone was talking about. George had stopped by Carly's office to give her an update.

The preliminary blood tests showed a blood alcohol level of less than .05, well below the legal limit, but enough to have been a slight factor in concentration and decreased reaction time. Based on the Florida Highway Patrol officer's report, her right wheels had run off the pavement onto the shoulder and she had overcorrected, jerking the car back up onto the pavement and causing it to flip. According to George, that wasn't unusual, and was responsible for a large share of single-vehicle accidents.

Such a shame, Carly thought. She felt guilty, even though it had been an accident. The problems with the IV pump had exonerated the young nurse, and everything was going to be expunged from her record. Although Darci's life had hit a bump, everything was on the mend and would shortly have been behind her.

She shuddered as she thought about Michelle's car. Too many people were still killed in automobiles. It seemed like a rash of incidents had plagued the hospital recently, and she hoped they were in for a reprieve. For a fleeting moment, she thought about Brian's accident. Different circumstances than Darci's, but she couldn't help but wonder if there was a connection.

The two men dressed in sports coats, but no tie, walked up to the door of the sprawling mansion overlooking the Caloosahatchee River just south of downtown Fort Myers. They looked around at the breathtaking view, one of the best in Fort Myers. The lot was huge, at least a couple of acres, they guessed. The house was steps away from the river. A dock and boathouse extended from the shore, and they could see a large cabin cruiser tied to the end of the dock. Two jet skis were hanging by davits on the other side of the dock. They looked at each other, shook their heads, and rang the doorbell.

Tonya Langford, still in her tennis outfit, opened the door and eyed the pair. She was tall and slim, with bleached blonde hair, blue eyes, and a tan that indicated a lot of time spent outdoors with little cover. The two men couldn't help but give her the once over—Tonya attracted that kind of attention. She was good-looking and knew it.

She looked at the pair with disgust, as if they were panhandlers who had somehow breached the gate at the end of the driveway.

Before she could dismiss them, the younger, heavier man held up his badge for her to see.

"Fort Myers Police Department. I'm Detective Karl Larson. Are you Ms. Forrest Langford?"

She had a look of disbelief as she looked at the other man and returned her gaze to the one holding his badge up.

"Yes. What's this about?"

The other man, taller and almost bald, pulled out a document and offered it to her. "I'm Lieutenant Anthony Budzinski. This is a warrant to search your husband's computer, Ms. Langford. May we please come in?"

Normally, Budzinski wouldn't have been involved on something like this. He usually worked homicide. But due to the high profile of this case, the Chief wanted a senior officer involved and assigned him.

She looked at the piece of paper he was holding as if it were toxic, then back at him.

"What? For what? I'm sorry, I'll have to call him first. There's been some kind of mistake. You can wait here." She started to close the door, but the younger detective put his foot out to stop it.

"I'm afraid that's not an option, ma'am." This time his voice wasn't as friendly and had more of an edge to it. "This warrant is signed by a judge and gives us the right to search his computer and related items without his or your permission."

It was then she noticed a Fort Myers Police Department car parked behind the plain dark blue sedan with tinted windows in her driveway. A young man in uniform was standing at the bottom of the steps, his thumbs hooked on the front of his belt, looking bored, but watching the encounter at the front door with interest. She took the document without bothering to open it, turned loose of the door handle, and stepped back into the house without saying a word.

The two officers walked through the door. "Would you please take us to his computer?" It was not a question.

She hesitated for another moment as she looked at one, then the other, as if she couldn't believe this was happening.

"This way, but I'm calling him and our attorney right now."

"You're free to do that, ma'am," the bald guy said.

She had her phone in hand and pressed the number for Forrest's cell phone as she walked the agents into her husband's study and pointed to the computer over on the desk.

They walked over to the desktop computer. The younger man started to turn the computer off.

Budzinski held up his hand.

"No, just leave everything on and unplug it." He shrugged. "That's what the IT forensic guys say."

The younger detective started unplugging wires as Tonya was latched on to Budzinski, like a Chihuahua.

"I thought you said you had the right to search it, not take it," she said, trying to assert herself in some small way.

Again, the bald one spoke. "The warrant in your hand gives us the right to take it back to our office to search it. That way we don't have to sit in your house for hours, which I'm sure would not be your preference." He gave her a thin smile as he turned back to the task of helping the younger officer unplug everything.

Tonya's call went straight to her husband's voice mail. "Shit. Call me ASAP," she said, as she disconnected and immediately called Michael Wentworth, their attorney.

"This is Tonya Langford. I need to speak to Michael."

She was tapping her foot as she watched the officers finish unplugging Forrest's computer.

"I don't give a damn if he is busy. There are two people from the Police Department in my house as we speak and I need to talk to Michael. Now!"

She tapped her tennis-shoe clad foot for another minute, holding the still-folded search warrant in her other hand.

"Michael, there're two police officers here who say they have a search warrant and they're taking Forrest's computer and they say I can't stop them. Can you tell them to leave?" She quit talking long enough to listen to her attorney.

"Hold on." She turned to the agents. "Will one of you talk to my attorney?" She held the phone out as if to say *now you're in big trouble*.

The older agent sighed and took the phone from her hand.

"This is Lieutenant Anthony Budzinski. I'm with the Fort Myers Police Department, badge number FM482456. I have a search warrant, document number—" He took a piece of paper out of his pocket and read it to the attorney, "FL9587326, dated today's date and signed by Circuit Court Judge Martha Bowes. You can call her office to verify it if you'd like. Here's Ms. Langford."

He handed the phone back to Tonya without waiting for a response.

She flashed a phony smile at the detective and pulled her hair back as she put the phone up to her ear.

"So, did you tell him to leave?" She tightened her face as she spoke. "What do you mean, you can't? As much as we pay you, you have to do something," she screamed into the phone. She threw the search warrant down onto the desk, slammed the phone on top of it, glared at the detectives, and folded her arms.

"You're making a huge mistake," she said. But the bravado was missing from her voice.

The two agents ignored her. They finished unplugging everything and searched through the desk for any electronic media. They gathered those items and put them into a bag she didn't realize they had with them. The younger man made notations on a piece of paper and, as they got ready to leave, he handed the sheet of paper to her.

"This lists the equipment and media we're taking. It has our phone numbers and information on it, should you have any further questions. We appreciate your cooperation, Ms. Langford. Have a nice day." He did his best to keep a straight face.

She took the piece of paper and tossed it onto the desk without even looking at it.

Determined to get the last word in, she said, "You'll be hearing from our attorney, probably before you get back to your office. And I can tell you, we're going to sue you for . . . harassment." She turned and flounced away.

The two detectives just looked at each other, rolled their eyes, and shook their head; nothing they hadn't heard before. The younger one picked up the computer while the bald detective took the bag with various USB drives and other digital media. They took one more glance around the office. Satisfied they had what they had come for, they walked out, not waiting for Ms. Langford to escort them to the door.

* * *

Carly and Eric were out on the lanai, having just finished dinner. Bo was lying on his side, content to be near the two of them.

"I still can't believe that about Darci. So tragic. And I almost feel responsible, in some crazy way," Carly said.

He shook his head. "Don't be silly. You had nothing to do with it." He started to add, *you can't be responsible for everyone*, but let it pass.

"I know that, on an intellectual level. But still . . ."

"You could go to San Francisco with me. Would do you good."

Eric was going to San Francisco in a few weeks for a conference. It was one of their favorite cities, and he'd tried to persuade Carly to go out with him, even for a couple of days. But she felt she needed to stay close. He understood, but was still worried about her.

She reached over and put her hand over his.

"I'd love to, you know that. But the timing couldn't be worse. We've got the mediation coming up."

"You could come out for the weekend, then fly back?"

"Tempting, but I'd want to stay. Besides, I probably wouldn't be good company."

Eric laughed, a big smile stretching across his face, and squeezed her hand.

"You're always good company. Maybe we can plan a trip out there later this year, spend a week."

Carly nodded. "I'd like that. Hopefully, things will settle down at work."

"Thank goodness you've not had anymore problems at the hospital. Well, except Darci's accident, but you know what I mean."

"Yes, apparently, the issue with the IV pumps was an isolated one. As my grandmother always said, 'This too shall pass.'"

Chapter 19

Tuesday morning, Carly was in her office checking email when Sandy walked in.

"Good morning, Sandy."

"Morning, Carly. Did you see the news this morning?"

"No. Why?"

"I should've brought you the paper. Forrest Langford was arrested."

"You're kidding, right?"

Sandy shook her head.

"For what?" Carly asked.

Sandy lowered her voice. "They found child pornography on his home computer."

"No! Are you sure?"

"Go to the *News-Press* website." She turned and walked out.

Carly clicked on the web address for the *Fort Myers News-Press*. Sure enough, in big headlines, "Local Surgeon Arrested." She skimmed the article.

Just as Sandy had told her, Forrest Langford had been arrested yesterday evening after the police had found child pornography on his home computer. Acting on a tip, they had gotten a search warrant and taken his computer out of his house earlier. After searching it and finding numerous copies of child pornography, he was arrested last night. His attorney, of course, maintained his client's innocence.

She couldn't believe it. As much as she despised the man, she had a hard time believing he was into something like that. It was just so out of character.

Carly's cell phone buzzed. It was Eric.

"Carly—"

"I know. I just heard. We spoke too soon last night about no more problems at the hospital. Does Michelle know?"

"No, I don't think so. She's still asleep. I'm home, doing a little work here before going into the office."

She thought a minute. "Would you wake her and put her on the phone? I'd rather her hear it from me."

"Okay. Hold on."

Carly could hear him walking through the house, then knocking on Michelle's door. A few minutes later, Michelle's sleepy voice answered.

"Hey Mom, what is it?"

"I wanted to tell you something." She paused, searching for the right words, but failing. "Your dad's been arrested."

There was a silence on the other end, then, "For what?"

Carly took a deep breath. There was no other way to say it. "According to the news, they found child porn on his computer at home. All I know is what I just read."

"Child porn? On Dad's computer? Mom, that's disgusting! Was it really his?"

"I don't know, Michelle. I just found out and wanted to tell you before you got hit with it. Go look up the *News-Press* on the computer. As soon as I hear anything else, I'll let you know. But I have a hard time believing it, just like I know you do."

The line was quiet for a moment. "Thanks for telling me, Mom. I've got to get ready and get on the road back to Gainesville. Love you."

"Love you, too. Be careful driving. Give me a call tonight, okay?"

"I will."

Carly put the phone on her desk. What the hell was going on? She really did have a hard time believing it was true. But they would not have arrested him if they didn't have something pretty convincing. Langford was well-known in Fort Myers and widely respected. She had to believe that every *I* was dotted and *t* crossed if they were going after him on something like this.

Later that morning, her cell phone rang again. It was Eric.

"You heard anything else on Forrest?" he asked.

"No, other than what's in the news. Looks bad, doesn't it?"

"That's all everyone out here on campus is talking about, for sure. But you know how the media is—they love to sensationalize everything. What do you think?"

Carly sighed. "I don't know. Part of me refuses to believe it's true, but then the other half wonders. Got to be something there somewhere. What are your thoughts?"

"Probably like yours. I don't know him well, but doesn't sound like his style. I did talk to a guy out here who teaches criminal justice and has a lot of contacts at the Police Department. He thinks it looks bad for Langford. According to his sources, they have a pretty damning case."

"My God, Eric. I know I sound like the typical moron on the six o'clock news interview. 'Well, I've known Doctor Langford for twenty years and he's a fine, upstanding man. He would never do anything like that.' I mean, the prisons are full of innocent people, right? I know better, but when it hits this close to home . . . How's Michelle?"

"She seems okay. After you hung up earlier, she talked to me a little. She's in shock right now, doesn't know what to believe. Tried to call her Dad, but didn't get an answer. Hey, love, this will get sorted out. Don't worry. I've got to run to a meeting. See you later."

"Okay. Thanks, Eric. Love you." Carly hung up the phone.

She thought George might know something and picked up the phone to call him.

"Hi, Carly. I suppose you're calling about Langford."

"Just wondering what you'd heard," she said.

"I'm over in the office tower now. I'll stop by in a few minutes if you're free."

"Sure, that'd be good. Thanks, George."

Carly was having a hard time concentrating on her work. It was creepy, even the thought that Forrest would be involved in something like that. Maybe she didn't know him as well as she thought. Perhaps it was true that everyone had a shadow side. *Who said that? Jung?* Maybe Forrest Langford did have a dark side.

George knocked on her office door and walked in.

"What a way to start off the day, huh? Our top admitter gets arrested for child pornography," Carly said, shaking her head.

George sat and looked at her. "What do you think?"

She let out a muffled laugh. "Everyone's asking me that. As if I have the answer because I was married to the man for eight years. The honest answer is, I don't know. I don't think he'd do something like that, but you probably heard that a lot when you were with the Sheriff's Office."

George just nodded.

"So tell me. How bad is it? This is serious, isn't it?" she asked.

He nodded and collected his thoughts before speaking. "Afraid so, at least from what I've heard. I don't know a lot, mind you, they're keeping pretty tight wraps on this one because of who it is. But, yes, the evidence is damaging. And lots of it."

"But realistically, couldn't someone have put those pictures on his computer? I mean, I don't know everything that's on my computer," she said, pointing to her computer screen.

"True, but there's more to it than that. This is off the record, Carly." He waited for an affirmation from her before proceeding.

"I understand. You know I won't repeat it."

"Apparently he'd been communicating electronically with an undercover agent posing as a minor. He sent the agent nude photos of himself. And copies of pictures they found on his computer."

Carly inhaled and put her hand over her mouth. She felt sick as she thought of that pervert living under the same roof with her daughter.

George continued, "They're keeping a lid on that for now, but it'll be out before long. Sorry to be the bearer of bad news, Carly. For what it's worth, I find it hard to believe, too. But I've been fooled many times before. You just never know."

"But dammit, George, I was married to the man. You know how that makes me feel?"

He shook his head. "No, but I know you're being too hard on yourself. You're human—you can't read minds any better than the rest of us. And you're not responsible for what he does."

"What do I tell Michelle?"

"Not a lot you can tell her. Your daughter needs your support right now. She's a bright girl. She'll come to her own conclusions over time. It's not up to us to judge him, Carly."

She considered his words and nodded in agreement. There were so many feelings racing through her mind right now.

"Thanks for sharing, George. And for your counsel. You're a wise man."

George laughed. "Don't know about that. Martha would argue with you on that point." He rose. "Call me if you need anything." He turned and walked out the door.

"Hey, George?"

He stopped and turned around.

"Do you know anything about identity theft?" She told George what had happened to her credit card. He gave her basically the same advice as Breanna. He did give her the name of a contact at the Police Department to call and file a report.

After he left, she pulled out her wallet and removed her credit cards.

Sandy buzzed her. "Paul Leggett is on line two for you."

Shit. What a morning. She was going to have to get Sandy to hold her calls while she checked on this credit thing.

"Thanks." She pressed the button for line two.

"Paul."

"What the hell is going on down there?" He continued without waiting for a response. "First, the thing with the incompetent nurse, now this? Do you realize how this makes HealthAmerica look? It looks like we don't have control over our own damn hospital."

He finally stopped to catch his breath. "Carter called me already and chewed me out until he found out that I hadn't yet promoted you. I have to be honest here, Carly—now I'm concerned about potential blowback from this mess over Forrest Langford." There was an uncomfortable silence on the line.

She was already in a bad mood and chose her words carefully. "Forrest and I divorced ten years ago. Exactly what sort of *blowback* are you concerned about, Paul?"

'That's just it—I don't know. All I know is he's your leading admitter, you were married for eight years, and you have a child by him."

Carly gripped the phone tighter, wishing it was Paul's neck.

"It's not your fault, Carly," he continued, striking a more conciliatory tone. "You're just in the wrong place at the wrong time. I'm just being frank here. But unknowns bother me. Corporate's concerned that somehow it may end up tainting you. HealthAmerica has enough image challenges as it is. We don't need this."

"So . . ." She didn't trust herself to say anything else.

"I'm prepared to make you acting CEO. I ran it by Carter and he agreed, though it wasn't an easy sell. It'll buy us time, let things get sorted out. When it settles down, we'll look at promoting you. Your bonus will be retroactive. What do you think?"

She started to say you're a chicken-shit bastard, but decided that wouldn't be a career-enhancing move. What choice did she have? She noticed he said *look at promoting you*. Bastard was leaving himself an out and trying to buy her loyalty to get through the issues at hand.

Carly knew the game too well. They didn't want to get rid of her now and put someone new in the position. If it didn't work out, then they would have to fire the new person. So they needed her. With Carly as acting CEO, she would be the scapegoat and fired. If things did work out, then promote her. It was a win-win for HealthAmerica.

"That's fine. But you need to publicly announce it pronto. This place needs someone in charge," she said, knowing she had no choice but to play their game. But it helped make her decision about leaving an easier one.

"Agreed. I'll get something out this afternoon. Thanks, Carly. I knew you'd understand. It's going to work out, don't worry." He hung up.

Carly slammed the phone back onto its cradle. "Asshole," she said a little louder than she wanted. She realized he didn't even acknowledge Darci's death. What a jerk.

Sandy heard her comment and buzzed her.

"Want me to hold your calls?"

Carly had to smile. Sandy knew her too well. "Yes, please. And thanks, Sandy."

Fortunately, Carly only had two personal credit cards and a debit card. She called the telephone number on the back of the other credit card, and as feared, it too had been compromised. She spent thirty minutes on the phone with them.

Next, she called her bank about her debit card, hoping for a break. Not a chance. Someone tried to withdraw six hundred dollars last night from an ATM in Miami. The bank had put a hold on it until they could contact her to verify her account. Thank God for small favors, she thought.

She asked Sandy to check with accounting and see if there was a problem with the hospital credit card Carly carried. Less than an hour later, Sandy buzzed her.

"Accounting said there were no unauthorized charges on the hospital account. But they're closing it as a precaution and sending you a new card up tomorrow."

"Thanks, Sandy." Damn, Carly thought. You'd know the one card that didn't get screwed up was the hospital credit card. That figures.

Shortly after Carly got her day back on track after lunch, Sandy walked in and laid the copy of the press release on her desk. "Congratulations," she said, with not a lot of enthusiasm. "Although I don't get the acting part."

"You know how corporate is, always wanting to hedge their bets. Apparently Atlanta is concerned about Forrest's little issue, so they're sticking their toe into the water."

Sandy nodded. "Figures. Leggett has no backbone." She turned and walked out.

Carly smiled. Sandy was protective of her boss and, though she usually held her tongue, on occasion she spoke out. Like then.

Later that afternoon, Sandy buzzed her. "There's a Jim Wallace Kitchens on the line. Wants to speak to you. Says he's Doctor Langford's attorney."

Carly wrinkled her face. She didn't recognize the name. Either he was new to Fort Myers or not from around here.

"Thanks, Sandy. I'll take it."

Carly pushed the button for the blinking line.

"This is Carly Nelson. May I help you?"

"Ms. Nelson. Congratulations. I see where you've been named acting CEO of Rivers Hospital."

The voice on the other end was practiced, with a deep Southern accent. That was quick, she thought. "Thank you, Mr. Kitchens. What can I do for you?"

"As you may know, I've been retained as Doctor Langford's attorney. I'm in Fort Myers for a couple of days and was wondering if I could come by your office in the morning. I wanted to meet you and have a little chat. I promise I won't take more than an hour of your time."

Carly looked at her calendar for tomorrow. It was pretty packed, but she could probably squeeze him in around eleven.

"How's eleven fifteen? I can give you forty-five minutes."

"Fine, thank you. Eleven fifteen it is. I look forward to meeting you."

Carly typed in Kitchens's name for the time slot and moved on to her other work, trying to catch up before she went home for the day.

Michelle looked at her phone to see who was calling. Josh. She debated not answering, but what the hell—she needed a break. And though things had cooled between them, they were still friends as far as she was concerned.

"Hey," she said.

"Hey. How are you?"

"Okay. Studying for a big test tomorrow."

"You sound down."

"Mom called earlier. I guess you've heard the news?"

"No, I've been busy at work. Not much of a news-type anyway. What happened?"

She took a deep breath. "My dad's been arrested."

"Arrested? What for?"

She paused again. "Apparently they found child porn on his computer at home?"

"What? You're kidding!"

"I wish I was. I'm sure it's all over town by now. Surprised you haven't heard. Mom said it was on the front page of the paper."

"Geez. You talked to your Dad?"

"No, not yet."

"You think it's true?"

"Don't know. Not sure what to believe. Just glad I'm in Gainesville right now. I may not ever come home."

"Sorry, Michelle. Anything I can do?"

"Make it all go away."

"Wish I could. Listen, I wanted to apologize for the other night."

Michelle didn't say anything and waited for him to continue.

"I was a jerk, okay? And I'm sorry. I have no right to be jealous. It's just . . . well, you're the first person I've cared about in a long time. I still want to see you, and I promise I won't act that way again."

She was impressed. She liked Josh, except for the possessive part, and liked hanging around with him. Deep down, she wanted to see him again and was glad he called.

"Okay. I'll probably be coming home this weekend, all this shit going on with my dad. Give me a call—maybe we can go out."

"I will. And thanks for giving me another chance."

"Well, I better get back to studying. Later."

She put the phone down and looked out the window of her apartment. Wayne would want to see her if she came home. She liked both of them, and for the first time, she didn't want to commit to one person.

Wayne didn't seem like the jealous type. Guess she'd find out. She wanted to continue seeing both of them and wondered if that was possible in Fort Myers.

Oh well, she thought, they would have to sort it out. She turned her attention back to her books.

Chapter 20

A few minutes after eleven the next morning, Sandy walked into Carly's office with Mr. Kitchens. He was shorter and heavier than Carly pictured, though well-dressed in an expensive-looking dark blue suit, white shirt, and red-striped power tie. His complexion was ruddy, which contrasted with his head full of silver hair. She guessed his age in the late fifties or early sixties.

He strode over to her desk with an air of confidence and extended his hand. "Jim Wallace Kitchens, Ms. Nelson. Everyone calls me Jim. I'm pleased to meet you. Thank you for seeing me on such short notice."

His Southern accent was well polished and pleasant. She suspected he used it to his advantage whenever possible.

"Call me Carly, please. Have a seat."

Kitchens sat in one of the chairs in front of her desk. They made small talk for a few minutes, but he soon got down to business.

"I know your time is valuable, Carly, and I promised to take no more than forty-five minutes. Since I'm a man who tries his best to keep his promises, I'll get right to the point of my visit.

"First, I'd like to ask if you would put out a public announcement regarding Doctor Langford's privileges. I've taken the liberty of preparing a draft of what I had in mind." He handed her a sheet of paper containing only two short typed paragraphs.

It basically reaffirmed the Florida Medical Board's statement, saying that Langford was innocent until proven guilty and, since the charges had no relationship to his competency skills, his privileges to practice were unaffected at this time.

She read it twice and placed it on her desk. "I have no problem with it, but I'll, of course, have to run it by our attorney."

"Yes, yes, I understand. I'd appreciate it. And if TJ has any questions, please ask him to call me directly. We're trying to move quickly to protect Doctor Langford's livelihood. As you can imagine, these preposterous charges have already severely impacted his practice."

She smiled at his casual mention of TJ. He wanted her to know he had done his homework and was on a first name basis with the hospital attorney.

Kitchens moved on to ask her questions about her relationship with her ex-husband. Making copious notes the entire time, he also asked about Forrest's relationship with Michelle.

At noon, he opened his briefcase and placed his notebook in it. "I believe I've used my allotted time, Carly. Since I want to stay on your good side, I'll leave with that last question."

He closed his briefcase and rose to shake her hand. "It was a pleasure meeting you. Thank you once again, and I trust that I can call you later with additional questions?"

"Certainly. And I appreciate your punctuality, Jim."

"Have a good day," he said as he turned and walked out of her office.

She called Sandy and asked her to take the press release down to TJ's office for his review.

Her cell phone rang, and she picked it up to see who was calling. It was Forrest. For a moment, she debated whether to answer or not. She pressed Answer.

"Hello?"

"Carly. It's Forrest." There was a slight pause. "I was wondering if you'd have dinner with me tonight." Another pause, then he said, "I need to talk to you."

She hesitated. "I'm not sure that's—"

"Please."

Carly was stunned. She couldn't remember the last time she'd heard her ex-husband use that word. She didn't realize it was in his vocabulary. She had to admit, she was curious and wanted to get his side of the story, but she wasn't sure if it was a good idea to meet him for dinner.

"I just want the chance to explain and to talk about Michelle. My treat."

His tone and the mention of their daughter made up her mind.

"When?" she asked.

"Around seven. At L'Auberge?"

She wasn't sure she wanted to see him, but part of her wanted to see his face when he explained. She wanted to believe she could tell if he was lying.

"I'll be there." She started to hang up.

"If you don't mind, I'll make the reservations in your name. It's become a little difficult for me recently, as you can imagine."

Fort Myers was still a small town at heart. Bad news traveled fast, especially when it involved the rich and famous.

"That's fine. I'll see you there."

Later that evening, when she walked into the restaurant a few minutes before seven, she told the hostess she had reservations for Nelson at seven. The hostess didn't bother to look it up. She gave Carly a quick look up and down and said, "Follow me please." Without waiting, she turned and walked toward the back of the restaurant.

Carly was surprised to see Forrest sitting at the table. The hostess pointed to the table, then turned and walked back to the front without saying a word.

He stood as Carly approached. She pulled her chair out and sat without as much as a handshake, skipping the perfunctory kiss between them.

"Thanks for coming," he said as he sat.

He looked smaller, she thought. And older. The confidence he normally exuded was gone. In its place was a frightened boy in the body of a tired, middle-aged man. She'd never seen him like this, and could almost feel sorry for him.

"How're you doing?" she asked, watching him closely, looking for clues.

He shook his head and laughed, but it was hollow.

"I've had better weeks. I wanted to talk to you about Michelle. But first, I want you to know that I did *not* do what they're saying." He leaned across the table and looked her in the eyes.

"Look, I know I can be an ass. And my people skills leave a lot to be desired. I didn't give you and Michelle the attention you deserved. I'm guilty of all those things, Carly. But I did *not* put those pictures on my computer. I knew nothing about them."

His expression was earnest. She thought about her conversation with George and started to ask him about his chats with the minor, but remembered her promise.

"So that was it? They're hanging you out because they found dirty pictures on your computer? I'd say you're hardly the first to do that. But children?" She shook her head in disgust.

He looked down at the table, then back up at her, shaking his head. His eyes were moist.

My God, she thought, who is this person sitting across from me? This was a side of Forrest she'd never seen.

"They're saying I had conversations with an underage girl online." His voice was stronger now and, again, his eyes met hers.

"Carly, I swear to you I didn't do any of this. I don't know what's going on, but I did *not* do any of it. Those pictures they've showed me, they're disgusting. I know I'm no angel, but I've never seen those before or anything like it. And I swear I had no interaction with any girl, online or otherwise."

She looked deep into his eyes, wanting to believe him. He didn't look away, as if welcoming the examination. All she could see was truth, but she couldn't keep from thinking about her conversation with George. She blinked and changed the subject.

"What is it about Michelle?" she asked.

"She won't talk to me. I've tried calling her and she refuses to talk to me or to call me back. I need to talk to her, to explain."

Her rage exploded. "Explain what, Forrest? All you've told me is that you're innocent, but I haven't heard any explanation, just you saying you didn't do anything. That's what they all say."

She realized she was angry and talking louder. Taking a deep breath, she got a grip on herself and lowered her voice.

"I don't know what to believe right now. But you've got to do more than just sit there and tell me you're innocent. And Michelle's going to want more than that. She deserves more than that. Why don't you give your explanation a test drive with me?"

He held up his hands. "I'm sorry. You're right."

Damn, Carly thought, there's something else I don't think I've ever heard him say.

"Look. I don't know what's going on here. They've accused me of chatting online with an officer who was impersonating an underage girl. They claim that I sent 'her' pictures that were on my computer. All I can tell you is what I told them—I know nothing about any of this. I haven't been chatting with anyone online, and I had no idea that crap was on my computer, the pictures of kids. All they have is shit they found on my computer, stuff I didn't even know was there. Do you know what all's on your computer? They haven't found one shred of evidence anywhere else, because it didn't happen!"

"The only thing I can figure is someone hacked into my computer and planted the pictures and made it look like I was chatting with someone."

Carly swallowed when he mentioned hacking. Until a few weeks ago, she would have thought what he said preposterous. But after her conversations with Wayne, she wasn't sure.

"But why would someone do that?"

Forrest snorted. "You of all people know that I'm not the most popular person around. I'm a damn good surgeon, and I know it, but I'm not naïve enough to think I would win the 'Most Likeable' award. There's probably a long list of people who'd like to see me disgraced, doubtless including you."

She ignored his jab.

"Surely the computer types can figure all that out?" she asked.

"Maybe. I certainly hope so. And I've got people working on it. But that takes time. Meanwhile, my reputation has cratered. I can't even get a restaurant reservation in my own name anymore. Patients are cancelling appointments and surgery as fast as they can call the office. The judge pulled my passport and they locked up my plane. The district attorney convinced her I was a potential flight risk—literally." He shook his head and slammed his hand on the table.

"I'm not going anywhere. I want to clear my name. I didn't do this."

Carly looked at the man across the table from her and wondered if he was telling the truth. She thought she knew him, but wasn't sure anymore. She wanted to believe him, for Michelle, but was afraid she was wrong.

"I'll talk to Michelle. But I can't make her talk to you. She's twenty-two now, and you know how independent she is."

He calmed down. "Thank you, Carly. That's all I ask. Just talk to her. Just ask her to please let me explain to her in person."

"I'll do what I can."

As they finished dinner, they talked about work. Forrest was still doing surgeries, but his case load was half what it had been. On the advice of Michael Wentworth, his local attorney, Forrest had retained Jim Wallace Kitchens from Tallahassee, a noted criminal attorney in Florida. While his partners were supportive, in private, they were also encouraging him to keep a low profile. People in Fort Myers were distancing themselves from Forrest, just in case.

He asked Carly whether or not his privileges were in jeopardy. She had spoken to Dr. B, the Medical Director at the hospital, and his position was the same as that of the State Board—Forrest was innocent until proven guilty. Since the charges didn't have anything to do with competence in his area of expertise, there was no immediate threat.

Forrest insisted on paying for dinner and thanked Carly again for seeing him. They left the restaurant together under the watchful stares of the patrons and walked opposite directions once outside.

When Carly got home and walked into the kitchen, Bo was waiting for her. She scratched his ears and talked to him a minute before heading to the bedroom, Bo right behind her. Eric was sitting up in bed reading.

"How was dinner?" he asked.

"Good. But I think aliens have abducted Forrest." She chuckled. "I know it's not funny, but he's a humbled man. I swear he's aged ten years. And he actually said *please* and that he was *sorry* and agreed I was right about something.

"He wanted me to talk to Michelle. He wants to explain, but she won't talk to him. And he swears he's innocent."

"What do you think?" Eric asked, putting his book down.

"I still don't know. If he's not innocent, he's either pathological or should consider Hollywood."

"Sounds like he convinced you."

"Nudged me that direction is more like it. He claims someone hacked his computer and did everything. A few weeks ago, I would've thought that ridiculous, but after the incident with the IV pumps and all, well, let's say I'm not as skeptical about things like that happening.

"As George said, not my place to judge. Thank goodness. I did tell him I'd talk to Michelle. He just wants to talk with her. I think he deserves that much, but I told him it was her call."

Eric nodded. "I think you're doing the right thing."

"What do you think about it all?"

"Probably like you—torn. The mathematician in me says he's just as capable as anyone and there's no discernable profile for people like that. I mean, we think they look sleazy and wear trench coats, but the reality is not. I have to say, though, the emotional side of me doubts that he's guilty of something like that. And you're right, that kind of stuff with computers does happen."

She nodded.

"I worry more for Michelle than anything. But nothing I can do. I'm beat. It's been a long day."

Thursday night, Michelle was over at a friend's apartment when her phone buzzed. It was Josh, again.

"Hey, what's up?" she said.

"Nothing, just wanted to call and check on you. Doing okay?"

"Yeah, I guess."

"Still coming home this weekend?"

"Yeah."

"Want to do something Saturday night?"

"Sure. Why don't you come over around seven?"

"I'll be there. Hey, I was on the computer last night and got to thinking. Maybe somebody put that stuff on your Dad's computer."

She considered what Josh was telling her. "Why would someone do that?"

"Don't know. I was just thinking about it last night. Who knows? No offense, but after asking around, your dad does have a reputation for being an asshole."

Michelle couldn't help but chuckle. "Yeah, he can be pretty abrasive. But why would someone do something like that? I mean, could they?"

"Hell, yeah, not as hard as it seems. Happens all the time. Anyway, just thought I'd mention it. Might want to get somebody to check it out. Just trying to help."

"Thanks, Josh. I appreciate it. I'll mention it to him— if I talk to him. I still haven't decided on that."

"Okay, I'll let you go. Call me if you need anything. Be careful driving, and I'll see you Saturday."

"Bye."

Michelle held the phone and thought about calling her dad. She'd talked to her mom, and Carly told her how he wanted a chance to talk to her. Her mom thought she should at least give him the opportunity.

She was angry with him, but the adult in her wanted to give him the benefit of the doubt. And she loved him. He was her father, but this wasn't a conversation she wanted to have over the phone.

She texted him, knowing he always had his phone nearby. This way she could avoid the conversation until she could see his face.

Dinner Fr nite?

A few minutes later, her phone buzzed.

Would love 2, u name it

She smiled. She loved sushi, but couldn't afford it often on a student's budget. She texted him back, saying she would meet him at Taberu around seven.

Chapter 21

The next morning, Carly was fast asleep when the alarm clock sounded. She reached over and fumbled with it, trying to find the Snooze button. Pressing it, she rolled on her back and tried to wake up and clear the cobwebs. She looked next to her, and Eric wasn't there. Then she remembered he had an early morning staff meeting.

Her brain was starting to wake up, and she thought about her conversation with Forrest yesterday evening. How could someone impersonate another person on a computer? If it wasn't so serious, it would be laughable. Carly wished she could ignore it. But the idea, as ridiculous as it sounded, was just plausible enough. And she still couldn't get the thought out of her mind that the cause of Brian's untimely death hadn't been an accident.

The alarm sounded again, and this time she was awake enough to find the Off button. She stumbled out of bed and went to get dressed, determined to drag into the gym.

After her workout, when she got to her office, Carly pulled out her cell phone and dialed the number she had scribbled on the piece of paper. Wayne answered on the second ring.

"Hi, Ms. Nelson."

"Hey, Wayne. I've been thinking and was wondering if you could come by my office this morning."

"Yeah, I guess." Wayne was reluctant. "When?"

"How about now?"

Wayne exhaled. "Okay, I'll be up in a few minutes."

As soon as he shut the door in her office, Carly started talking as he sat.

"I keep thinking about what you said—about Sorcerer indirectly referring to Brian Jenning's accident. How do you know Sorcerer wasn't just talking about stuff that everyone knew? Maybe he watched the news that morning."

"So you don't believe me?" Wayne looked hurt.

"I'm just saying, I need something more substantial."

He looked out the window and said nothing for a long time. Finally, he looked at Carly and spoke.

"Because Sorcerer made that comment online early Wednesday morning. Before the accident was called in."

A chill ran down Carly's spine. "How do you know that?"

"The news said the accident happened at 1:40 a.m. and Sorcerer made the comment before that."

"You're telling me that you knew about the accident before it happened? Why didn't you tell me that earlier?"

"Because I was scared. I didn't know if I could trust you. And I didn't want you going off all crazy on me! And I didn't want you to think I had anything to do with it! 'Cause I didn't!"

Carly considered the possibilities. "Maybe he picked it up off the police scanner? People do that, right? Maybe the news report had the wrong time for the accident. What time were you online?"

"Dunno, around one thirty Wednesday morning. I remember logging off around then. Hadn't thought about that; maybe he did get it off the scanner. Maybe he was just jerking Huffin's chain, playing with his head."

"Any way to find out the exact time? Do you have a log of the conversation?"

Wayne shook his head. "This is a smart group, Ms. Nelson. We aren't that dumb! I mean, I can find out what time I was logged on to my computer and when I logged off. But a log of what was entered from someone else's end? No way! We use an encrypted, firewalled chat room. I could use a screen capture, but that doesn't tell you anything. I could've typed that in myself."

"I can verify the time the accident was reported, which would give us a time for anything on the police scanner. We can compare that to when you were online, go from there," she said.

"Ms. Nelson, you can't tell anyone about this."

"I'm not, Wayne. Not yet. I told you I'd talk to you first and I will, okay?"

Wayne nodded, but not convinced. "I'll try to find out what I can."

"And I'll get the time the accident was reported. Let me give you my cell phone number in case you need to call me outside of work." Carly wrote down her number on the back of a business card and handed it to Wayne. He looked at the number and put the card into his pocket.

"Thanks, Wayne. I appreciate you sharing this with me. Hopefully, it's just posturing on the part of this

Sorcerer. As soon as I get the time, I'll let you know. Maybe this will be the end of it."

"I sure hope so. But I have a strange feeling about this." Wayne got up to leave. "Talk to you soon."

"Wayne?" Carly asked.

He stopped and turned around. "Yes?"

"Would it be possible to hack into electronic equipment on an airplane?"

He looked puzzled as he considered her question, then shrugged. "I don't know why not. I'm sure they're just like everything else—loaded with computers. Like I said, if it's got a computer, it can be hacked."

"Has Sorcerer ever mentioned anything about hacking an airplane?"

"Not that I recall. Why?"

"Could you ask him, I mean, you know, in a way that wouldn't arouse suspicion?"

"I suppose. Anything specific?"

"Doctor Langford's plane had a problem with the autopilot the other week. He mentioned that the mechanic said it was a software problem."

Wayne shrugged.

"I'll see if I can toss something out there he might hook on."

"Thanks."

Carly sat there as she watched the young man walk out of her office. Her intuition was starting to sound alarms.

She picked up the phone to call George. He answered after two rings.

"Hi, Carly. What could I do for you?"

"I was finishing up a report to corporate and was wondering if you could get me the exact time that Brian's accident was called in. You know me, a stickler for details, and I just wanted to make sure I had it right." She hoped that George would buy her story.

George hesitated and Carly held her breath. "Sorry, I was looking for my copy of the accident report. I can make you a copy if you'd like."

She exhaled. "That'd be great, George. Thank you. How's Dorothy doing?"

"Not bad, under the circumstances. She's stronger than she looks. I know she misses him—we all do, but she'll make it."

"Please tell her I asked about her."

"I will. Thanks. And I'll drop the copy of the accident report by on my way to lunch if that's okay?"

"That would be great. Thanks, George." Carly hung up the phone.

She had a meeting outside the hospital and, when she got back, the copy of the accident report was lying on her desk. When she picked it up, her hand shook slightly. She glanced over the information and noted the time the accident was called in. 1:37 a.m.

She picked up her phone and called Wayne. She got his voice mail. "Wayne, this is Carly. I got that time for you. It was 1:37 a.m. Let me know what you find out. Thanks."

She hung up the phone and stared again at the accident report. The description was so clinical. She understood it had to be that way, but still it was disturbing. This was her friend and mentor, not some anonymous stranger. She wondered how responders could detach themselves like that. They had to, she guessed, in order to survive.

Her cell phone buzzed. She picked it up and looked at the caller ID. It was Wayne. She clicked Answer.

"Hello, Wayne."

"The times don't match."

"What do you mean, don't match?"

"The discussion occurred before the reported time." Wayne was being cryptic in his response, as if he thought someone were listening in.

Carly caught her breath. "Are you sure?"

"Absolutely. Six minutes earlier. I gotta go. Can I come by your office later?"

She looked at her calendar. "Anytime after five thirty. I usually leave around seven."

"Okay, I'll see you later." Wayne hung up before she could respond. He wasn't taking any chances.

Damn. Her mind started racing. So Sorcerer either had something to do with it or knew it was going to happen. That's the only way he could have mentioned it before it was called in. She tried to think of another explanation, but there was none. So Brian's death wasn't an accident. But who? Who would want him dead? He was one of the few people she knew who didn't have enemies.

Around six, Wayne knocked on her office door. Sandy had already left for the day.

"Hi, Wayne. Come in."

The nervous young man stepped inside her office and closed the door.

"I checked. I logged off that morning at 1:31 a.m., six minutes *before* when you said it was reported."

"How could Sorcerer have posted his comment about Jennings before it was called in?" she asked.

"He had to have known about it."

"Assuming the times are accurate," she said, thinking back to Eric's comments, trying to be logical. "For the sake of argument, let's say the times are correct. So he had to know about it, but it still doesn't prove he was responsible. Maybe someone else did it and told him about it?"

Wayne considered her point. "Possible. I'll try to push him on it a little, see if I can get more information. He was online last night. He said *the fun had begun.*"

"The fun had begun? What's that supposed to mean? What else did he say?"

"Nothing much. He was pretty cryptic, as usual. I asked him a few questions without being too obvious. All he would say is that we'd know what he was talking about."

Carly frowned. "Any ideas?"

"Not a clue. But Sorcerer likes to brag. He'll say more."

"Any luck on tracking him down?"

Wayne shrugged. "Not much. I told you I have to be real careful. I don't want him after me. But I've been trying to trace some addresses and stuff." He looked at Carly as if to say you wouldn't understand.

"Did you ask him about airplanes?"

Wayne nodded. "I asked someone else in the chat room, but I knew Sorcerer was in there."

"And?"

"Huffin said that sure, it was possible, but he didn't know anyone who had done it. Sorcerer said *Oh yeah, I know it can be done.* I asked if he could tell me how, but he backed off and said some other time."

She looked at Wayne. "You think he was bluffing?"

He shook his head. "I told you, Sorcerer doesn't bluff. He's the real deal. If he says he knows it can be done, he knows it for a fact. I'd bet the farm on it."

Carly thought back to her conversation with Forrest last night and changed the subject.

"Is it possible to take over someone else's computer and make other people think they're the owner?"

"Sure. That's easy. Why?"

"And do it without leaving any trail?"

"More difficult, but yeah, definitely doable. You asking about Doctor Langford?"

"I guess you heard?"

"Who hasn't? It's all over the hospital."

"I talked to him, and he swears someone planted those pictures on his computer, chatted with someone, and made it look like him."

"If the computer is connected to the Internet, it could happen."

"Could you look at his computer and tell?"

Wayne thought for a minute. "Probably. Would take me a while, but I think so."

"Would you be willing to look at his computer?"

Wayne thought for a minute. "Yeah, sure, would be a challenge. When?"

"This evening?"

Wayne laughed. "It would take more than a couple of hours, Ms. Nelson. I'd probably need it for at least a couple of days."

Carly called Forrest and asked if the police had returned his computer. He was surprised when she told him she had someone she wanted to look at it, someone who might be able to get to the bottom of things. He told her the police still had his computer and he didn't know when he could expect to get it back.

She hung up the phone and looked at Wayne. "The police still have it. He doesn't know when he's getting it back. I'll let you know when he does."

"No problem." Wayne rose to leave.

Carly laughed. "Maybe I should be getting you to look at my computer."

Wayne look puzzled. "You having computer problems? Dancing bear back?"

"No, not that. More serious. Somebody's stolen my personal information. The last few days I've been busy canceling credit cards, getting police reports and that kind of fun stuff."

He sat back down. "What happened?"

She told him about trying to use her credit card and all that had gone wrong since. He asked a few questions and sat back in his chair.

"Would you mind if I took a look at your computer?" he asked.

"Are you serious?" She was worried now.

"From what you've told me, it sounds like someone has hacked into your computer. That's the only thing that makes sense."

Carly shook her head. "You've got to be kidding me, right?"

"Well, you told me none of your things have been stolen. Even if someone boosted your card number, like at a restaurant or something, that wouldn't give them the personal information."

She thought for a moment. What Wayne was saying did seem logical.

"I'd appreciate that. When could you come over?"

"I can't come tonight. How 'bout tomorrow night? Say around seven?"

"That'd be great. Why don't you just plan on having dinner with us?" She didn't add that Michelle would be there.

Wayne didn't argue. "Okay, see you then. In the meantime, I'd unplug your computer from the Internet."

Forrest was standing in the tiny lobby of the Japanese restaurant when Michelle walked in. His face lit up when he spotted her, and he gave her an affectionate hug, more tender than his usual greeting.

The hostess led them to a booth in the corner, away from the other tables. It was early, and only a few tables and several spots at the sushi bar were occupied.

"You look nice. When did you get home?" he asked

"Thanks. About an hour ago."

"How was your drive?"

She shrugged. "Boring. I've made it so many times, I think I could do it in my sleep."

He laughed. "Please don't try it. I-75 is way too busy."

"You got that right." She looked at her dad, close. His face seemed to have more wrinkles and he looked older. She realized that she never really looked at him when they were together. He was Dad. Though he hadn't been an intimate part of her life, she loved him and was concerned about him. She wanted to know if the allegations were true.

"How are you?" she asked him. The simple question conveyed more than three short words, and Forrest seemed to pick up on what she wanted to know.

"Okay," he said as he leaned over the table, looking directly into her eyes.

"Michelle. I didn't do it. I swear to you, I've never seen any of those pictures, and I never had any type of relationship, online or otherwise, with a minor." He paused to let her search his eyes.

She looked at him for what seemed to be a long time. At last, satisfied he was telling the truth, she nodded and asked, "So, what happened?"

He sat back in his seat and exhaled. He turned his palms up and shrugged.

"I don't know. The only thing we—my attorney and I—can figure is someone planted that stuff on my computer and somehow took control of it and initiated online correspondence with a police officer posing as a minor. But I don't have a clue as to who would do such a thing, and the how of it is way beyond me."

"Josh told me that was possible. In fact, he suggested it the other night when I talked to him."

Seeing the confused look on his face, she explained.

"Josh, the guy I've been seeing. Works at the Toyota place. I told you about him when we were in Key West. He's a computer whiz."

Remembering, Forrest nodded.

"Anyway, Josh said it was entirely possible. Suggested you get someone to check your computer."

The server came over to take their order, and when she walked away, Forrest asked, "Could he do it?"

Michelle shrugged. "I'm sure he could. I'm going out with him this weekend. I'll ask, if you want."

He nodded. "Yes, that'd be good. Kitchens, my attorney, was planning on hiring someone, but if this Josh is as good as you say, we could hire him. We're supposed to get the computer back, or at least a copy, early next week."

"Okay, I'll check with him."

With some effort, Michelle asked her dad how Tonya was doing. He said it had been hard on her, but she was supportive. They all just wanted it resolved, but Forrest wanted more than resolution; he wanted the satisfaction of vindication and having his name cleared.

"Speaking of computers, did you ever figure out what happened with your airplane?"

He nodded. "Speaking of damn computers. They said it was a software glitch, a computer bug. What they don't know yet is how it got there. Apparently that takes a while to track down. But they fixed it and sent out a software upgrade."

His face turned down as he continued.

"Since my plane's been impounded and they've taken my license, I can't fly. Don, the mechanic, has taken it up a few times and says it's working fine."

Michelle nodded, sympathetic to her dad. She knew how much he loved flying.

She was tired of talking about it. Convinced her dad was innocent, she changed the subject and started talking about school. He seemed relieved to talk to her about normal things, and his disposition improved.

The sushi was wonderful, and he hugged her again when they left, promising to do it again before long. He thanked her for giving him the opportunity to explain. She was surprised at how emotional he was, a huge change for him, and wondered what was going on.

George, Lieutenant Budzinski, and Carly were seated around the conference table in her office.

"The lieutenant wanted to talk with us about the case. Tony?" George turned the conversation over to his friend.

"Thanks for meeting with me on such short notice. I wanted to ask you a few more questions. Like I told you, we've made the IV case a priority. We've interviewed most of the staff here at the hospital whom we needed to talk with, and I've been racking my brain trying to figure out some link on this.

"Then, as you know, we arrested Dr. Langford. I can't go into any details on that, but our computer guys took a close look at his computer. Long story short—it looks like it had been hacked. So, now I'm trying to figure out if the IV case and this are related, Langford being the common denominator."

Carly looked at George, then back at Tony. "You think someone is trying to . . . go after Forrest? Make him look bad?"

Budzinski shrugged. "Don't know, but it's the best angle we've got right now. Both patients were his. Then, his home computer is hacked. Too much coincidence for me."

"But why?" she asked.

"Well, that's why I'm here. Anybody you can think of with a grudge against Dr. Langford?"

Carly laughed, then said, "Sorry—I shouldn't have, but that's probably a long list. Don't get me wrong. He's a brilliant surgeon, one of the best. If I had to have neurosurgery, he's the one I'd want. But," she looked at George, "let's just say his people skills are pretty much non-existent."

George raised his eyebrows and nodded in agreement.

Tony continued, "I gathered that from everyone we talked to. But is there anyone in particular, you know, like a recent altercation, a colleague, employee, even someone outside of work?"

Carly shook her head. "No one I know of. Of course, my only involvement with him outside of work is fairly limited. We have dinner occasionally and obviously a mutual interest in our daughter, Michelle."

She thought about the episode with Keith, but wondered whether or not to mention it. Keith didn't seem capable of anything like Budzinski was suggesting, but she concluded that was for the lieutenant to decide.

"The only recent incident involving an employee that I'm aware of was Forrest went ballistic because he was late two days in a row getting out of the OR. He pitched a fit with Keith Davis, our OR manager. Came to me and wanted me to fire Keith, which was nonsense."

Budzinski made a few notes.

"That's the only incident I'm aware of. Like I said, I'm too far removed from the day-to-day stuff."

"What about your relationship with the doctor?"

Carly was startled at the sudden change in questions from the lieutenant. For a moment, she wondered if he thought she had anything to do with it. Shaking her head, she realized he was just trying to complete the picture of Dr. Forrest Langford. At least she hoped that's all it was.

"Cordial. I think that's a good way to sum it up. As I'm sure you know, we were married for eight years and have the one daughter. He's a difficult person to live with."

She chuckled. "I probably shouldn't say this, but to be honest, there were times I would've liked to strangle him. But again, that's a long list of people. But I strive to be civil. He's my daughter's father. And he's responsible for a lot of business for the hospital."

Budzinski made no comment, jotted down a few more notes.

"Do you think whoever did this is finished?" she asked.

He turned his hands over on the table, palms up. "Hard to tell. We don't even know for sure they're connected. Just seems to be a logical angle to pursue at this point."

Sensing the meeting was over, George shifted in his chair. "We'll get out of your hair, Carly." He looked over at Tony. "Unless you've got anything else?"

Tony shook his head. "No, I think we're done."

The men gathered their things and rose to leave.

"We'll be in touch," Budzinski said as they walked out.

Chapter 22

Friday afternoon, on her way home from work, Carly decided to stop by the shooting range. It had been a tough week, and shooting was a great stress reliever for her, getting her mind to focus on something else, even if just for a little while.

She shot her usual hundred rounds and was sitting at the table on the other side of the glass windows from the range, looking at her five targets. The first one was a little sloppy, but by the time she got to the last one, it was more like it. All twenty shots were in a tightly grouped pattern, clustered within a few inches of the target center.

Studying the target, she looked for areas of improvement, as always. She chuckled to herself as she thought, if they all went through the same hole, then she'd be happy. Of course, then she'd have a hard time connecting the shots fired.

Her mind drifted back to the events at the hospital. Maybe they were connected as well. Maybe she just couldn't see it. Everyone had been thinking of them as isolated, random events, but what if there was a connection or pattern? What was that she'd read recently, about there being patterns to everything, but sometimes we just couldn't see it? But how?

Obviously, Lieutenant Budzinski was thinking along the same lines. He's the one who brought up the idea about someone trying to get at Langford.

She shook her head. Now she was starting to sound like those conspiracy nuts, seeing patterns where none existed. But the thought kept nagging at her. What if they were somehow connected? But where did Brian's death fit in? That had nothing to do with Langford. Maybe it was just an accident, as George had suggested.

She'd talk to Eric about this when she got home. He was good at this sort of thing, logical enough to analyze data, but disciplined enough not to see things that weren't there.

It was late Friday afternoon, and Carly had just got home from work. She had just told Michelle that Wayne suspected her computer had been hacked.

"So, he's going to check it out?" Michelle asked.

Carly nodded. "He's coming over to look at it tonight, so I asked him to have dinner with us."

"That's cool. What's for dinner?"

Carly had put a pan of lasagna in the oven, something she had made yesterday.

"Lasagna. Will you fix the salads, please? I'll get the bread ready."

Before long, Eric got home and a few minutes later, Wayne showed up. They had a nice, leisurely meal out on the lanai, Eric entertaining them with stories about his classes out at Gulf Coast.

After dinner, Carly took Wayne back to their home office so he could check her computer while Eric and Michelle cleaned up. She came back to the kitchen to help, and by the time they were sitting out on the lanai with coffee, Wayne joined them.

"Everything's fine on your computer," he said. "My guess is that whoever put the db virus on it probably hacked your information. But it's secure now, no sign of any problems."

"Thanks for checking it," Carly said.

He turned to Michelle. "Want to go out for a bit?" He looked at his watch. "We could catch a movie, if you'd like?"

"Sure." Michelle rose, and they turned toward the door.

"Thanks for dinner, Ms. Nelson, Professor," Wayne said.

Later that evening, Wayne was bringing Michelle home from the theater.

"Wanna do something tomorrow night?" he asked, as they pulled into her driveway and he switched his truck off.

"Uh, no, sorry, I've got plans."

Wayne looked at her, a puzzled look on his face. There was an awkward silence.

She took a deep breath, reached out, and put her hand on his before speaking.

"Look, I like you a lot, Wayne. We get along good, and I enjoy doing things with you."

"So . . ."

"I'm just not ready to limit myself to seeing one person right now. Nothing personal, okay?"

He nodded. "So you've got another date tomorrow night? Josh?"

She answered both questions with a single nod.

"Hey, that's okay," he said and shrugged.

"You sure?"

"Yeah, really. Thanks for being honest with me." He looked at her and gave her a thin smile. "Hey, I'm not like that—you know, possessive. Don't worry about it."

"I'll probably be back home in a couple of weeks. We can do something then, if you want?"

"Sure. Let me know."

He walked her to the door. They kissed goodnight, and everything seemed fine.

Sunday, Tonya Langford was anxious to work on her tan. The last several days had been overcast, unusual for Fort Myers, and her tan needed touching up. She got lots of compliments and was obsessed about keeping it year-round.

She had a 48-lamp, professional-quality bed installed in her "spa room," a large room in the house that Forrest had let her equip as her own personal retreat. The futuristic brown and silver clamshell-shaped device was the latest in tanning technology and represented the top-of-the-line bed. It boasted facial lamps, shoulder lamps, deluxe audio system—the works. At over twenty thousand dollars, it wasn't something the average household could afford, but the Langford household wasn't close to average, with Forrest making almost two million a year just from his practice.

Her spa room was perfect. Situated on the side of the house, it had windows on one wall, letting in lots of natural light, giving the feeling of exercising outside. It contained all of her preferred exercise equipment she'd picked out. This way, she didn't have to go to the gym with everyone else, sharing inferior equipment with sweaty strangers. Plus, she could tan in the nude, as she preferred.

She finished her workout, pulled her drenched workout clothes off, and put them into the hamper next to the door. She could see the river through the windows as she walked over to the tanning bed, stopping in front of the full-length mirror on the wall. It never bothered her to be naked in front of the windows. Their lot was private, and besides, she wouldn't have cared if someone had seen her without clothes. She had a nice body and was proud of it.

She placed her hands on her hips and posed, shifting her weight from one foot to the other, looking at the reflection in the mirror. Putting her hands under her generous breasts, she lifted them, tweaking her nipples in the process. Having the larger boobs was nice, but they would definitely be sagging before long. She'd have to keep a close eye on that.

Not bad, she thought, as she ran her hands down each side of her body. The tummy was starting to develop a little pooch, something that Dr. Mendoza would have to take a look it.

Dr. Raul Mendoza was the best plastic surgeon in southwest Florida, *her* plastic surgeon. In fact, he was one of the best in the southeast. People came from all over for implants, tummy tucks, facelifts, lipo, all of the make-me-beautiful kinds of things. He was a gifted artist.

These were his work, she thought, as she lifted her breasts once more. She had gotten many compliments since the surgery, but the best part was the stares from strangers. Of course, she dressed to show them off as much as possible and pretended not to notice, but inside, she was pleased at the reaction she got everywhere she went. She had wanted to go one size larger, but Dr. Mendoza convinced her that would be too disproportionate for such a lithe, petite figure as hers.

She walked over to the tanning bed and stretched out on the bottom platform on her back. She adjusted the goggles and looked up at the electronic control panel above her and punched the menu button. This model was capable of duplicating current conditions at any of over fifty different popular sunbathing locations around the world. It had a built-in computer connected to the Internet and received the latest weather information. It then electronically duplicated the chosen locale.

She thought for a moment, then scrolled through the choices. Cabo San Lucas, the French Riviera, Rio de Janeiro—that was it, Rio. Forrest had taken her there last year for Carnival, her first trip to Rio, and she had fallen in love with the place. She liked the carefree attitude of the Cariocas, the Rio-born citizens, and the fact that women there wore the skimpiest bikinis in the world, leaving little to the imagination. It was the first beach she went to after her surgery and she would have been happy to go topless, but the locals frowned on that. So she bought a bikini there that barely covered her nipples, proudly displaying the results of Dr. Mendoza's fabulous work.

Rio would be perfect. Since she only wanted a touch-up, she selected five minutes and medium intensity.

When she punched the start button, the electrically operated lid closed over her. She hated wearing the goggles, because they had a tendency to leave those tell-tale raccoon-shaped circles around her eyes, but everyone insisted on them for safety reasons. When the top reached the full closed position, she saw the glow of the lamps and heard the hum of the unit as it kicked on.

Usually, five minutes breezed by, but today it seemed to drag. She felt sure it had been longer, but the lamps were still on and she could still hear the cooling fans. Normally, at the end of the pre-selected time, the unit cut off, a chime sounded, and the lid raised automatically, signifying the end of the session.

She glanced up at the electronic display and it still showed two minutes and thirteen seconds left. That couldn't be right. Damn thing probably broke, she thought. She'd have to call the people out from the place where she bought it and have them check it. They'd get a piece of her mind.

She stared at the timer display and realized that the seconds were taking much longer to count down. 2:12. She counted in her head. *One Mississippi, two Mississippi, three Mississippi, four Mississippi.* 2:11. Four seconds went by before it clicked to 2:11. She counted again and realized in horror that it was only recording one second for every four. Quickly doing the math, she figured she'd been under the lamps for twelve minutes.

She pushed up on the lid to get out, but it was stuck. That was strange. That had never happened before, even on the old one. Pushing a little harder, she wasn't able to budge it.

This made no sense. As far as she knew, there was no locking mechanism on the lid. She pushed again. Still, it wouldn't move. Now she started to panic. Her skin felt warm, and she pushed with all of her strength to open the damn thing. Nothing. It wouldn't move an inch.

She punched the large red Stop button on the control panel. It was supposed to shut all power off to the unit. Nothing. She punched it again, harder. Again, nothing.

Now she was frightened. She banged on the control panel with both fists, hitting all the buttons as hard as she could. But with the lid closed, it was difficult to generate much force in the tight space. She thrashed about, banging her elbows on the thing, trying to get the lid open. On the old one, both ends of the device were open and she could just crawl out, but on this model, the cooling fan blocked the end at her feet and the shoulder lamps blocked the head end.

She was smart enough to know this wasn't a good situation. Her skin felt hotter than normal, as if the lamp setting had been turned up to its maximum position. She tried turning over onto her stomach, but there wasn't enough room inside to do it.

She yelled, hoping somebody would hear her, then realized how hopeless that was. Forrest had gone to his office, and no one was in the huge house but her. With the nearest neighbor several hundred yards away, no one could hear her. She had to get out on her own.

With no way to leverage herself, she could only move a tiny bit at a time. Kicking at the fan was futile. She was sweating profusely and still banging at the control panel. At last, she must have managed to jar something loose in the control panel, and the lamps went off. She pushed the top lid up and lay there, weak and sweating profusely, unable to move right away.

She tried to swing her legs free and tumbled out onto the floor. Still trying to regain her strength, she looked down at her body. It was already red from the overexposure. She looked up at the wall clock and realized she'd been in it for almost twenty minutes.

Shaky, she stood and walked over to the mirror. Her skin was tender to the touch. Great, just fucking great. They were supposed to go to a benefit ball this weekend, and now she'd look like a lobster. Her new Vera Wang she bought over in West Palm Beach for the occasion was cut down to the waist in the back and almost as far in front. Tonya failed to realize the severity of what had just happened.

Thirsty, she walked over to the cooler and drank several cups of water. Where was her phone? The people at the spa store were going to catch hell for this. They'd be lucky if she didn't sue them.

Carly was sitting out on the lanai after dinner when Michelle walked out.

"Guess what happened to Barbie?" she asked.

Carly looked up from the newspaper and shook her head. She had given up on getting Michelle to refer to Forrest's wife by her name.

"The bimbo fell asleep or something in her new tanning bed. She's got first-degree burns over all, and I mean all, her body."

"How did that happen?"

"She claims it wouldn't open and malfunctioned, but my guess is she just fell asleep or couldn't figure out how to open it. I couldn't figure out why she needed a tanning bed in Fort Myers anyway."

Carly ignored the last part of Michelle's comment. "Is she going to be okay?"

Michelle nodded. "Dad says she won't be going out of the house for a week or two. They're going to miss the City of Palms Benefit Ball this weekend. He said her skin is so sensitive that she can't wear anything. That's going to be lovely. I sure wouldn't want to be stuck there with her. Can you imagine?"

She started to say she doesn't wear much as it is, but decided that would be too catty. She couldn't help but chuckle as she pictured Forrest at home with a nude, toasted Tonya.

"I'm sorry, that's not funny," Carly said. "I shouldn't be laughing. That could've been dangerous."

Michelle said, "I know. The funny part is thinking about Dad stuck with her. She's such a princess. I feel sorry for the people she bought the tanning bed from."

Later that evening, as they were lying in bed, Carly asked Eric, "Something's been bothering me." Michelle had gone out for the evening, so they had the house to themselves.

"I know this sounds crazy, but do you think that these incidents at the hospital are related in some way?" she asked.

Eric put his book down and looked at Carly.

"What do you mean?"

"Everyone's looking at what has happened as random, unrelated events. What if they're related some way?" She wrinkled her forehead. "What are the odds? You're the mathematician."

He thought about it for a minute, then said, "Possible, yes. Why?"

She shook her head. "I don't know, something I read about events being related, but we can't see the pattern. Maybe it was something you told me." She laughed. "And, no, I'm not one of those conspiracy theory nuts in the tabloids! I would only mention this to you. There just seems to be a rash of things happening."

Eric chuckled. "I'm not dismissing you, love. And you're right, sometimes there's a pattern and we just can't see it. But there have to be some common elements, and that would be the place to start. Find the common elements in these events and go from there."

"Well, the detective thinks it may be a vendetta against Forrest. But I don't see a link between Forrest and Brian."

"You still think Brian's crash wasn't an accident?"

"I know, it's crazy, but yes, my intuition says it was no accident. But I can't find any relationship, other than the hospital, between Brian and Forrest."

"Nothing obvious, or else you wouldn't be asking. But assume for a minute that Forrest is on someone's list. Then, maybe the *why* is what links him and Brian."

She thought about what he said. *Nothing obvious.* But if they truly are related, there has to be a common link. Different people were the target, so what linked those people together, other than they all were related to Rivers Community Hospital?

The logical answer to that question was a patient. That was the only thing that could link such disparate lives together. A patient.

"Like a patient?"

Eric shrugged. "Maybe. Maybe Brian was on the list simply because he was the head of the hospital. As long as we're speculating. We're starting to pile assumptions on top of assumptions, you realize that."

"Maybe a patient who wasn't satisfied with his outome. So he blames Forrest, as his doctor, and Rivers, with Brian representing the hospital."

"Plausible, for a movie plot. Have you told the detective about your suspicions on Brian's death?"

"No, I haven't said anything since George sort of rejected it. But he doesn't know about the times."

"Give that to George and the detective. Let them sort it out."

But each of those people had hundreds of interactions a week with patients. That would be like looking for a needle in a haystack. No, there had to be some way to narrow it down. She shook her head. *If* there was a connection at all.

"Maybe someone *is* after Forrest," she said. She thought about the incident with his airplane and Wayne telling her that Sorcerer knew how to hack airplane computers. Her mind started racing.

"Maybe he's the common denominator. A patient who blames him for a bad outcome. Remember me telling you about Wayne's comment on this Sorcerer person knowing how to hack into airplane computers? You have to admit, there seems to be a lot of things happening to Forrest, too much to be coincidence, don't you think?"

Eric pondered her words and raised his eyebrows. "Could be. That would explain a lot of things. Why don't you run this by George? It doesn't sound as crazy as you might think."

She nodded. "I will. First thing in the morning."

Eric looked over at her. She was sitting up in bed, wearing one of his shirts. He could see that she had on nothing else.

"You don't play fair, you know?" he said.

Carly was still thinking about possible connections to Forrest when Eric reached over and ran his hand up the inside of her leg. She jumped when he got past her thigh and he didn't stop.

"I'm done reading. Why don't you turn out your light and let's get comfortable?" He moved his head over to her lap, his hand still in place between her legs.

She smiled and looked down at his face. "I'm pretty comfortable right now, especially if you keep doing what you're doing."

"Oh, I'm just getting started," he said.

The last thing she remembered was his muffled voice saying something about taking her mind off work.

The next day, Carly met with George.

"Remember when I asked you a few weeks back if you thought Brian's death was an accident?"

George nodded.

"Well, what if I told you that Sorcerer person mentioned it *before* the accident happened?"

"Go on."

She was in a jam here. She had promised Wayne she wouldn't tell anyone about his suggestions before asking him. This was too important, she decided. He'd understand.

"I got my information from an employee here at the hospital. Wayne Jensen, in IT. He was the one who told me about the Sorcerer."

"That's why you wanted a copy of the accident report."

Carly had a sheepish look on her face, embarrassed.

"I didn't want to bother you, and besides, I thought you'd think I was nuts. Plus, I promised Wayne I wouldn't tell anyone what he'd told me. He's afraid of this Sorcerer."

"So . . ."

"Wayne said Sorcerer mentioned Brian's accident at sometime before 1:31 a.m., which was six minutes before the time of the accident listed on the police report."

George put his hand on his chin, thinking.

"And all this happening to Langford. What if it's a patient, or former patient, trying to get back at him?"

"That occurred to me. I need to call Tony. He needs to talk to Wayne, find out what he knows. You're right, this could be important. Can I use your phone?"

Carly turned her desk phone around to face George. He dialed the number, got Tony on the line, and put him on the speakerphone. They went over everything she told George, with Tony occasionally interrupting with a question.

"When's the last time you talked with Wayne?" Tony asked.

"Yesterday," Carly answered.

"Let me check on a few things. And please don't say anything to Mr. Jensen until I get back to you, George."

"You got it."

The line was disconnected.

"I'll get back to you soon as I hear from Tony," George said.

"Okay. George?"

He stopped and looked at Carly.

"I'm sorry. About the accident report. I just didn't want you to think I was some flighty female. It was wrong, and I apologize."

George nodded. "Accepted. And for the record, I'd never think that of you. I have way too much respect for you, Carly. But no more secrets, okay?"

"Okay."

Chapter 23

George had been uncharacteristically quiet, but finally spoke up. "After Tony and I talked, we came up with one person who might bear closer scrutiny."

Lieutenant Budzinski, George, Helen, TJ, and Carly were at the conference table in Carly's office, summoned at George's request. They all looked at him, awaiting his response.

"Wayne Jensen. In our IT department."

Carly looked shocked and sat back in her chair. "Wayne? Why him?"

"He's been working here for a little over a year. He's from Fort Myers," George said.

TJ spoke, "So, being a computer-genius from Fort Myers makes him a suspect?"

George held up his hand. "Hold on. Let me finish. I'm not accusing anyone, okay? As Tony pointed out, just looking for candidates, if you will. That's how these kind of investigations solve cases.

"Wayne's got the ability, no doubt, and in his position, the opportunity. What's interesting is he may also have motive," George said.

Everyone perked up in their seats and leaned forward.

"His mother was a patient here a little over a year ago. And ..." George paused. "She was a patient of Dr. Langford's. She had a stroke, was admitted here, and Dr. Langford did surgery. She died in surgery."

There was a collective gasp around the table. George continued.

"The odd thing about it is Wayne has told no one about that connection, at least that I've been able to determine. He even lied to Carly about where he was from."

Carly thought, there's the link. The common element.

TJ jumped into the conversation. "But that doesn't explain Darci's involvement. Maybe I could buy that Wayne has a grudge with Langford, but both errors were committed on her watch. Coincidence?"

"I know, lots of questions, and I haven't got that far," George said.

Before Carly could say anything, Helen said, "Darci worked with Langford in the OR."

TJ whistled. "Holy shit!"

"Do you think Wayne is on a vendetta? That he holds Langford and Edwards responsible for his mother's death?" Carly asked.

George shook his head. "Let's don't leap to conclusions here. But, we have to admit, there is means, opportunity, and potential motive. He needs to be checked out."

He continued. "Having said all this, it's important we keep this in perspective. All of this is circumstantial, and if any of this gets out, could come back to haunt us if this kid's reputation is unfairly damaged. So again, nothing leaves this room. Understood?"

"What about Brian? And Langford's plane?" Carly asked.

"We're checking that out," answered Budzinksi. "We're confirming the time on the accident report with the officer on the scene."

Helen and TJ look puzzled. Budzinski explained.

"There is some indication, not yet proven, that an online person known as Sorcerer, may have had knowledge of Brian Jennings's accident—before it happened."

There were gasps on that side of the table.

"We're going back through the accident report to see if anything was missed. Also, there was apparently an incident involving Forrest Langford's private plane, something about a software problem with the autopilot that caused it to take an unexplained nosedive on the way back from the Keys."

Helen looked shaken. "So you think that one person is behind this? Someone trying to get back at Dr. Langford?"

Budzinski shrugged. "Not sure, but that seems to be our best direction at the moment. We're seeing if it holds water."

"You think it's Wayne Jensen?" TJ asked.

Budzinski shook his head. "Like I said, not sure. But he is, as they say, a person of interest. We're investigating any potential information he might have related to it."

They finished the meeting, and afterwards Carly cornered George.

"My God, George. You realize Michelle is seeing Wayne?"

He shook his head. "Didn't know that. But we don't know anything for certain at this point, Carly. Just brainstorming."

"But George, I can't let her go out with him if he's a suspect in something like that!"

He held his hands out, palms down. "Let's don't jump to conclusions, here, okay? We have no proof whatsoever. It just looks a little curious is all. That's why we're turning it over to Lieutenant Budzinski. Let him check it out."

Carly leaned forward and looked at George, locking onto his eyes. "If she were your daughter . . ."

He thought for a minute, then shook his head and said, "No, you're right. I wouldn't want her going out with him until this was settled."

She sat back in her chair, wondering how she was going to handle this with Michelle. It wasn't like she could just tell her she couldn't see Wayne anymore. Michelle would want an explanation. At least she had left this morning to go back to Gainesville. That would buy Carly a little time.

"Do you think he could've done it?" she asked.

"Could have or did? I believe almost anyone is capable of almost anything. Whether he did or not, I honestly don't know. I believe someone did. I don't think it was Darci, and I don't think it was an accident."

That evening at home, she was telling Eric about the meeting with Budzinski.

"What am I going to tell Michelle? Any suggestions?" she said, as she leaned back in her chair at the table on the lanai. Bo was in his usual spot between them, lying with his head on his paws as if he were listening to the conversation and considering what Carly had said.

Eric shook his head. "Whew, that's a tough one. This is why I like math—it's easier."

They both laughed.

"Michelle's a big girl, and she's mature. Just level with her. Lay it out for her. She'll figure out how to deal with Wayne. I agree, I don't want her seeing him until this is resolved."

She nodded. That was what she thought, but it helped for Eric to say it as well. She smiled as she pondered the way he said *I don't want her seeing him*. He was just as concerned about her as her real father.

Carly decided she would wait until Michelle came back home. That was a conversation best had in person.

The next morning, George, TJ, and Ron were in Carly's office.

"I just talked to Budzinski. He's going to pick Wayne Jensen up for questioning this afternoon, after work. Thought I'd give everyone a heads-up," George said.

He'd already explained to the group what was happening, and Carly thought it would be good to get everyone together and make sure they were all on the same page.

Ron spoke up, "Is there anything we need to do in IT?" He was concerned about the exposure, given that Wayne worked on a lot of sensitive systems at the hospital.

"We need to be careful here," said TJ, "from a legal perspective. He hasn't been charged with anything, and, as I understand it, is only being called in for questioning, nothing else. While we need to be prudent, any whiff of changing or restricting his job at this time could come back to haunt us."

Ron nodded.

"Among us, I'd say just exercise caution and keep an eye on him. If he's done anything, he'll know we're watching him, so the likelihood of him trying anything else is pretty remote. If he's innocent, then, as TJ says, we don't want to give anyone ammunition," George said.

"What about Darci's attorney? Soon as they get wind of this, which probably won't be long, they'll be at our doorsteps wanting whatever we have. Same goes for Langford's attorney, too," TJ asked.

Darci's attorney hadn't dropped the lawsuit, even though Darci was dead.

"What do you suggest?" Carly asked.

TJ shrugged. "It might be better to call them in and share with them upfront. We could stonewall them, but I'm afraid they'll find out anyway, and when they do, my guess is they'll go straight to the press. If we're open with them, we might have a chance of keeping it out of the daylight for a little longer."

Carly thought for a moment. She trusted TJ and was inclined to go with his suggestion. For a moment, she considered running it by corporate, then thought, *the hell with it*.

"Go ahead, TJ. Let me know how it goes. Anything else?"

Everyone shook their heads, and Carly declared the meeting over.

Michelle had come back to her apartment by herself from dinner. Anna was still out with a couple of their friends, but Michelle had to finish a biology paper and passed. She had her earbuds in, listening to Jack White, trying to get in the right frame of mind without a lot of success. Her phone rang and she looked to see who was calling. Wayne. She took her earbuds out and picked up her phone.

"Hey," she answered.

"You talked to your mom?" he said, without even saying hello.

"No, not lately. Why?"

"I just spent three hours at the police station."

"What? Why?"

"They picked me up after work, took me downtown to ask me a bunch of questions. Michelle, they think I had something to do with hacking into IV pumps at the hospital!"

"What are you talking about?"

"Remember that patient who sued the hospital for medication errors? It was in the news a few weeks ago."

"Vaguely."

"Well, apparently someone tampered with the IV pumps, hacked them, and changed the settings. Almost killed the patient."

"What's that got to do with you?" she asked.

"Nothing! But someone's got it in their mind that I did it."

"Oh my God! Why you?"

"Cause I work at the hospital and everybody thinks I'm a computer whiz."

Michelle paused, her mind racing. She still had the earbuds in her hand, winding the wires around her finger.

"I didn't do it, if that's what you're wondering," Wayne said, anger in his voice.

"I wasn't thinking that, okay? Just trying to figure out why anyone would think it was you."

"There's something I need to tell you."

She opened her mouth to respond, but closed it before saying anything. He just said he didn't do it. So what was it? Michelle held her breath and didn't say a word, waiting for him to continue.

He hesitated, then spoke, "Remember me telling you my mom died a year ago?"

"Yes," she answered in a voice just above a whisper.

"She died at Rivers Hospital. Your dad was her doctor."

She dropped the earbuds she was holding. "What are you saying?"

"That's part of why they picked me up. They think I have some kind of grudge or something against your dad."

She didn't say anything for a few seconds. This was a lot of information to absorb over the phone. A part of her wondered if Wayne was being truthful. Omission was lying, too. Confused, she asked, "Why didn't you tell me before now?"

"I didn't tell anyone, okay?" he said, exasperated. "I was afraid they wouldn't hire me at the hospital, so I never told anyone. And I was going to tell you, but then we hit it off so well, and . . . I was afraid. Afraid you wouldn't go out with me once you knew."

Michelle could hear the sadness in his voice and felt sorry for him. She looked out her apartment window, seeing a group of students piling into a car, ready for a night out on the town. Shaking her head, she pushed the question of his truthfulness to the back of her mind and her voice took on a more gentle tone.

"Wayne, why would you think that? I don't even live with him, and I don't see him that much. That has nothing to do with us."

"I'm sorry. I should've told you."

"Does Mom know?"

"I don't know. I didn't tell her. You're the only one I've told, other than the police. Look, I know I screwed up and I'm sorry."

"Anything else you haven't told me?"

"No, I swear."

"So what happens now? With the police, I mean?"

"I don't know. I answered their questions. They told me not to leave town, they want to look at my computer and they probably will want to talk to me again."

"Did you get an attorney?"

"No. Can't afford one. Besides, I didn't do anything." His voice got a little louder.

"I know, but you might think about hiring an attorney. Anna's dad is an attorney. I can talk to her, if you want?"

"I guess. I'm just in shock right now, not sure what to do. You coming home this weekend?"

She hadn't planned on it, but now was considering it. "Not sure. I wasn't thinking about it, but I might now. I'm calling Mom. Let me see if she knows anything. I'll call you back after I talk to her, okay?"

"Thanks, Michelle."

She disconnected and sat there, digesting everything. She was hurt that Wayne hadn't been up front with her, but his explanation made sense. She pressed the button to call her mom.

As soon as Carly answered, Michelle launched into her. "What's going on, Mom? Why didn't you call me?"

Carly's delay in answering confirmed what Michelle had heard from Wayne.

"I didn't want to have this conversation over the phone. You talked to Wayne, I take it?" Carly said.

Michelle shook her head and didn't respond, waiting for her mom to continue.

"There're some things going on at the hospital, and the police wanted to question Wayne. He's not—"

"Did he do something, Mom? Why did they question him?"

"Michelle. Listen to me, please. This is why I didn't want to have this conversation on the phone. He's not being charged with anything. They just wanted to ask him some questions, okay? Remember that patient who's suing the hospital for a medication error?"

"Yes, but what does Wayne have to do with that?"

"Probably nothing. But someone apparently tampered with the IV pumps and the police are trying to figure out who did it."

"I still don't see what that has to do with Wayne."

"It had to be someone good with computers. He's good, and he works here at the hospital, so they just wanted to ask him some questions. That's it."

"Did you know Dad was his mom's doctor?"

"I just found out this afternoon. That's all I know. On paper, Wayne would be a logical person for the police to talk to. But if they know anything else, I'm not aware of it.

"Michelle, what happened was serious. A patient almost died. The police are just doing their job, trying to get to the bottom of it."

"I'm coming home this weekend," Michelle said.

"It'd be better if you didn't see Wayne until this is settled."

"What happened to innocent until proven guilty?"

"I'm not saying he's guilty of anything. Look, we've had these conversations before. I don't agree with it, but appearances can be misinterpreted. All I'm saying is it would be better if the two of you cooled it a bit until this blows over, that's all."

They talked for a few more minutes with Michelle asking if Wayne could come over to the house. Carly was not receptive to the idea, but Michelle insisted, saying that Wayne was her friend and needed her support. They ended up compromising, with Carly agreeing to Wayne coming over and Michelle agreeing not to go out with him.

"You sure you don't want to go to law school?" Carly asked, trying to defuse the tension.

Michelle laughed. "Positive. The last thing the world needs is another lawyer. I'll see you Friday. Love you."

"Love you, too. Be careful driving."

That evening at home, Carly told Eric about her conversation with Michelle. When she got to the part about Wayne coming over to the house, Eric shook his head, but didn't say anything.

"What could I say? She had me. She was right, and you know it, too."

Eric laughed. "Not disagreeing, love. Just marveling at how much alike you and your daughter are. Talk about two peas in a pod."

She laughed when she realized Eric was agreeing with her. "I know. I asked if she was sure she didn't want to go to law school. That was one of those times when I felt like I was talking to my twin."

He reached over and put his hand over hers. "You should be proud. You've done well. You always said you wanted her to be independent."

She shook her head as she leaned over to kiss him. "Be careful what you ask for, huh?"

That Saturday evening, when Wayne walked in, everyone said their hellos, but Carly wanted to clear the awkwardness in the air.

"I feel like there's an elephant in the room, as the saying goes, so I'd like to say something," she said, looking at Wayne and Michelle. "Obviously, I know you were questioned by the police about the med error. That had to be upsetting, but I want you to know where we stand, so there's no confusion."

They nodded, and Carly continued.

"What happened at the hospital was a serious incident, one that almost killed a patient. It's apparent someone tampered with the IV pump, and we're going to find out who's behind it."

Wayne leaned forward to say something, but Carly held up her hand.

"Like it or not, Wayne, you're a logical person to talk to. You work at the hospital, you're a whiz with computers, and . . . there's a connection of sort. Nobody, including Eric and me, is accusing you of anything. But the police have to do their jobs.

"I appreciate you and Michelle staying out of the public eye for a while until this is resolved. Not fair, I agree, but in my position, appearances can be easily misconstrued. In the meantime, you're welcome here, and I apologize for any unease this may be causing."

She reached for her wine, hoping she chose the right words.

Wayne looked at Eric, then Carly. "Thank you, both. I appreciate your saying that. But I want you to know I didn't have anything to do with it. Nothing." He grabbed Michelle's hand and continued.

"And I realize I made a mistake for not telling you about my mom. That was stupid, and I apologize. Like I told Michelle, I was afraid it would keep me from getting the job at Rivers, and I needed a job, bad. But I'd never do anything to hurt anyone."

After pausing to make sure everyone was done, Eric said, "Well, now that we've got that out of the way, can we move on to dinner? The burgers are almost done."

There was a collective laugh around the table, the tension diffused.

That night, in bed, Carly asked Eric, "So, what do you think?"

"I believe him. Don't have anything to base it on, other than gut feeling, but I don't think he did it. But it wouldn't be the first time I was fooled. You?"

"I agree. Like the thing with Forrest—I just don't see him doing it. But I still don't want him and Michelle too far from my sight, not until this is settled."

He pulled her close. "Agreed." He ran his hands down her body, causing her to shiver. "And I don't want you too far from my reach."

She started at his chest, then slid her hand all the way down his body. "Show me," she said.

"Dad? I was wondering if Josh and I could come over so Josh could take a look at your computer?"

Michelle and Josh had gone out to get pizza. While they were waiting, she called her dad.

"Sure. Not going anywhere, so come on. Have you had dinner yet?"

"Yeah, we just ordered pizza. Thanks. We'll be there in about an hour."

"Okay, see you then."

She disconnected the call and looked over at Josh.

"I told him we'd be over in an hour."

Josh nodded. Michelle told him about Wayne, leaving out the part about Wayne coming over to the house last night.

"Sounds like he's in a lot of trouble. You think he did it?"

She looked at him and shook her head. "No, I don't. We're talking about trying to kill someone, Josh. I don't think Wayne could do that."

Josh shrugged. "You never know. The police wouldn't have picked him up if they didn't have something."

"Listen at you! So, you're saying my dad's guilty?"

He held up his hands in surrender. "Hey, sorry, just making conversation, not trying to start a fight. You're right."

Their pizza came, and the conversation shifted to his work and her classes as they ate. They finished dinner without anymore discussion about Wayne, then drove over to the Langford's house.

Just as they got to the door, Tonya opened it and welcomed them. She was still peeling from the tanning bed incident, but she had on a low cut blouse, exposing as much of the tops of her purchased boobs as she could without leaving much to the imagination. Maybe she thought the distraction would divert attention from the sunburn.

Michelle looked over at Josh, caught him looking, and shook her head. Men. They were all alike.

Tonya gave her an air kiss and shook Josh's hand. She led them back to the sunroom where Forrest was waiting.

"Hi, hon. Thanks for coming over," he said as he gave Michelle a big hug.

Michelle introduced Josh, and Tonya went to fix them something to drink. They sat and chatted for a few minutes, making small talk, with Forrest quizzing Josh about his background. Finally, Forrest asked Josh to come into his office and take a look at his computer.

Michelle, not wanting to be stuck alone in the den with Barbie, followed them into the study.

"This is not my actual computer, but a clone. The police wouldn't give me back mine, so I had to buy another one and copy everything over to this one," Forrest said.

"That should work fine," Josh said. He sat at Forrest's desk and started tapping away on the keyboard. "It's going to take me a while," he said, hinting that they didn't have to stay in there while he worked.

"Why don't we go back out to the den," Forrest said to Michelle. "Let me know if you need anything, Josh."

She shrugged and followed her dad back out to the den, where Tonya was sitting.

They talked about school, and Michelle asked her dad what was going on with the charges against him.

"My attorney is getting ready to file a motion to try and get the charges dropped. The computer experts he hired have determined that it was possible that someone hacked into my computer. Maybe Josh can find something."

"I still think we should sue them or something," Tonya said.

Forrest ignored her and continued, "I just want to get this mess behind me and back to some semblance of normal."

After an hour or so, Josh emerged from Forrest's office.

"I think I found something," he said.

"Yes?" Forrest swiveled his head around to focus on the young man.

"I found a piece of code that was inserted into the operating system. With the right key, it would allow someone outside to take control of the computer."

"Are you sure?"

"Absolutely. It's pretty state-of-the-art stuff. Whoever did it was good."

"Unbelievable! Why didn't the people my attorney hired find this?" Forrest asked.

Josh shrugged. "Like I said, clever and hard to find. The only reason I found it is I was looking for it. I heard about it online. Very new. It's called Mira, after a variable star in the constellation Cetus."

"What's a variable star?" Tonya asked.

"One where the intensity changes. In Mira's case, it seems to disappear at times. It's Latin for *astonishing*."

"You seem to know quite a bit about astronomy," Forrest commented.

Josh shrugged. "A hobby of mine, along with computers. Anyway, it takes a while for everyone to catch up. It's like a chess game—the hackers get out ahead, then everyone catches up, then they come out with something new. Another few weeks, and this one will be old school."

"Any way of tracing where it came from?"

"Maybe. It'd take a while. But tell your technical guys that Mira is on your computer. That'll save them some time, and if they're any good, they can probe further."

Forrest had his cell phone out and was pressing buttons.

"Jim. Forrest. Get your computer guys to look for Mira. Mira, it's a—" He looked at Josh, and Josh mouthed *Trojan horse*. "Trojan horse. My daughter's boyfriend found it. He said they'd know what it was."

He clicked the phone off and said to Josh, "Thank you. I appreciate your taking a look at it."

"More lucky than anything. Hope it helps."

"Michelle told me you've already had dinner, but we need to plan on going out soon."

"That'd be nice."

"Well, Dad, we're going out to the beach."

They stood to leave.

"Thanks again," Forrest said as he shook Josh's hand.

He hugged Michelle. "Good to see you. Let me know when you come back to town. I love you."

Michelle was surprised. It was unusual for him to say that, especially in front of people.

"Love you, too, Dad."

Tonya came over and gave them both an air kiss. This time Josh didn't stare at Tonya's chest, Michelle noticed. He's learning, she thought.

Budzinski sat in the chair next to George. They were in Carly's office, and she was curious as to what was going on. George had called less than half an hour ago and told her they needed to meet. Something important had come up.

"Our computer guys found something on Doctor Langford's computer. Actually, your daughter's boyfriend—" Tony looked down at his notes, "Josh— found it. It's a program called Mira. Apparently, it's the latest in hacker circles. It gives someone unauthorized and hidden access to another computer."

Carly was intrigued. So Forrest was telling the truth.

"I thought Forrest had his computer back?" she asked.

"Nope, we still have his. He has an exact copy that we gave him."

"Any idea who did it?" Carly asked.

The lieutenant looked at Carly, then back at George. "Our technicians have traced an IP address back to Wayne Jensen's computer."

Carly's jaw dropped and she shook her head. My God! Wayne? Wayne was behind this?

"We've got a warrant for his arrest. They're taking him in right now. I just wanted to give you a heads-up."

"So, do you think he was behind changing the IV pumps, too?" George asked.

Tony shrugged. "Don't know. We've also got a warrant to search his computer, so we'll see. And we don't quite know the relationship to the stuff on Doctor Langford's computer. All we have is something that linked his computer to Jensen's. It doesn't prove Jensen actually did it."

All Carly could think about was Michelle. She had to get to her and tell her. No way was she going to continue to see Wayne, even if he did get out on bail. Over her dead body, she thought.

"But the evidence is starting to pile up. I mean, I'm no detective, but this seems pretty damning to me," she said, looking at the two men.

"Definitely starting to take shape. But far from concrete," Tony said.

George was shaking his head. "Right here in front of us, the whole time."

As soon as they left her office, Carly called Michelle's cell phone. It went straight to voice mail, typical. She texted Michelle to call her.

Ten minutes later, Carly's phone buzzed.

"Hey, hon," she said when she answered.

"What's a matter? I was in class when you called."

Carly took a deep breath. "They're arresting Wayne. They found—"

"What?"

"They found something on your dad's computer that pointed to Wayne's computer. So they're arresting him and searching his computer."

There was a pause on the line. "Mom." The voice sounded like a little girl. "Wayne did that?" she said.

Carly could sense the hurt in her voice. She wished she could hug her little girl. She remembered the lieutenant's words.

"It's not proof, okay? But suspicious. And," she added, "it doesn't look good."

"I can't believe this shit, Mom!" Her voice was angry now. "That son of a bitch!"

Carly felt so sorry for her. Michelle reminded her of a younger version of herself, naïve and trusting, before she became calloused by the world. She was tempted to remind her of the line about innocent until proven guilty, but she couldn't bring herself to do it.

"Sorry to be the bearer of bad news, but I wanted to let you know. Give me a call later?"

"Yeah, I will."

Michelle disconnected, and Carly started to put the phone on her desk. She decided to call Eric first.

"Hey, love. What's up?" he answered.

She told him about Budzinski's visit and talking to Michelle. Eric was as surprised as she.

"I guess at least we don't have to worry about Michelle seeing him now?" he said.

"I think we're safe on that. I just feel so bad for her."

"I know. Not much you can do, though."

Chapter 24

Wayne Jensen was not in a good mood. He'd just spent two nights in jail, his first such experience, and one he wasn't anxious to repeat. His cell mate, a veteran of the facility in Fort Myers, slept like a baby, snoring the entire night.

This morning, they released him with no explanation, other than an anonymous person made bail for him. Although he was glad to get out, he wondered who and why.

He had met with a public defender, who had convinced him of the seriousness of the charges. He was being charged with twelve counts of child pornography, based on the twelve pictures found on Doctor Forrest Langford's computer, and was also being investigated as a "person of interest" in relation to the manipulation of the medical data on Robert Willis's IV pump.

Wayne knew the pictures weren't on his computer and hadn't come from him. But how did they link back to his computer? Somebody was screwing with him, and he needed to find out who. Fast.

He got back to his apartment and saw that his computer was gone. His attorney said he probably wouldn't be getting it back, at least anytime soon, as it was considered evidence. Without a computer, he was lost.

What the police didn't know was that he had a complete mirror image of his computer, stored in the cloud on a secure backup site. Thank goodness for the benefits of modern technology. He looked around and noticed that not only had they taken his computer, but his external hard drive and various USB drives he had around his apartment.

The first order of business was to get another computer. He looked at his watch. Still time, and he was anxious to get on the trail.

Fortunately, he had a little cash saved up and would go to the computer store later to pick up a nice laptop. Then, he could sign on to the backup site and download the mirror image of his computer.

He had to be careful. He figured the police would be monitoring his broadband Internet connection, so he'd have to make other arrangements that would be untraceable and difficult for anyone except perhaps the National Security Agency to trace. But he wasn't worried about NSA, only the Fort Myers Police Department, with not nearly as sophisticated and extensive resources.

He sat down and thought about his situation. There was a good chance they would be following him, so he didn't want to get picked up and lose his new computer. Maybe it would be better to wait and drive up to Tampa tomorrow and get one. There'd be a better selection there, and it would be easier to lose anyone following him.

Since he'd been suspended, with pay, at work, he had nothing better to do. Someone had set him up for Langford's porn charges and they would pay dearly. They were messing with the wrong person, as they would soon find out.

He was guilty of hacking, and hoped that anybody looking at his computer would be solely focused on the link to Langford. If they cast a broader net, there could be more problems.

He picked up his phone and thought about calling Michelle, then put it down, knowing she probably wouldn't talk to him. By now, she knew that he'd been arrested. Plus, that snake Josh was probably whispering in her ear, glad Wayne was out of the picture.

Maybe he could throw some water on that. When he got his computer up, he was going to do some snooping on the smooth-talking Josh, see what he could find out.

The next day, Wayne drove to Tampa to the largest computer store there. He was careful to watch for any suspicious cars behind him, and even then, he parked in the parking lot of a store one block up Dale Mabry from the computer store and walked back, figuring it would be easier to spot someone following him.

He paid cash for the computer, raising some eyebrows at the checkout, but he explained that it was a gift from his grandmother. Since it was less than $10,000, he knew there was no legal requirement to report it, and after a brief consultation with the manager, they accepted the money and allowed him to leave with the computer.

When he got back to his truck, he drove to the nearest Starbucks, got a latte, and signed on to the Internet. The connection at Starbucks wasn't as fast or secure as he would have preferred, but he needed to get back online fast. The first order of business was to set up the basics on his computer. He knew he couldn't use the broadband connection in his apartment, so he was going to be stuck with other options for a while.

When satisfied that the computer was secure, untraceable, and able to access the Internet, he left Starbucks and drove north on Dale Mabry until he came to an upscale apartment complex. Seeing that the gate was open, he drove in, watching the notebook computer open on the seat next to him. He circled through the complex, looking for a Wi-Fi connection that he could glom on to. Although more people were careful about securing their wireless routers these days, it didn't take him long to find a network that he could use.

He pulled into a parking place and connected to the Internet through the stranger's wireless network. No one was on the connection, so the owner must be at work.

Much better, he thought. It was nice to have an unrestricted broadband connection. The first thing he did was to download the mirror image of his computer that had been confiscated by the police. Even with a broadband connection, that took a while.

As soon as it was done, he left the complex and went to another Starbucks. He didn't want to push his luck by staying at the apartment complex too long, and he didn't want to go to the same public place twice in a row. No need, since there was wireless Internet available on almost every corner these days.

At this Starbucks, he got what he needed off the Internet, then headed back to Fort Myers. He didn't need to be online to search his computer for clues as to who had breached his computer. Now that he had the proper tools downloaded, he could do that anywhere. When he found out, they were going to pay. He smiled as the phrase *the fun has begun* popped into his head. Damn right, he thought. Just wait.

Michelle looked at her phone; another call from Wayne, the third one in the last couple of hours. She slammed it down on her desk, hoping he wasn't going to be a pest. She had nothing to say to him, and if he called again, she was going to call her mom and see if she could get the police to make him stop.

Her phone buzzed. A text message. From Wayne. She started to delete it, but clicked on it to read it first.

B careful w Josh-ask him about his mom

She stared at the phone. What kind of bullshit was this? She deleted the message, but it kept nagging at her. Josh had told her his mom was dead, but nothing more. She couldn't get it out of her mind.

She picked up her phone and called her mom.

"Hey, sweetie. What's up?" Carly answered.

She decided not to mention the phone calls. "I got a text from Wayne."

Carly jumped on it. "If he's bothering you, I can call the detective and I'm sure he can do something about it."

"No, not really. He just sent me a text telling me to be careful with Josh and to ask him about his mom."

Carly thought about it, then said, "That's weird. What does he mean by that?"

"I don't know, but it's bothering me. Josh hasn't told me anything about his family. He did tell me his mom was dead, but that was it."

"Sounds like Wayne's just jealous and trying to start something. I wouldn't give it too much thought. Consider the source."

"I guess you're right."

"Let me know if he starts bothering you, okay?"

"I will."

After Carly hung up the phone, she kept thinking about Wayne's message. Why would he send that to Michelle? Josh had been evasive about his background, but so had Wayne.

She called George. "Hey, could you come by my office this afternoon, say around three?"

"Sure. See you then."

A few minutes before three, George walked into her office and Carly motioned for him to close the door. He closed it, walked over to her desk, and sat in front of her.

"What's the matter?" he said.

She told him about her conversation with Michelle and Wayne's message.

"He's not harassing her, is he?" George asked.

"No, but I could tell it upset her. Josh hasn't said much about his family. Eric tried to pin him down on a few things, and he deliberately dodged any discussion about it."

"Interesting. If you'd like, I can make a few calls and check things out, discreetly of course."

Carly nodded. "I'd appreciate it."

"You don't know his mother's name by any chance?" he asked.

"No. All I know is his last name is Mills and he works at Gulf Toyota in the service department."

"That's fine. Let me see what I can find out."

She nodded. "Thanks, George."

The next morning, George called Carly and wanted to come up to her office. She told him to come on, and in a few minutes, she heard a knock on her door and looked up to see him.

"Come on in."

He closed the door behind him and walked over to her desk.

"I was able to find out a little about Josh Mills."

She saved the file she was working on and gave George her undivided attention.

"Apparently, he's a computer genius. I made a few inquiries and that came up several times. His father died some years ago, and he lived with his mother here in Fort Myers before he went off to the University of Florida. Graduated with honors, worked in Orlando a while, then came back here and went to work at the Toyota place."

"Sounds pretty harmless," Carly said.

George frowned. "There's more. About a year ago, his mother was brought to Rivers through the ER, an apparent suicide attempt—an overdose. She died in the hospital."

"My God!" Carly said. "No wonder he doesn't want to talk about her."

"There's more. Guess who the doctor on call was?"

She was puzzled for a second, then her eyes got wide, her mouth dropped open, and she shook her head.

He nodded, confirming her thoughts. "They called Langford in, but there was nothing he could do."

She didn't speak as her mind raced to fill in the blanks.

"She was Forrest's patient? You don't think—"

George held up his hand. "Let me finish. After his father died, his mother took back her maiden name, that's why nothing showed up anywhere. Her name was Irene Keisler.

"To answer your question, I don't know. A lot of coincidence there, which always makes me nervous."

"So, what do we do?"

"I've passed it along to Tony, see what they come up with. In the meantime, I'd keep a close eye on him."

Carly's mind was racing. What was she going to tell Michelle?

"Damn, George, this is a mess. What do I tell Michelle?"

George raised his eyebrows and exhaled. "That does complicate things, doesn't it? Well, you can't tell her what I've just shared with you. Probably get some people in hot water. And we don't have anything solid. But I'd be wary, keep a close eye on him, maybe push him for some answers to questions, that sort of thing."

She nodded, thankful Michelle was in Gainesville. She'd definitely have to talk to Eric about this one.

That night, at home, she cornered Eric.

"We need to talk about something. I need your advice."

Eric put his book down and looked up at Carly, waiting for her to begin.

She told him the story about what George had uncovered about Josh Mills.

"Now I don't know how to deal with Michelle. I mean, I don't want her hanging around with him either, but I can't just come out and say why. You know her— she'll want more information. Any suggestions?"

He shook his head. "Geez. This is getting complicated. I keep thinking back to how evasive he was talking about his family. I can understand him being embarrassed by it, but makes you wonder if he's hiding something.

"You said anything to Forrest? Maybe he could shed some light on things."

Carly's face lit up. "Maybe so. But how could I explain to him—"

"Don't explain, just say you were looking into a case involving a hospital patient, ask him what he remembers about it, what he has in his notes."

She smiled. "Good idea. I'll call him tomorrow."

As soon as she got to work the next morning, she called Forrest, left a message asking him to call her back as soon as possible.

Fifteen minutes later, her cell phone buzzed. It was Forrest.

"Thanks for calling me back so soon," she said.

"No problem, what's up?" Just like the old Forrest, no small talk, right to business.

"A case came up internally on a patient who died about a year ago, just a routine review. Anyway, it was a patient who came in through the ER, an apparent suicide attempt. According to our records, you were on call and you came in to see her. Irene Keisler. You remember?"

There was a pause, then, "Keisler, Keisler. Yeah, I remember. It was a weekend, a busy one. I had three calls. She was an overdose, loaded up with Xanax, and booze, if I recall. Damage was done by the time they brought her in, nothing we could do. As I recall, she died less than twenty-four hours later. Why? Don't tell me they're suing, too?"

She was almost relieved the old Forrest was back.

"No, nothing like that. Just an internal review on our side, I just wanted to touch base with you and see what you remembered. That's all."

"No problem. Hey? Thanks for talking to Michelle. She called me, you know?"

Carly smiled. Maybe the aliens tweaked him a little before they brought him back.

"Yeah, she told me. How you doing?"

His tone softened a bit. "Okay. Trial date hasn't been set yet. I'll be glad when it's over. But things are settling down some. And Kitchens is good, seems to be making some progress."

"Good. Thanks for the info on Keisler."

"Sure."

That evening, she replayed her conversation with Forrest for Eric.

"I've got to tell Michelle. She needs to know what's going on."

Eric nodded. "I agree, it's only fair."

When Carly got home from work the next day, Michelle's car was in the driveway. She was on the lanai, in front of her iPad, with Bo lying at her feet.

"Hi, Mom."

Carly went over, gave her a hug and a kiss.

"Hi, hon. When did you get in?"

"Only about thirty minutes ago. How was your day?"

Carly shrugged, then sat at the table across from Michelle.

"Not bad. At least as far as the past month has been. How's school?"

"Good. I met with my advisor this week. Looks like I'll be done in May."

Carly smiled. "Great, congratulations. So we need to plan on coming up for graduation?" She was hopeful.

Michelle nodded. "As far as I know."

Carly adopted a more serious tone. "Can we talk for a few minutes?"

Michelle shifted her glance away from the iPad and looked at her mom. "Sure, what's up?"

"How are things with Josh?"

Michelle crinkled her nose and eyes. "Good, I guess. We're going out tonight." She cocked her head. "Why?"

"We've always had an open relationship with each other. So please take what I'm about to tell you in that vein, okay?"

Michelle had a puzzled look on her face. "Okay."

"I found out some things about Josh that I wanted to share with you, things I thought you need to know."

"Great, so here's where you tell me he's an axe murderer, huh?"

They both laughed.

"No, just that I'm not sure he's being totally honest with you and I think you should know. If I were you, I would."

"Great. Another one. Maybe I'll just stay in Gainesville."

"Sorry. Anyway, his mother died about a year ago, right? But that's all we know, at least all I know."

Michelle just nodded.

"I found out that his mother committed suicide and died at Rivers."

Michelle frowned and said, "My God . . ."

"Your dad was her doctor." She let that sink in.

Michelle's look turned to confusion. "You've got to be kidding me! I date two people in Fort Myers and both of their moms were Dad's patients and died at your hospital? What are you saying, Mom?"

Carly shook her head. "Nothing, just information I thought you should know. Josh had to know that your dad was his mother's doctor. And I'm just surprised he didn't tell you. He knows who your dad is, right?"

Michelle nodded as she digested what Carly told her.

"I love you, and I just don't want to see you get hurt. I don't know how serious you two are, but I thought it was something you needed to be aware of."

"Who told you? Wayne?"

Carly shook her head. "No, not Wayne. I'm sorry, I can't tell you. Most of what I told you is covered under patient privacy regulations and I could get in a lot of serious trouble. But you're my daughter, and I'll always do anything necessary to protect you, even if it means breaking the law. But I can't put other people at risk if I don't have to."

Michelle considered what her mother said and nodded. "So Wayne was right?"

Carly nodded. "I don't know what he knew or how he found out. I hate to dump this on you, but again, I felt strongly that you should know."

"Thanks, Mom—for telling me."

Michelle and Josh were out at the The Hut, sitting out in the old building. The band had taken a break.

"You're kinda quiet tonight. Everything okay?" he asked.

"I guess. Just been thinking a lot."

"Anything in particular?"

She studied his face. "I like you, Josh, a lot."

He smiled. "I like you, too." He waited for her to continue.

"But I don't feel like you're letting me in. I mean, you've been over to my house, met my parents, but I know nothing about your family."

His smile faded. "I told you, I don't like to talk about my family. Nothing to say. My mother and father are dead, no brothers or sisters. End of story." He took a swallow of beer.

She looked down, then out at the beach. "Sorry I brought it up. Never mind."

The band came back up on the small stage and started tuning up for the next set.

Josh finished his beer, grabbed Michelle's hand, and said, "Can we go for a walk?"

She didn't answer, but let him lead her out to the beach. He was still holding her hand, but they were both silent.

The moon was almost full, reflecting off the calm waters of the Gulf as they walked down the beach. Lots of people were out on the beach around the Hut, enjoying the nice evening and the break. The opening guitar strains of "Statesboro Blues" drifted across the sand as the band broke into the old Allman Brothers's tune.

As they walked farther down the beach away from the Hut, the number of people thinned out. Before long, they were alone on the beach, only scattered condos on one side and the Gulf on the other. Clouds had covered the moon and it was surprisingly dark.

He led her closer to the water's edge, stopped and turned, facing her. The gentle waves of the Gulf were lapping up on the beach only a few feet away.

"I like you a lot, Michelle, okay? Enough to tell you everything, something I've never done before with anyone."

She looked up at him, nodded, and felt his grip tighten.

"My dad died when I was nine, so I don't have a lot of memories of him. Mom told me that he had heart problems and that's all I know."

He looked around, grabbed her other hand, and took a deep breath before continuing. "A year ago, my mom committed suicide. Overdosed on Xanax. They took her to Rivers, but it was too late. She died there."

The sadness in his eyes was obvious, even in the dim light, and was evident in his voice.

"I'm sorry," she said.

He shook his head. "She was all I had. I never understood why she did it." Tears started coming down his cheeks.

"In the ER, they called your dad in. He got there, did all he could, but . . ."

Michelle pulled him close to her, his head on her shoulder. She just held him, not saying a word, feeling his tears trickle down on her neck.

The next morning, when Michelle got out of bed and went into the kitchen for breakfast, Eric and her mom were already at the table.

"Good morning," Eric said.

"Morning," Michelle answered as she poured a cup of coffee. She took a sip, then sat at the table with them. "Josh told me about his family last night. Everything."

Carly looked at Eric, then back at her daughter.

"Don't worry, I didn't tell him anything. All I said was that I didn't know much about him. We went for a walk on the beach and he broke down and told me."

Carly reached over and put her hand over Michelle's. "I'm sorry, sweetie."

Michelle shook her head. "No, it's okay. I'm glad you told me. And I'm glad he told me about it, on his own. I was going to ask him about it."

"That's good."

"I like him a lot. But I don't want to get serious about him right now, especially after what happened with Wayne."

Carly nodded, proud of her daughter's newfound maturity. "That's probably a good thing. Things have a way of sorting themselves out if you're patient."

"I know." She rose and took her coffee. "Going to check my email. Anna and I are going out to the beach later."

After she left, Eric looked at Carly and said, "She's growing up. You did the right thing, telling her."

Carly raised her eyebrows. "I never know. Kids don't come with a manual."

He laughed. "No, but you should be proud. You've done well with Michelle. She's a good kid."

Carly smiled. "Thanks, I need to hear that."

Chapter 25

Michelle's break went by too fast, Carly thought, as she sat in her office. Michelle was already back in Gainesville and, though she wasn't home much, it was still nice to spend a little time with her and catch her coming and going. At least she'd be back in Fort Myers this weekend. There was a wedding, so she and Anna were coming back for that.

Eric was headed to San Francisco for a conference the day before Michelle was scheduled to come home. Carly wanted to go with him, and seriously considered going out just for the weekend. But, with everything going on at work, she decided she couldn't afford to be away. A shame, she thought. She always enjoyed San Francisco.

The intercom buzzed and snapped her out of her daydreams.

"Paul Leggett on line one," Sandy said.

"Thanks," Carly answered and pushed the button for the blinking line one.

"Hello, Paul." She wondered what he wanted. Paul Leggett never called to chat.

"Carly. I'm sitting here looking at a press release from the *Fort Myers News-Herald*. What in the hell were you thinking?"

His opening salvo caught her off guard for a minute. Then she remembered—the press release she'd sent out regarding Forrest Langford.

"Not sure I follow you, Paul. It was basically a repeat of the press release that the Florida Medical Board issued. What's the problem?"

"The problem is that it relates to a doctor, your ex, by the way, who's a pedophile. I thought I made it clear when I was down there that HealthAmerica didn't need any adverse publicity from this Langford thing."

Carly felt her face flush and her blood pressure rise.

"Now wait a minute, Paul. First of all, he's been charged, not convicted. Matter of fact, the detective told me that the charges are probably going to be dropped. Second, there's absolutely nothing inaccurate about the statement—his privileges are intact. And last, the fact that he's my ex-husband has nothing to do with anything." She took a deep breath.

"Appearances, Carly, appearances. You know who sent me this? Fucking Carter Freeman! His little note on the bottom says, and I quote, 'Maybe we should keep a lower profile on this?' Well, I can tell you this, you can kiss that promotion goodbye. No way that's going to happen now."

She was stunned. That ass-kissing, brown-nosing bastard! He was just covering his own rear. She didn't trust herself to respond.

Paul continued, "No more press releases on anything unless you clear it with me first. Got it?"

Carly was squeezing the telephone handset so hard she was surprised it didn't collapse under the pressure.

"Yeah," she said, slamming the phone down on the base so hard she thought she might have broken something. She was so angry, she considered calling Leggett back and telling him to stick it where the sun doesn't shine. It took a lot to make her angry, but her temper was not to be trifled with. And Paul Leggett had pushed all the right buttons.

Sandy stuck her head inside the door with her hand on the doorknob.

"Want me to shut this?" she asked in a tentative voice.

Carly turned and glared at the voice until she saw the look on Sandy's face. She could tell Sandy had overheard the conversation and knew something was wrong. Sandy seemed to retreat a few inches. Carly exhaled and tried to relax her face.

"No, but thanks, Sandy. Leggett just made my day. Said the promotion was a no-go, thanks to that damn press release I sent out on Langford."

Sandy relaxed but kept her distance. "It was just a repeat of the Florida Medical Board statement. What's the big deal?"

"The big deal is Paul Leggett has no balls, that's what."

Sandy stifled a laugh. "You've known that for a while."

"Yes, but Brian usually dealt with the corporate bullshit. I don't know how he managed. Maybe I'm not cut out for the top position."

"Not true. Don't lose too much sleep over it. Leggett's a willow in the wind. It's not over yet."

Carly smiled. "Thanks, Sandy. Just leave the door open, I'll be fine."

Eric was packing his suitcase for the trip tomorrow. Carly knew he was excited about going and wished she was going with him. Bo lay on his rug with his head between his paws, watching Eric. He knew somebody was leaving and was trying to figure it out.

"I wish you were coming with me," Eric said.

Carly smiled. "Me, too. Don't remind me. Just too much going on. Don't want to give Paul another reason to fire me, though that might be a good thing." Over dinner, she had told Eric about her conversation with Leggett.

Eric shook his head. "What an ass. I agree with Sandy. It's not over yet. Don't forget, several of your board members have some good contacts with HealthAmerica, board members who support you."

"I know. I've decided not to worry about it. Do my job and let things sort out. Only so much I can do anyway.

"Where are you staying? With Frank?" Frank was Eric's old college roommate and still lived in Berkeley. Frank was lost in the sixties, still looked about the same as he did when they were in grad school together; maybe a few more pounds and a little less hair. Frank was a professor at University of California, Berkeley.

"I'm staying the first two nights with Frank, then moving to the Marriott in the city where the conference is. Just too much of a hassle commuting from Berkeley when I don't have to."

"I hope you and Frank don't get in to too much trouble." She laughed. "You've told me too many stories about your adventures."

Eric walked over to the bed and leaned over to kiss her. Not just a peck, either. He pulled away, holding her hand and said, "You have nothing to worry about, love. I know what I've got here." He looked right at her with those blue-gray eyes that she loved so much.

She kissed his hand. "I'm teasing, you know that. Tell Frank I said *Hi*."

He turned to finish packing. "At least Michelle is coming home tomorrow, so you and Bo will have some company."

Carly nodded and laughed. "If we get to see her, right, Bo?"

At the mention of his name, he got up and walked over to the bed for some scratches. They both laughed.

"Five nights without you? Maybe you should finish packing later," she said, as she pulled him down on the bed on top of her.

"You've got on too many clothes," he said, as he helped her get out of his shirt she was wearing. "But we can fix that."

They didn't bother to turn the light out. They both enjoyed looking at each other's bodies.

After he got her shirt off, he kissed one nipple, then the other, watching with interest as they got harder. She complained, mostly in jest, that her boobs were too small. And he always insisted they were just right.

"What about you?" she said, as he continued kissing her. Without waiting for an answer, she pulled his t-shirt over his head, then moved her hands down to his shorts.

She wanted him, and could tell as she removed his shorts that he wanted her, too.

Bo went back to his rug to lie down, ignoring the commotion on the bed. He seemed to know there would be no attention to him for a little while.

Chapter 26

"Hi, Mom," Michelle said when Carly answered her cell phone.

"Hi, hon. Where are you?" Carly looked at her watch and saw it was three fifteen.

"On our way to Tampa. We're going to have an early dinner with Anna's dad, then head to Fort Myers."

"Well, be careful. Give me a call when you leave Tampa."

"Will do. Love you."

"Love you, too."

Carly put her cell phone back on her desk. It had been a long week and she was glad it was Friday. She still had a few more hours to work, but that was fine, since no one was home but Bo. Eric had called earlier from San Francisco. Frank had met him at the airport, and they were going out for dinner at Zuni Café in the city before taking BART back over to Frank's house in Berkeley.

It was just getting dark as she pulled into the garage after six. Bo was waiting at the door when she unlocked it. She entered the alarm code, then took him out through the pool area to the back yard.

Bo walked around, sniffing everything as if he were checking. He decided which area of the small lawn needed fertilizing, stopped, and took care of business. After checking a few more things on his way back to Carly, he ran in ahead of her.

She went into the bedroom and changed into shorts and one of Eric's long-sleeve dress shirts. Carly loved wearing his shirts and had appropriated several that now resided in her closet. She rolled up the sleeves and went out into the kitchen to fix something for dinner.

The first thing she did was pour a glass of chardonnay. She normally didn't drink during the week, but it was Friday and, after the week she had, she deserved it.

The glass of wine in hand, she opened the refrigerator door and waited for something to speak. She spied some leftover shrimp from a couple of nights ago and decided that, with a salad, would make a nice dinner for one. Taking the plastic container out, she pried open the top and gave it a quick sniff. Pronouncing it still good, she set it on the counter while she made a small salad to go with it.

The doorbell rang. At first she thought Michelle may have lost her key, then looked at the clock and realized she was still in Tampa. Bo walked toward the front door as Carly followed. She looked through the viewer. It was Josh.

She unlocked the door and opened it.

"Ms. Nelson, hi."

"Josh, come in." She grabbed Bo's collar, opened the door, and let him in.

"Michelle's not home yet," she said as Josh walked past her and she closed the door. "She and Anna were going to have dinner in Tampa with Anna's dad."

Carly turned around to see Josh pointing a black, semi-automatic pistol at her.

"Yes, I know exactly where she is. Don't let the dog go or I'll shoot him." He pointed toward the back of the house with his free hand. "Put him in your bedroom."

She was confused, wondering what was happening. She came close to releasing Bo, who was straining under her grip, but was afraid Josh would make good on his threat to shoot him.

"What's going on here, Josh?" Her heart was racing and she was trying to remain calm and in control, which was hard to do when someone was pointing a gun at you.

"Just do what I said. I'll explain soon enough." He motioned with the gun toward the hall leading to the master bedroom, never taking his eyes off her.

Bo's ears were back and he bared his teeth, positioning himself between Carly and Josh as if he knew something was wrong.

Carly reached down to pet him. "Come on, Bo." She kept her eyes on Josh as she started toward the bedroom, almost pulling the large dog with her.

Josh followed, but far enough behind to avoid giving Carly any chance to do anything. "I know you're desperately thinking of something to try. Don't. I know how to use a gun and won't hesitate to shoot you if I have to. As long as you do what I say, Michelle will be safe."

At the mention of her daughter, Carly stiffened. What in the hell was going on here? Her mind was racing, trying to make sense of it all.

Josh stood back as she put Bo in the bedroom and closed the door. He pawed at the door on the other side.

"Back in the kitchen." Josh motioned the gun toward the other room. He backed to the side of the hall, still pointing the gun at her as she walked past. She could hear Bo scratching at the bedroom door as she walked down the hall.

When they got to the kitchen, he pulled a chair out from the breakfast table. "Sit," he said and backed away from the chair.

She sat and noticed a laptop on the table. Did he have that with him at the door? She couldn't remember. Things were happening too fast to process. What did he want?

He was still pointing the gun at her, but far enough away that she knew she couldn't make a move.

She saw four thick black plastic cable ties on the table in front of her. Josh pushed two of them across to her. "Put these around your ankles and the chair legs."

She hesitated, not wanting to constrain herself and reduce her chances of getting away.

He raised the gun and pointed it directly at her head. "I'm not going to tell you again, Carly. Put the ties around your ankles, now!"

His hand and voice were steady, she noticed. At this point, she wasn't prepared to find out if he was bluffing. Carly bent over and put the first tie around her ankle and the chair leg, then the other one, careful not to pull them too tight. She sat back in her chair.

He pushed another plastic tie toward her. "Now, take this one and tie your right wrist to the chair arm."

Instinctively, she reached out with her right hand to pick it up and started to tie her left wrist.

"No—I said tie the right wrist."

She stared at him, then slowly complied. It was awkward, since she was right-handed, a fact that Josh had observed.

He sat on the other side of the table where he could watch her. Josh turned the laptop around to face him, opened it, and turned it on. He still held the gun in his hand.

"I'm going to give you a little demonstration. Then I won't need this anymore," he said, holding up the gun.

"What's this about, Josh?"

"Shut up. Don't distract me. You'll have the answer to that soon enough." His look gave her chills. There was nothing in his eyes; nothing human.

Satisfied that the computer was where he wanted it to be, he slid it to one side.

"Here's the deal, Carly. You remember how Brian Jennings died, right?"

At the sound of Brian's name, her face tightened.

Josh noticed.

"Thought so. Except it was no accident. Your little nerd friend figured that out for you, didn't he?"

She forced herself not to give him the satisfaction of anymore expressions.

"It's okay. I know all about it. He's pretty clever, actually, just not as clever as I. He was right. I hacked into Jennings's truck computer. I drove him off the Sanibel Causeway. He was my test drive, so to speak." He laughed a sick laugh, as if he were making a joke. "He had to go, but I wanted to make sure the program worked properly. It did, didn't it?"

Carly's mouth opened and a chill went down her spine as she realized who was sitting across her breakfast table. Sorcerer.

He studied her face as he watched the tumblers fall into place. "You're pretty clever yourself. So you know I can hack into a car's computer. Remember when Michelle's car had the problem with the stuck accelerator?"

She gasped when she realized what this maniac was saying.

"What you don't know is I hacked into Michelle's car computer. I can control it completely from here." He tapped the laptop with the gun and paused for what he said to sink in.

As if reading her mind, he went on. "Now, I know you're probably sitting there wondering if I'm bluffing or not. I would be. Here's where the demonstration comes in. You asked her to call you when she left Tampa, right?"

The look of surprise on Carly's face gave her away once more.

"Oh, I forgot to explain that part." He grinned, proud of himself. "I've hacked your phone and hers, so I've been monitoring all of your calls. And I know Eric's in San Francisco. Having dinner with his friend Frank. Want me to tell you where he's staying?"

He watched her for a reaction. Satisfied she understood, he continued.

"Anyway, back to Michelle. Let's listen in on her cell phone." He clicked the mouse a couple of times, then turned the computer around so she could hear.

"Don't bother to scream or say anything. The microphone on our end is muted. We're just listening."

Carly could hear the noise in the background, then she could pick out Michelle's voice coming from the speakers on the laptop.

"I'll go ahead and call Mom. We're about ready to leave, right?"

Then Anna's voice. "Yeah, probably in the next thirty minutes."

Josh could tell that Carly was visibly impressed. "Not bad, huh? But that's nothing. Here's the part you need to listen to closely." He turned the screen back around to face him.

"When she gets into her car, I'll be able to control her car from here. I can accelerate, turn it, disable the brakes, basically everything. Think about that for a moment."

He just sat there grinning while Carly digested what he said.

"Now I want you to think about where she's going to be driving. She'll be on I-75, going down to St. Petersburg. You've lived in Florida a long time. How does she get across Tampa Bay?"

Carly felt a wave of nausea sweep over her. The Sunshine Skyway. A sick look came across her face that she couldn't hide.

Josh's twisted grin got bigger. "Give the woman a prize, she figured it out. That's right, Carly. The Sunshine Skyway Bridge. Want to know how high it is? Although the total length is five and one-half miles, the center span is 191 feet high and spans 1,200 feet. Pretty scary, huh? You're starting to get my drift. It would be tragic if her accelerator got stuck, brakes failed and the car took a hard turn on top of that section, wouldn't it?

"Now, you're wondering, could he do that? GPS is only accurate down to ten feet or so. Throw in a couple of seconds delay and I could be off as much as four or five times that. Let's round it up to one hundred feet. So, I miss the peak by a hundred feet. With a 1,200 foot span, I don't think it matters, do you?"

She started shaking from fear and anger and a feeling of helplessness. Her eyes narrowed and her glare filled with hatred at the psycho in front of her. The words came out through clenched teeth.

"What do you want?"

"Patience, Carly. Almost there. By now you're probably getting some crazy idea that you could disable me and call Michelle and tell her to pull over. But here's the thing. I've set up what's called a *deadman* control. Know what that is?"

He waited for her to answer, but she wouldn't give him the satisfaction.

"I've programmed it so that if I don't enter my code every five minutes, then the computer will automatically call for full acceleration, no brakes and when the speed hits eighty, take a sharp left turn. Can you imagine? May not be as dramatic as going off in the bay, but the end result will probably be the same. So if you do manage to knock me out, then you've just sentenced your daughter to a gory death. Sure you want to do that, Carly?

"Oh. One last thing. Maybe you think you could take my gun and force me to enter the code to buy you time."

He slid the gun across the table. "Go ahead, pick it up."

Carly looked at it carefully for the first time. It was a Glock 19, same as the one she had in her nightstand in her bedroom. Looked to be a nine millimeter, a carbon copy. She extended her free hand, wondering what the catch was. Letting it rest on top of the gun, she considered her options. She looked directly at him. It was as if he were reading her very thoughts.

"Pick it up. I don't care."

She picked it up. It felt heavy, but not heavy enough. She pointed it directly at him, even though she knew the magazine wasn't full. But maybe there were one or two shots. All she needed was one.

The sick grin never left his face. "Now what?"

"Move the computer over to me."

"I don't think so."

"Move the damn computer over here to me. Now." She pointed the gun directly at him.

"Nope." He crossed his arms.

"I will shoot you, you son-of-a-bitch."

"Go ahead. I don't think you can."

She pointed the gun at his head and pulled the trigger. The gun clicked. It was empty. She released the magazine and it fell onto the table. She didn't have to look at it. She could tell by the sound it was empty.

"That was just a prop to give me time to explain my collateral," he said, tapping the top of the laptop screen, "your daughter."

Carly threw the pistol against the wall next to the table, where it left a hole in the wall before falling onto the tile floor.

"Careful. You don't want to damage my computer here, do you?"

She was furious. Anger burned deep inside; anger at him, anger at herself for letting him trap her.

"What do you want?" she asked again.

"I think I've got your undivided attention now. Good. So you're not going to do anything stupid, are you?"

He slammed his hand on the table, startling her. "Answer me, dammit. Now!"

She shook her head. "No."

He sat back in his chair. "Good. So here's what you're going to do. Call Dr. Langford and get him over here. ASAP. Because if you don't get him over here before Michelle crosses the Skyway, it'll be too late."

"So this is what it's all about. Forrest Langford? You're trying to get back at him?"

Josh's left eye twitched as he ignored her question, then looked at his watch. "You're wasting time, Carly."

"How in the hell am I supposed to get him to come over here?"

"Your problem. Figure it out. Clock's ticking." He leaned back in his chair and folded his arms across his chest.

She could see he was going to be no help. Glancing up at the wall clock, she tried to calculate how much time she had. An hour and a half, max. Josh handed her the cell phone. With her left hand, she pressed Langford's number.

The call went to Forrest's voice mail. "Call me as soon as you get this, please," she said, leaving a message.

She ended the call and held the phone. "I got his voice mail. He didn't answer."

"Not my problem," Josh said again.

Shit. She decided to call his office, knowing it would go to his answering service.

"Hi. This is Carly Nelson. I need for Dr. Langford to call me as soon as possible. It's an emergency."

She listened as the operator tried to triage her call and refer her to the physician taking call that evening.

"This is personal. I'm Dr. Langford's ex-wife, and it has to do with our daughter. I need him to call me as quickly as he can."

Josh leaned forward and slowly shook his head.

"Thank you," she said into the phone and hung up.

"I don't think you should mention anything about Michelle."

"I'm just trying to get him to call me back, you–" She started to say *idiot,* but didn't want to risk making him mad.

He nodded. "Good. I want him here."

In a few minutes, Carly's cell phone buzzed. She took a deep breath and answered.

"Forrest? No, nothing's wrong. Michelle's fine. She and Anna are on their way here from Tampa. It was the only way I could get your service to page you. Sorry if I worried you."

She listened for a few seconds while he talked, then interrupted. "I need you to come over. It's about your computer. I think you need to see this as soon as you can."

Carly shook her head. "No, it can't wait. The computer guy is over here right now and he'll be leaving to go out of town in the morning." She paused, not wanting to sound too desperate.

"Hold on." She covered the phone for a few seconds, stared at Josh, then spoke into it. "I'm sorry, Forrest. He's actually leaving tonight. He has a flight leaving in a couple of hours and he won't be back for a week." She was making everything up as she was going, trying to get Forrest to drop what he was doing and come over.

"He said it won't take long, but you need to see it," she added.

"Okay, I'll see you in a few." She hung up the phone and exhaled a deep breath.

Josh still wore that bitter smile. "You did good, Carly. How long?"

"Thirty minutes."

"Good. That gives us time to get ready. Now, put your left hand on the arm of the chair. And be real careful that you don't even twitch."

Josh held the gun with one hand and put the tie around her left wrist. He pulled it tight, then checked and tightened all of the others, making sure they were secure. Her skin crawled when he touched her ankles. His fingers lingered just a little too long.

"You know, you're an attractive woman." His hand was still on her ankle as she felt her hand make a fist. "We might have a little fun after Langford gets here. He'd probably like that, after looking at those pictures on his computer."

She strained against the ties binding her and felt them cut into her flesh. He looked up at her and grinned, and in his eyes was nothing but pure evil.

Chapter 27

Josh held up a roll of duct tape. "I don't need to gag you before the good doctor gets here, do I? If I hear as much as a peep from you, I swear I'll throw the computer into the pool."

Carly shook her head.

"Let's see if Michelle is in her car yet." He tapped a few keys on the laptop and once again, Carly heard Michelle's and Anna's voices.

"Traffic sucks," Michelle said. "It's going to take us forever to get home."

"Did you call your Mom?" Anna asked.

"Yeah, but it went straight to voice mail. I left her a message."

Carly could hear the radio blaring, some rap music in the background.

Josh looked at Carly. "About now you're still trying to decide if I'm bluffing or not. I lied about the gun. Well, technically, I didn't lie. You just assumed it was loaded, right? So, maybe you're thinking when doc gets here, maybe we can overpower Josh and save our daughter. I know you know how to use a gun and that you're a good shot."

He watched her closely for a reaction. Carly tried not to show any recognition or emotion and keep her facial expressions neutral.

"Well, another little demonstration is in order, to prove I can control her car. Let's accelerate, shall we?"

He clicked the mouse and almost instantly she heard Anna's voice.

"What the hell are you doing? There's a car in front of us!" Anna screamed.

"I don't know, accelerator—"

Carly's hands tightened around the end of the chair arms. Josh noticed. He clicked the mouse again.

"Damn. That was scary." Michelle talking. "I don't know what happened. That was the same thing it did that other time. But before I could switch the ignition off, it quit doing it. I guess my foot slipped and hit the accelerator or something."

Anna, laughing nervously, said, "You scared the shit out of me, girl! I thought you were going to smack that car. Want me to drive?"

Josh turned the volume back down. "Believe me now?" He watched for acknowledgement in her eyes. "I thought so. By the way, switching the ignition off won't have an effect this time. I fixed that when your husband brought the car in."

Carly nodded. "Just don't hurt Michelle."

Josh laughed. "I don't want Michelle. I want the doctor. Not a peep out of you when he gets here, okay?"

"Why?" she decided to ask, "What do you want with Forrest?"

He ignored her. The doorbell rang. "Remember, not a word." He walked over to her and put a piece of duct tape over her mouth. He picked up the pistol, inserted a full magazine in it, and stuck it under his belt behind his back.

Her eyes got big.

"Not taking any chances," he said. He pulled out a Taser and also put it behind his back as he walked to the foyer.

She could hear them talking at the front door. She strained to loosen the ties, but it was no use. They were too strong and too tight.

"Doctor Langford. Hi, I'm Josh, remember? Ms. Nelson's busy in the kitchen and asked me to come let you in."

She saw Forrest walking into the kitchen. Josh was behind him. He stopped as soon as he saw Carly with duct tape over her mouth, but before he could assimilate the scene, Josh pointed the Taser at him and zapped him. Forrest convulsed and collapsed into a heap on the floor.

Josh looked at Carly's wide eyes. "What are you looking at? I didn't want to have to shoot him—too messy."

He switched the device off and Forrest lay on the floor.

"Get up and sit in that chair," he said, pointing to the other arm chair.

"Fuck you," Forrest said, rubbing his arms.

Josh fired the Taser at Forrest, and once again, he convulsed. He walked over, put his hands under the still twitching arms of Forrest, picked him up, and put him in the other arm chair. He tied his wrists and ankles to the arms and legs similar to Carly. Then, he slid the chairs around so they faced each other and tied them to the table legs with the remaining plastic ties.

"Carly? What the hell?" Forrest said. He was still confused.

Josh turned the computer screen around so Carly and Forrest could see it if they turned their head sideways.

For the first time, Carly noticed a rectangle in the upper right hand corner of the screen. There were two rows of numbers, one above the other, in the box. The top row showed 72:34 and seemed to be counting down. The bottom row displayed 4:27 and was also going down. She gasped when she realized what the numbers signified.

Forrest was straining at the ties as he regained his facilities. "What the hell is going on here? Who are you?" he demanded of Josh.

Josh walked over and backhanded the doctor. "Shut the fuck up. You don't ask the questions here, *Doctor* Langford. I do." He ripped the duct tape off Carly's mouth, walked back to his chair, and sat down.

"Carly, why don't you explain to this asshole what's going on," Josh said.

Forrest spit blood out of his mouth. "You're in big trouble, you punk."

"Shut up, Forrest," Carly said. In a firm, but slightly kinder tone, she continued. "Please be quiet and let me explain."

She gave him the condensed version in a hurry, to get to the part she thought most important—their daughter.

"That's bullshit," Langford said. "I don't believe it."

"Carly, maybe I need to give the doctor a demonstration," Josh said, reaching over to the laptop.

"No!" she answered too quickly. "Forrest, listen to me. He's not lying. He showed me before you got here. He made Michelle's car accelerate. I heard her and Anna's reaction. It's not bullshit. Plus, he made Brian Jennings's truck go off the Causeway. It wasn't an accident. It was him. He's Sorcerer."

Langford paused and considered what Carly said.

"Okay. So what do you want? Money? What, tell us," Langford asked.

Josh leaned across the table. All eyes were on him. He spoke clearly and deliberately.

"What I want, you can't give me. Tell me, *Doctor* Langford," he said, emphasizing again the word *doctor*, saying it with disgust. "Do you remember a patient of yours? Irene Keisler? About a year ago."

Langford's eyes widened and he shot Carly a glance before he recovered. He shook his head. "I see hundreds of patients. I can't remember all of them."

Josh slammed his hand down on the table so hard, Carly was afraid he was going to knock the laptop off. "That's your problem, Doctor. You don't remember. And you don't give a shit. Well, I'll refresh your memory. Irene Keisler was my mother. And you killed her. Sunday was a year ago."

At first Langford look confused, then a look of horror crossed his face. He looked closely at Josh.

"But . . . you're not the . . . your hair?" Forrest stammered.

Josh laughed. "Yeah, I had long brown hair then. But after that, I cut it short and kept it blond. Nice change, don't you think?"

Langford answered him in a calm, deliberate voice, no edge to it now. "Your mother had a stroke. It was an emergency, I was on call that night. I did all I could, but she didn't make it." Then to Carly, "He was there. I went out and talked to him after, told him the news."

Carly's heart sank. *So this is what it was all about. A child loses his mother. Forrest was the surgeon. A case of revenge.*

Forrest continued, "What do you want? Michelle had nothing to do with this. I don't care what you do to me, but leave her and her mother out of this. They've done nothing to you."

Out of the corner of her eye, Carly saw Josh get up and walk over to them. He leaned over inches away from Forrest's face.

"She. Was. All. I. Had! You took her away from me. Now I'm going to take something away from you!"

He turned and walked over behind Carly. He reached out and ran the back of his hand down her face. She recoiled at his touch and turned her face as far away from him as she could, straining against the ties that bound her.

Josh looked at Forrest, smiled, and said, "Doc, did you enjoy those pictures I put on your computer? They were some of my better ones."

His eyes still on Forrest, he ran his hand down inside the front of her shirt, squeezing one breast, then the other.

She closed her eyes, trying to pull away from him, impossible while tied in the chair.

"I was thinking I might have a little fun here with the ex. She's got a nice body, plus she doesn't have those fake boobs your current princess has. I might even let you watch. What do you think?"

"Leave her alone!" Forrest said.

With his free hand, Josh gripped the placket of her shirt and yanked it down, ripping the top two or three buttons off and exposing her breast. He covered it with his hand and squeezed it, hard, making Carly whimper.

"Leave her the fuck alone, you coward!" Forrest said.

Josh froze and looked up at Forrest. Slowly, he left his position behind Carly, walked over to Forrest, and punched him in the gut, a solid blow, knocking the wind out of him. Forrest was doubled over, groaning, trying to get his breath.

"You may be king at the hospital, but you don't call the shots here. I do. And I promise you I'm gonna do whatever I damn well please with her. And you're going to watch. When I'm done here, I'm going over to your house and take care of the blonde bimbo. It's going to hurt a lot more than the sunburn I gave her."

He went back to his chair at the table and sat, glaring at them both, typing on the keyboard of his laptop.

Carly's mind was racing. She was frightened, not for herself. It was a primal fear roiling deep within her very being. Now she realized what Josh planned. He was going to drive Michelle's car off the Sunshine Skyway Bridge while Carly and Forrest listened to her die. And there was nothing she could do to stop him.

Chapter 28

Wayne Jensen was at a Starbucks in Fort Myers, working on his computer. He was still afraid to use the Internet connection at his apartment, so went out to various places to avoid detection. He had Doctor Langford's log file from his computer up on the screen in one window and was looking through it. When he found what he wanted, he looked back at the other window on the screen.

The IP addresses matched. He thought it looked familiar, and now he was sure. The person who had hacked Langford's computer was the same person who hacked into Carly Nelson's computer—Sorcerer.

He turned to his keyboard and typed in several commands. Last night he'd made progress tracing Sorcerer. He was so close. Just a few more pieces and he'd have a location.

He scanned the list, then stopped. Sorcerer had logged on in Fort Myers. Once again, the IP address looked familiar. Where had he seen that address? He couldn't place it, but knew it was something recent. He opened another window on his screen and scrolled down through a list of numbers. It was Carly's Internet address! That couldn't be right—Sorcerer was logged on through Carly Nelson's Internet address? Which meant he was coming in through another address or . . . ?

His fingers flew over the keyboard. After checking a couple of other things, he sat back in his chair. Sorcerer was logged on through Carly Nelson's router at her home.

He pulled out his cell phone and pressed the entry for her cell phone number. It went straight to voice mail.

"Ms. Nelson. This is Wayne Jensen. I've found some information on Sorcerer. Please call me as soon as you get this. It's important."

He looked at his watch. Seven o'clock. Maybe she was on her way home. He needed to talk with her. What if Sorcerer had broken into her house and was waiting on her? He tapped his fingers on the desk for a moment, then went on the Internet to look up her home phone number. In less than a minute, he had it and was dialing it on his cell.

It rang and rang, then an answering machine picked up.

"You've reached Carly, Eric, and Michelle. Leave a message and we'll get back to you."

It was Michelle's voice.

At the tone, he left a message, "Ms. Nelson, this is Wayne. Please give me a call as soon as you get this message. It's important."

In Carly's kitchen, Josh heard Wayne's voice leaving a message and looked at Carly.

"Well, well. Your little geek friend is calling. Wonder what he wants? He's a moron, you know that, don't you? He's been trying to figure out my identity for weeks and he's not even close. But I know who he is. I even bailed him out of jail, anonymously, of course, just to screw with his head. I'll deal with him after I've finished with you and the good doctor."

With a sick feeling, Carly realized she would never get to tell Wayne who Sorcerer was. If he was saying this much, then he had no intention of letting them live.

Wayne paced the floor of the coffee shop. Carly Nelson hadn't called him back. He couldn't stand the inaction. To hell with it, he'd drive over to her house. If no one was home, he'd wait. He shut down the computer, grabbed everything, and walked out.

Fifteen minutes later, he pulled into Carly's driveway. There was another car there, one he didn't recognize, and a pickup. He got out, looked around, and saw no sign of anyone at home. He walked up to the door and rang the bell.

At the sound of the door chime, Carly's eyes opened wide.

Josh was up in a flash. "Who the hell is that?" he asked.

"I don't know. I wasn't expecting anyone," Carly said.

He took a piece of duct tape and taped Langford's mouth shut first, then Carly's.

"Don't want to take any chances." He picked up his gun and the Taser and walked out of the kitchen.

He tiptoed to the front door, and peered out the view hole. He grinned when he saw who it was.

He opened the door. "Yes? Can I help you?"

* * *

Wayne recognized the young man standing in front of him. It was Josh Mills. He looked relaxed, as if he belonged there, with his left hand in his pocket. Now he was confused. What was Josh doing there?

"Yes, I'm Wayne Jensen. Aren't you Josh?"

Josh reached out to shake Wayne's hand. "That's right, I remember. We met out at the beach. I'm Josh Mills."

Wayne stumbled over his words, still trying to sort things out. "I work at the hospital and I needed to speak with Ms. Nelson. Is she home?"

"Sure. She's in the kitchen with Doctor Langford. Come on in."

Wayne walked in and Josh closed the door behind him. Josh pointed to the kitchen and walked a few steps behind Wayne.

Wayne's mind was racing. Doctor Langford? Josh? What was going on? He was beginning to wonder if he'd made a mistake, but no, the IP address was definitely the router at Michelle's house. He was trying to figure it out as he walked toward the kitchen.

Josh pulled out the Taser and switched it on with his thumb. He was talking to Wayne so Wayne couldn't hear any sounds from the tied up couple. He raised his arm to fire it at Wayne. Unfortunately, he never heard the sound of Bo finally chewing his way through the flimsy bedroom door and the click-click of paws on the tile floor as Bo raced up behind him.

The eighty pound lab was running full speed when he left the floor and hit Josh from behind, flattening him on the hard tile floor. The Taser and the Glock skidded down the hall past Wayne.

Startled at the commotion behind him, Wayne saw the weapons slide past him on the hard surface. He was about to turn and see what happened when he saw Ms. Nelson and Doctor Langford tied in their chairs, trying to yell at him through the duct tape covering their mouths. When he turned, he saw Bo on top of Josh, teeth gnashing and snapping at Josh.

His first reaction was to try to get the dog off Josh, then realized with horror that Nelson and Langford were probably tied up as a result of Josh. He looked again at the Taser and handgun on the floor and figured they belonged to Josh.

Josh had his arms up, trying to protect his face and neck from the angry dog snarling at him. He tried to kick the dog, but didn't dare lower his hands.

Wayne reasoned that Josh was occupied trying to defend himself, so he ran over to pick up the Taser, then hurried over to pull the duct tape off Carly's mouth.

Carly gasped, in a rush to get the words out. "He's trying to kill us, Wayne. Untie us, quick."

Leaving Langford still trying to scream through his taped mouth, Wayne ran to the kitchen and retrieved a knife. He glanced over at Josh, still battling the furious black dog.

He cut the ties binding Ms. Nelson, then moved over to Doctor Langford and cut his as well. Langford reached up and ripped the duct tape off his mouth.

Carly grabbed the pistol off the floor, released the magazine to check it, then slammed it back up into the grip. She racked the slide, chambering a round, and walked over to Josh, still on the floor trying to defend himself.

"Bo," she said in a firm voice. "Relax."

Bo looked up to see his master and started wagging his tail. He looked back down at Josh, still shielding his face, as if to say *you were lucky,* then walked over to Carly and sat next to her.

"Good boy," she said, petting Bo with one hand and keeping the Glock pointed at Josh.

He finally realized the dog was no longer trying to kill him, moved his hands down, and looked up at Carly, who was pointing the pistol right at him.

"Don't even think about moving, asshole," she said. "Yes, this time it's loaded and I won't hesitate to shoot you. If you don't think I will, just try me."

Never taking her eyes off Josh, she said, "Wayne, bring those plastic ties over here and tie this scum up."

Without the dog in his face, Josh was starting to recover his composure. He looked up at Carly and that sick smile crept across his face. "You've forgotten about your daughter, haven't you? You might want to check the timer on the screen."

In her rage and anxiousness to get Josh, she had forgotten about his deadman's program. Shit, now what?

"Wayne, give Forrest the ties and take a look at the computer. What are the numbers in the box on the upper right hand part of the screen?"

Wayne handed the ties to Forrest and turned the computer around so he could see the screen.

"The top says 21:42 and the bottom says 3:18. They're both counting down."

"Josh said he's programmed his computer to control Michelle's car. She's on I-75 on her way home, headed toward the Skyway Bridge. He says he has some type of deadman control program, that if he doesn't type in his code every five minutes, the program will automatically crash her car." She heard Wayne typing on the keyboard, but never took her eyes off Josh.

"Did he say how he was controlling her car?" Wayne asked.

"Yes, through her cell phone. We can listen to her, but she can't hear us."

Josh started to sit up.

"Don't move. Now what's the code?" Carly pointed the pistol right at Josh's face.

He still had that twisted grin on his face. "He'll never crack that program in time. She should be almost to the bridge by now. There's not a thing you can do."

The roar was deafening. The shot hit the tile floor about a foot to the right of Josh's head and ricocheted through the sliding glass door to the lanai, shattering the glass. Everybody jumped except Carly and Bo.

"What the fuck are you doing?" Josh yelled, covering his head.

"I didn't miss—that was where I aimed. The next one is going through your crotch. If you live, you'll be singing soprano for the rest of your life."

Langford finally spoke. "Damn, Carly. That scared the shit out of me. Give us some warning next time, would you?" He tore off a piece of duct tape and handed it to her.

She looked at him quizzically, then when he pointed to her chest, she realized her breast was still exposed.

Turning red, she pulled the two pieces of the shirt together and slapped the duct tape over the gap.

Forrest carefully moved closer to Josh. "Put your hands behind your back. And Carly, make sure you don't shoot me by mistake."

Josh put his hands behind his back and Langford put the ties around his wrists, pulling them tight.

Her gaze was flat and she stared straight at Josh. "Give Wayne the code—now! Or I swear I'll shoot you."

Josh watched her closely, regaining his composure. He was studying her face for clues.

"You won't shoot me. Not until after she crashes, then you might. But not before. You may be a good shot, but you can't afford to take the chance. If your aim is off by a few inches, you might kill me and that'll lead to your daughter's death for sure. Right now, you need me." He yelled at Wayne in the kitchen, "How much time, Wayne?"

"One minute thirty."

"Tell her. Tell her you can't crack it in time. Tell her the truth."

"Wayne?" Carly said.

"He's right. No way I can crack it in a minute and a half. We have to have the code."

Josh sneered. "Told ya. Wish I could see her car go off the bridge. It'll be much more spectacular than Darci Edwards's crash."

"You killed Darci?" Carly asked.

Josh snickered. "Of course. That was a piece of cake."

"Can you talk to Michelle? Ring her phone or something?" Carly asked Wayne.

Josh answered for him. "Sorry, Carly. It's locked out. All you can do is listen." He laughed a silly, high-pitched laugh.

She was running out of time and knew it. Josh was never going to give her the code. He was right. She couldn't afford to shoot him, not as long as there was a chance.

"Wayne, call Anna's phone."

Josh's smile tightened just the tiniest bit. He recovered, but not before Carly saw it. "It's locked out, too," he said.

"You're lying."

"What's her number? Is it on your phone?" Wayne asked.

Oh shit, Carly thought. She looked at her phone on the kitchen counter. I don't have Anna's cell number.

"It's not on my phone. Let me think."

Josh smiled that evil grin again. "Not enough time to look it up on the Internet, Wayne. Looks like you lose."

Carly heard Wayne tapping keys on the keyboard.

"Got it," he said.

Josh and Carly both looked toward the kitchen.

"Now who's lying," Josh said, without a lot of conviction.

Wayne had Carly's cell phone in his hand. "I looked it up on Michelle's phone. Since we're linked to it, that was easy. I'm dialing it now."

Carly smiled this time as she looked back at Josh. His eyes were darting from side to side. He hadn't thought about that possibility.

"Anna, this is Wayne Jensen, who works with Michelle's mom at the hospital. This is important. She needs to talk with Michelle, now. Here she is."

He looked at the numbers on the countdown screen as he jumped up to hand the phone to Carly. Twenty-four seconds.

"Michelle. It's Mom. I'll explain later, but you must do what I tell you. Pull off the road as soon as you can, switch off the car, and get out. Now!"

"But Mom, we just passed through the toll booth. We're coming up to the bridge. There's nowhere to pull off."

"Michelle," Carly said, trying to keep her voice calm and not scream. "Pull off in the emergency lane, anywhere, but pull off, stop the car, and get out. Do it now! There's no time!"

"Whatever. What's going on?"

"Just get out. I'll explain when you're out of the car!"

Wayne looked at the counter. Eight seconds.

Carly strained to listen at what was going on in Michelle's car. At last she heard the car doors open.

"Did you switch it—" Before she could finish her question, she heard Michelle swearing.

"What the hell?"

Carly heard the car engine revving and the scrape of metal. "Michelle! Are you and Anna out of the car?" This time she screamed.

"Yeah, Mom, but the damn car just took off. On its own! It's going up the bridge by itself!"

Carly took a deep breath. "Are you both okay?"

"Yeah, but this is too weird. What happened?"

"I'll explain. Just stay there until the police come, Michelle. I've got to make a quick call, then I'll call you right back."

"Sure, Mom. Nowhere to go anyway."

Carly disconnected the call and stuck the phone into her shorts. She put both hands on the gun, still pointed at Josh, and looked at him with disgust. Her hands didn't waver.

Forrest watched her closely and said, "Carly. Don't. It's not worth it."

Josh looked up at her, taunting her, daring her to pull the trigger.

She moved her trigger finger inside the guard, letting it rest on the trigger. Five and one-half pounds of pressure is all it would take. One shot would do it, and the world would be rid of this piece of shit. It would be justified, she knew. No jury in the world would convict her, even if it came to that. She wanted to wipe that perverted smile off his face—permanently.

"Carly. Please."

It was Forrest talking again. Him saying *please* took her out of the place she was in. With great effort, she moved her finger outside the trigger guard. Now her hands started shaking when she realized how close she had come to pulling the trigger.

With her free hand, she pulled out her phone and called George. Her hand was still trembling as she put the phone up to her ear.

"George, Carly. Hate to bother you, but can you call the police and get over to my house as soon as possible? I've got Josh Mills here, also known as Sorcerer. He's tied up and I have a gun pointed at him, but it's complicated."

Chapter 29

A few minutes later, George arrived with Tony Budzinski. Forrest met them at the door. George and Tony both walked in with guns drawn. They weren't taking any chances even though Carly had explained the situation to George as he drove out to her house.

As soon as they saw Josh tied up on the floor with Carly sitting in a chair pointing a gun at him, they relaxed, but kept their weapons out. Carly dropped the magazine, cleared the chamber on the Glock, and handed it to George. He noticed her torn shirt and the piece of duct tape keeping it together, but didn't say anything, taking the gun from her.

As Tony holstered his gun, he noticed the chunk missing out of the tile floor next to Josh and looked up at the shattered sliding glass door.

"Warning shot," Carly said. "Nobody was hit."

Tony nodded and pulled out his cell phone. He called the Police Department, asking for someone by name. As soon as he hung up, he found two more plastic ties and bound Josh's feet together.

"Not that I think he'd make it far, but better to be safe," he said when he finished.

"It'll be a few minutes yet. I told Chance lights and siren weren't needed, the scene was secure, and for them to come on in."

George's phone rang. He answered it, mumbled a few words, and said, "Thanks. Somebody will be there to pick them up in a couple of hours." He put the phone in his pocket and turned to Carly.

"Pinellas County Sheriff's Office deputies picked up Michelle and Anna and are taking them to the county complex. They're fine, but the car decided to drive off the bridge and is in the water."

"I can have someone from the department pick them up for you, Carly," Budzinski said.

Before she could answer, Forrest spoke. "No, thank you, we'll leave as soon as we can to pick them up. Can you get someone from there to take them out to St. Pete-Clearwater airport?" He turned to Carly. "We can take the plane; it'll be quicker."

"We can do that," Tony said, "but it's going to be a while. We'll need statements from both of you first. Why don't I go ahead and send someone up to get them?"

"Thanks, Tony, that would be appreciated," Carly said. She pointed at Josh. "He admitted killing Brian—and Darci."

Josh had that sick grin on his face again. "I didn't say anything. I don't have any idea what she's talking about."

Carly's face got red, and now she wished she'd pulled the trigger.

Wayne said, "Not to worry. I recorded it."

Both Josh and Carly looked at him.

He tapped the computer. "I activated the microphone on it, and it's been recording everything since I got here."

Carly looked at Josh and smiled as his grin faded away.

"That's bullshit! You're lying," Josh said.

George had enough, walked over to Josh, and stood over him. "Shut up, son. The detective here may have to put up with your mouth, but I don't. I'm retired and would be more than happy to slap a piece of duct tape over your mouth and my knuckles might slip in the process."

Josh glared at the big man, but kept his mouth closed.

Bo heard a car pull in the driveway and started for the front door.

"Bo. Stay," Carly said, and the Lab sat next to her.

The two uniformed officers came in with their hands on their guns. When they saw Budzinski, they relaxed and walked over. He filled them in on what he wanted, and they started processing the scene after cuffing Josh Mills.

Carly's hands started shaking as she realized how close she had come to losing Michelle. She looked over at the gangly kid with the brown ponytail and thought back to the first time she had met him in her office. Little did she realize he would save their lives.

She walked over to him and hugged him. "Thank you, Wayne. You saved my life, but more importantly, you saved my daughter's life. And thanks for recording this."

He blushed and started to say something, but closed his mouth.

"How did you know to come over here?" she asked.

He glanced over at Tony before speaking.

"Kid," Budzinski addressed him. "Based on what we've heard here, all charges against you are going to be dropped. I promise nothing you say will be held against you. We'll need a formal statement this evening, but right now we're off the record."

Wayne nodded. "I was cross-referencing IP addresses and tracked Sorcerer down. Then I realized he had signed on to the Internet through your router here. That's why I called."

Carly shook her head. "I still don't have a clue what you're talking about, but I know one thing."

Everyone looked at Carly, waiting for her to continue.

She looked at Wayne and smiled. "From now on, you call me Carly, got it? No more Ms. Nelson. Understood?"

"Yes, ma'am—Carly."

Acknowledgments

Once again, many thanks to all of my wonderful friends and family who continue to support me in my writing endeavors. I can't say "thank you" enough to the following people for taking time to read my manuscript and offer much-needed feedback and support: Mary Jo Burkhalter Persons, Otis Scarbary, Cindy Deane, Shirley Scarbary, Clara Blanquet, Fred Blanquet, and Barry McIntosh. Also, thanks to Lt. Karl Steele for many conversations on police procedures. Any mistakes that remain are mine.

My granddaughter Breanna continues to share my love of reading and I sense that she has that urge to write. I hope I inspire her as much as she inspires me.

To my wife June—thank you, thank you, thank you! You're letting me live my dream, and I couldn't do it without you.